GIRL
ANATOMY

rebecca bloom

GIRL
ANATOMY

a novel

WM WILLIAM MORROW *An Imprint of* **HarperCollins***Publishers*

HarperCollins books may be purchased for educational, business, or sales promotional use. For information please write: Special Markets Department, HarperCollins Publishers Inc., 10 East 53rd Street, New York, NY 10022.

FIRST EDITION

Designed by Shubhani Sarkar

Printed on acid-free paper

Library of Congress Cataloging-in-Publication Data

Bloom, Rebecca, 1975–
    Girl anatomy : a novel / Rebecca Bloom.—1st ed.
      p. cm.
    ISBN 0-06-621257-X (alk. paper)
    1. Los Angeles (Calif.)—Fiction. 2. Female friendship—Fiction. 3. Young women—Fiction. 4. Weddings—Fiction. I. Title.

PS3602.L66 G47 2002
813'.6—dc21

                        2002066045

02 03 04 05 06 WBC/RRD 10 9 8 7 6 5 4 3 2 1

to the rockin' JR's
I love you

GIRL
ANATOMY

two for the price of one

Sometimes I think I am schizophrenic. Well, maybe not schizophrenic. Casually assuming the moniker without proper medical diagnosis is slightly melodramatic and disrespectful of true sufferers of the disease. But I do sometimes feel like *Sybil* with two versions of me rattling and banging around in my brain, arm wrestling each other for dominance. There is the "Wannadoer" and the "Wishidinter": carefully thought out nicknames for my alter egos. The "Wannadoer" stares and watches the world with eager fascination, jonesing for a taste of the high life. The life of dark bars, dark-haired men, and leather-panted experiences worthy of a *Playboy* spread. The "Wishidinter" tosses and turns in bed, spitting out the taste of sour snogs and reddening at the memory of my ill-prepared ass trying to strut beautifully dyed cowhide

2   around town. The "Wannadoer" leaps into escapades, falls head over heels in love at a simple hello, ignores rational thought in favor of high-relief fantasy, and has a gold neon naive sign flashing on her brow in broad daylight. The "Wishidinter" scolds herself for childish romance, tries to prevent an immature heart from beating the tom-tom for the wrong guy, picks up the scattered pieces after the inevitable fall, and attempts to assimilate the failure into growth. Both creatures seem very normal, very human. What person does not have both the sage and the sucker lurking within? However, mine exist at the same time, all the time, and most of the time, they initiate conversation or argument with each other no matter the circumstance. In simple terms, I talk to myself, a lot, everywhere. I talk myself into things, out of things, around things, and through things.

A perfect example of this happened just the other night. It started out innocently enough, at dinner with Max, my older and sometimes wiser brother; Robert, Max's friend; and Josh, a friend of mine. We were celebrating Robert's new show of paintings at Gallery Downtown. Afterward, we hit a few bars, feeding off one another's good news and good vibes. At the pinnacle of our excitement, we ran into my good friend Danielle and a group of her friends from work. Amid the crowd of becoming familiar faces, a cute, skinny guy, with a black bar-code tattoo on the inside of his left wrist, an artsy computer-designer job, and vintage dark green glasses, caught my slightly buzzing eye. He was a friend of a friend, of a friend, and his name was Justin. At midnight we began talking.

"Those are great glasses." Smiling at him. "Where did you get them?" Looking closer.

"Thanks." Touching the frame. "There's this cool place in Pasadena that only sells unused vintage frames. They have the biggest collections of unique lenses."

"I think I know the place. I have been meaning to check it out." Smiling again.

"Do you wear glasses?"

"Only at night, in the movies, and when I really want to see." Smiling again and again.

"So, tonight you want to be a little blind?"

"Well, as my brother says, sometimes it's nice to see things a little blurry. All those sharp edges can get in the way of a true aesthetic."

Here is where my inner voice, the "Wishidinter," piped in.

"Uh, Lilly." (That's me.)

"Yeah?"

"What the hell are you talking about?"

"I thought I was being clever. It's always good to throw 'aesthetic' into the conversation. It's one of those hot words that make guys think you are brilliant."

"Yes, but one has to use it in an intelligent way to demonstrate brilliance. Sharp edges getting in the way? Please."

"Go away. You're distracting me from being witty."

"Fine! Wouldn't want to do that. You need all the help you can get."

I took a big drink of my vanilla Stoli and Coke, and tried to return to this cute boy, still grinning at me. Just for the record, no one else can hear the "Wish-I." Obvi-

4 ously no one else can hear my inner monologue, but whatever. I swallowed again, recouped, and continued with my version of peppy bar-talk minus, however, the employment of SAT words I apparently do not know how to properly use. We got to know each other a bit more, and by two when the lights glared, I thought my string of bad luck might have finally ended because I still thought he was cute despite increased illumination. In addition, we had begun the hand fondle thing. You know, squeezing and stroking palms, simulating what we want to do to each other's private parts. It's usually the precursor to the kiss. We extricated from the larger group and I heard myself saying,

"Are you tired?"

"Not really." Eyeing me. "You?"

"Nope." Eyeing him.

"Want to come over and hang?" Eyeing me lower. "I can play you that CD we were talking about."

"Sure."

"Cool. Follow me?"

"My car's just here."

I got in my car, started her up, and flipped on the radio. My cheeks burned at my brazenness, and as I pulled out, my stomach began to burn a bit too. By the time I got to the corner, and he was in front of me, waving through the rearview mirror, I was on fire.

"What on earth do you think you are doing?"

Oh no, here she is again.

"Nothing."

"Nothing, huh?"

"He's cute."

"Yeah, in a potential serial killer way. You don't even know him."

"He's a friend of a friend of a friend."

"Whose name is?"

"Justin, I think."

"Justin what?"

"Fuck off. I just wanna smooch!"

"But one thing leads to another and who knows what could happen."

"You only live once. And you know my things don't lead to others."

"Yeah, but come on. Look, I know it's been awhile and you are in need of affection, but this guy could be some psycho. Is that really how you want to go out?"

"You are such a drama queen! Chill out."

"Just turn."

"What?"

"Turn!"

And with that, before I could stop the "Wishidinter," I turned right onto a side street. I sped up à la *Speed Racer*, turned left, turned right again, and lost every trace of him. The "Wannadoer" had no chance, but as you will come to see later, she usually never ever has a chance.

That's the inherent problem with Los Angeles. You experience the walk of shame before you even get to do anything. All those questions about the person you are about to let flitter his tongue on your teeth and grope your left breast surface before any initial contact. Sure, great first line of defense, and in this day and age blah, blah, blah, but sometimes it's fun to let go and kiss the frog! In college, it always happened post-hookup. You

6 trudged home in the snow wearing your clothing from the night before, and inevitably you would run into every single person you knew who saw you the night before in your carefully planned outfit that now you wish wasn't so carefully planned. A chuckle here, a snort there, and you would creep home embarrassed by everyone's knowledge of your night of passion. However, you at least got the play!!! In LA, the walk of shame begins once you start driving home. In a city where everyone drives, there is always the "follow me home." Some stranger trailing you for fifteen minutes as you maneuver to your nest, trying to ignore your inner voice telling you how sketchy this all could become. Before there is even a tongue touch, or one that didn't happen against a wall in the bar, which does not count, you have yourself convinced as to what a horrible idea this all is, and you bail. Shame is a wicked cock block.

So, there you go. The constant dialogue between my wish-I-was-wild side and the I-wear-flannel-granny-nightgown side plays a key role in my life. It is the outline of everything I do, the system in which I operate. The duality extends to every aspect of my existence. I live a split existence. There are really two Lilly's floating around and tending to nudge people for attention. One of me lives in a world of cheap bars, thrift store furniture, and vintage clothes. The other resides in a pink palace dotted with contemporary art, Prada pillows, and movie stars. One is my life alone, sans grown-ups and bank accounts; the other is advised, influenced, and paid for by loving parental figures. I do have to say that these loving parental figures are somewhat responsible for my melodramatic behavior. I think it's slightly their fault that I am a little off center. I learned from the best. It is very easy to be nutty and open when your parents, from the minute you met them, beat to the sound of their own drums. Nothing fazed them. Whether it was my whip-smart-blue-jean-ponytailed-lawyer of a father or my organized-nice-to-everyone-civic-minded mentor of a mother, they both forged their own paths and made others listen to them without compromising. Max, my older brother, and I were always free to be you and me.

I have to admit that it wasn't always such a great thing to have parents who were so hip and cool. I remember wanting to murder my mother every time she came to pick me up from school in some shoulder-padded, Japanese, intellectualized jacket. The spiky hair, the crazy jewelry made me cringe. Echoes of "your mom dresses so weird" haunted me every time she bought some new Comme des Garcons deconstructed skirt. I wanted a mom who looked like a mom. A mom with soft hair, a pale beige velour sweat suit, and loafers. A mom who wasn't some fashion plate. Well, that was when I was seven and awkward. Now I admire her subtle rebellion and raid her closet whenever I can. I realize that I too like to go a little crazy myself, wearing leopard print and pearls to a bowling alley. I tell you it must be in the jeans . . . *oops,* I mean, genes. That's why we do end up inevitably like our parents. If I am blessed with just half of my parents' eye for excellence, detail, and style, I'll be a cultured, swinging, and cutting-edge gal for the rest of my life.

I have all these idiosyncrasies competing on the playing field of my personality. I am all over the place. I think

8   that is why I got this new task at work. My boss at *Chick,* a
new magazine for the too-cool-for-school girl, assigned
me the chore of testing every product that comes sailing
through the doors. Maybe my internal struggle to figure
myself out is a little more visible than I thought. Maybe
the right nail polish or superglue will put me together
again.

When I got to work this morning, there was a pile of
toothbrushes waiting for me. My dentist is smiling right
now and not knowing why! So besides my usual mundane
tasks of doing whatever my boss yells, I mean, tells, me to
do, I have to sort and categorize all these toothbrushes by
next Friday. I am going to have the best breath this week.
But, God, did I hate my boss. She was beginning to taint my
positive impression of the magazine. Plus, I dislike working
nine to five. I just don't think I'm cut out to work within
confined spaces or deadlines with psychos breathing down
my scrawny neck.

Why I thought this assistant, assistant, assistant editor
thing would be better than freelancing is beyond me. At
least when I was on my own trying to hash out small articles for any magazine that would toss me a few coins, I
could control my environment. Granted, snippets on
the best sakitinis in town and what bar attracts the most
soap stars weren't up there with Hemingway, and it wasn't
like I was writing a Pulitzer, nor really earning enough to
support my shoe habit, but I was independent. Furthermore, I didn't have to deal with people like my boss. She
held on to her meager position (just one step in front of
me) by means of personal espionage, intercepting faxes,
memos, and hacking into the other writers' e-mail to get

a juicy tidbit she could use in her tired advice column.
Why I put up with her shit is a question I continually ask
myself.

You know those times when an opportunity comes up
and you hear yourself in some voice you hardly recognize
saying yes? Like some imposter has invaded your throat,
thumped on your vocal chords, and made a decision for
you before you even have had a chance to think it through?
All of a sudden, you are behind a desk, in a pencil skirt,
with voice mail that has your first and last name recorded.
That's how this job thing went down. A friend of Mom's
higher up at *Chick* suggested I come on board since there was
a position open. This suggestion took place in front of said
Mom who was at that precise moment wanting said daughter to have a bit more structure and discipline in her young
life. All there could be was a "yes, sure, sounds great, when
do I start?" Smile, smile, swallow. So here I am with an
insane boss, and so much structure that I have begun coor-
dinating outfits at the beginning of each week, and matching my bags to my shoes!

Then again, on a positive note, my house was freely
being stocked with every gizmo, gadget, crème or crudité
known to modern man. And my boss knew I knew about
her deviousness. I guess that held its own power. I was
fairly confident I would never be fired, maybe chastised
and deafened by her shrill voice, but never fired. And she
did bring me Starbucks every morning, our own version
of graft. I felt guilty about not standing up for fellow
employees when she ripped into them or stole their stories, but who really wants to be Joan of Arc? All I wanted
was the flexibility the paycheck allowed, as well as the sigh

10 of relief from my mother I swear I could hear every morning wafting into my car on the way to the office. Also, with freelance, I never knew where the next buck was coming from, and there was way too much pressure in constantly creating witty wordplay that people would actually like enough to pay for. I figured a few hours dealing with conniving, catty bitches would sharpen my skills of observation, give me pages of material, and enough self-earned money to put food in my big ol' belly. The small sacrifice I made to my art, but damn was my mouth going to hurt this week!

AT SIX-THIRTY I packed up my perfectly matched bag and was headed for the door when the phone rang. It was my brother.

"Hey, Lilly."

"Hi, you just caught me. I have a long night of teeth brushing ahead of me. I need to get a jump on my new assignment."

"Toothbrushes?"

"Yep."

"At least it's not muscle-easing creams. You reaked for days."

"No shit. There is just so much BenGay a girl can take." Laughing. "What's up?"

"I got us on the list at Swallow tonight."

"Swallow?"

"That new club on Highland."

"Oh, okay. What time?"

"Ten. Meet you there in front."

"Sure, sure."

I headed home and thought about what I would wear. Of course that is my first thought. The outfit is the all-important aspect of an evening activity. If a girl hits the asphalt in a less than stellar getup, she is fucked and not in a literal sense. Clothing is armor: protection from the ever-present bombardment of self-esteem-reducing missiles. A quaint bar with a small crowd, a piano, and red vinyl couches can easily morph into a set from *Hellraiser II*, with knives flying from the wall, piercing confidence like a fork through mashed potatoes. Without the proper gear, hell is the handbag.

At this stage of my body life, black pants are my staple. Not just any pair of black pants, but my Katayone Adeli pinstripe light-weight wool trousers. They are the only ones that perk up the aforementioned ill-prepared ass. I throw them on, an overpriced Rolling Stones baseball T-shirt with a smattering of rhinestones, high-heeled black boots, and a long black coat. With my red hair long and shaggy, and my makeup smudged artfully on my freckled cheeks and around my brown eyes, a trick courtesy of my last meeting a few weeks ago with Tess, the perfectly shimmered Stila girl at the Barneys counter, I felt ready. I felt okay.

Luckily my brother has the same internal clock as me, and he was right on time. Decked in red bowling shoes, a long black leather coat, and dark jeans, my brother too had armed himself. We made a hot team. A few other friends met us and we entered beneath an archway shaped like a large pair of wings. Within the threshold came the usual forking over of twenty bucks for God

12 knows what because my six and seventh sense told me I was going to last all of about ten minutes. I get better long-distance rates than that. Anyway, once fully inside the bar, my armor started itching and chaffing like what you would imagine a spring break issue of bikini rash and crabs would. Slowly crawling out of my skin, I watch the parade of girls walking by in their Skyy shoes, low-slung stretch Earl jeans, and boob kerchiefs. Boob kerchiefs, a term coined by my brother, are basically tops with only fronts and a series of whips and ties that artfully secure them over the chest. They can be leather, lace, pleather, peacock, you name it, and here they were in full effect. Yet again, no matter how I try to break the pattern, I just can't get it right.

"Nice place." Eyeing a peacock who was eyeing my brother. "Your tongue is hanging out."

"No." Max, smiling at me, and closing his mouth. "Love this place already."

"I can tell. It is right up your alley. Pretty girls in pretty naked clothing."

"You are just bitter because . . ."

"Don't say it." Glaring at him in an "if you tell me I am fat I will kill you now even if we are related" way. "Please go get me a drink."

"Vodka Red Bull?"

"Why not?" Wrapping my coat around me tighter.

Max went to the bar and I continued looking around, feeling more and more uncomfortable by the minute. The mirrors on the walls began to stretch and slide, shifting into some wacky freak show à la *Something Wicked This Way Comes.* By the time Max returned with our drinks,

I had been looked through by enough guys to feel like a piece of vellum minus the shiny surface. I should have mauled bar-code boy because the chances of my getting another opportunity were slim to none if this was the scene in which I had to operate.

"I think I'm going to bail." Sucking back my beverage quickly.

"Give it some more time. We just got here."

"I don't think so."

"Party pooper." Pouting at me.

"You did not just call me a pooper? Are we, like, ten?"

"No, just stay a few more minutes."

"Okay. Fine. I gotta pee anyway."

I left Max with his buddy and wandered around the back of the club in search of the restroom. Behind a glazed glass wall were two doors with similar headshots adorning them. Another problem with LA, the attempt to be cool and kitschy prevents an average girl from being able to discern male from female. I closed my eyes and pushed the door with the picture of the best shoes, hoping I would avoid any penis sightings. Successfully, I did my duty and returned. Max and Robert were seated in a small silver booth surrounded by boob kerchiefs. I walked up to the table and pasted a fake grin on my face.

"Is there room for one more?" Asking my brother.

"Of course. Slide over." Gesturing to the pair of perfect blow-outs with bedroom eyes. "This is my sister, Lilly."

"Hi." Slithering in unison as they looked me up and down.

14   The girls slid over and I squeezed into a space big enough for one ass cheek. It was right then I heard a horrifying sound. There was a faint rip and pull that reverberated in my ears. Then there was a gentle give and the fabric covering my seat relaxed. My favorite pants had proceeded to tear right up the middle along the seam. You have got to be kidding me! I quickly downed the rest of my drink, and carefully slid back out of the booth knowing that I really didn't want to wait around and continue with this disastrous evening. Not only was I experiencing clothing catastrophe, I was being forced to endure my embarrassing brother's jazz hand pressing flirtatiously on the small of the girl's back beside me. Watching my brother get his groove on is something I try to avoid. I was living in a chorus of Aerosmith's *Misery,* and I had this sinking feeling it was only going to get worse if I stayed one minute longer.

"Have fun." Swirling my coat tightly around my free-floating bottom and setting my empty drink on the table. "I will talk to you in the morning."

"It's ten-thirty!" Groaning at me.

"I'm tired. I have some work anyhow." Lying. "Don't get into too much trouble." Winking.

"It's Friday night. There is no work tomorrow."

"Yeah." Staring at him. "Your point being?"

"Fine, bye." Leaning up and over and giving me a kiss.

"Later." Waving. "Bye, Robert."

"Lilly." Not looking away from his new girlfriend.

I walked into the bar sign—lit night and rode home with this pit in my stomach. If these are the places where people meet and greet, I am either going to have to fully

reconfigure my fleshy figure to ensure my clothing will
actual remain intact and not strain and bust at the seams,
or become a lush who will go home with strangers. By the
time I got home, I sunk even further into poor-me pity.
To think a fucking boob top could send me on a low ride
so quickly! Well, it wasn't just the boob top. Having your
favorite pants literally let you down was pretty much as
low as any young thing could go no matter how you look
at it. I threw off the carefully thought out outfit, ran my
hand down the foot-long tear, whimpered, then quickly
threw on my oldest, schlumpiest, ripped flannel nightgown. I grabbed an Arizona iced tea and sat down in
front of my computer with my toothbrushes at hand.
Absentmindedly, I picked up the phone and checked
messages. Josh, Danielle, Max from the bar saying good
night again, and Maya, my best friend from college who
now lives in San Francisco. I dialed her number and
listened for her voice.

"Hi." Maya, answering.

"Hey, it's me. Did I call too late?"

"Nope, we are up and a bit wired. I have actually been
waiting for you to get home. I think I have called you at
least ten times." Maya sparked.

"What's going on?" Carefully opening the packages
while taking a sip of tea.

"Well, we're engaged!!!!"

"Wow!" Dropping the tea all over the packages.

"Yep, Ted asked me tonight, flowers, dinner, the
whole nine yards. It was amazing."

"That's great." Trying to sop up the mess with the
sleeve of my nightie. "Getting married, huh?"

16   "Yeah. We're not sure when yet, but it is going to be sometime next fall."

"Terrific. I'm so psyched for you."

"Shit, my phone beeped. Look, I will talk to you to-morrow, okay? Everyone and their mother are calling us."

"Sure, I want details anyway." Hanging up.

Oh. Lord. Help!

the call of all calls

Last night, I got "the call." Okay, well maybe it wasn't "the" call, but it was a major call all the same. There are a few calls that can be classified as "the call." These are the ones that take your breath away, make you stutter, choke, and lose all your vocabulary even when you're the girl your friends have determined always has something to say. These are the calls that make you weak at the knees, chew the phone cord, tear up, sniffle, cough, blush, or get nauseated with anticipation. They rattle your worldview like a flamenco dancer's maraca, stand you on your head like an acrobat, and make you disco dance in a room full of rappers. Essentially, these are the calls that change your entire existence in one infamous second.

The first type is the worst possible a person can get. It's the call you get when someone near and dear is hurt and lying in

18 a hospital bed in a random city after being in an accident with a tractor and a deer and in desperate need of your blood or love or something else to get her through the next few hours. The second is not quite as do or die, but this call is potentially even more emotionally destructive. This is the call you get from the ex-love of your life who would have, could have, and you still want to be the one telling you he found his one and only, but she sure as hell ain't you, and they are getting married next summer. You crumble, you cry, and you try to figure out your next move now that your what-if is a what-not.

Another of these calls is the one I received. What can be worse for a very single, sometimes insecure, hopelessly romantic, occasionally here and there and everywhere kind of twenty-four-year-old girl than the call she gets from her best friend relating the news of her engagement. My best girl, Maya, is getting hitched and I'm decidedly flipping a lid. I think I maybe discovered a new shade of J. Crew catalog green: flaming jealousy. I don't want to marry her boyfriend, but what the fuck? How did she get so old all of sudden? How did she become a wife-to-be? Why aren't I?

Maya and I met in college, our freshman year. She lived with Emily down the hall and around the corner. We could never quite pinpoint the exact moment when we all became inseparable, but by second semester it didn't matter. For the first time in my life, I had the type of friends I had always wanted. We goofed around, told stories, got drunk, treaded through the snow in plat-forms singing Phish songs, and mended one another's broken hearts. Maya and I also found a trust so complete

that a disastrous trip to Europe didn't sabotage our
bond. For our graduation present, we set off to do the
whole backpack Eurail thing. I was looking for adventure,
and she was pining for the boy back home. It was a lethal
combination that left us both feeling totally annoyed,
alienated, and alone. We called it quits after only one
week. Luckily, after months of not speaking to one
another, we made our way back to each other and became
even stronger. She's always the first person I call whenever I do something silly, or mischievous, or important.
Nothing seems real until she knows. She is the one who
gives validity to my escapades and grounds me.

Those are the things I am afraid of losing. Will she still
take the three A.M. panic calls, or the I'm hyper as hell
and need to gossip calls? Will she care about my stupid
little crushes? Will she listen to my Jewish guilt trips?
These are the things I am so worried about. I'm not sure
exactly how to come to grips with becoming a little less
important to someone I hold in such high regard. Your
family has to stay with you always. They are your blood,
and no matter what, you are connected. With friends,
even best friends, a little thing can sever the tie and make
you walk down separate paths. Without a word, friends
can go silently into the cool dark night and never return.
That just can't happen here.

I never really had a friend like her in high school.
Danielle, my other best girl, always was there on the
periphery, but she went to a different school and had
totally different friends. Danielle and I were extremely
close but not day-to-day. I needed someone loyal and
interested in my life who was present all the time. I spent

20 so many lonely nights in high school wishing for a real kind of friend. One who would have plans and ask me to hang out. One who wouldn't pretend to be there for me and then tease me relentlessly in front of others because I was awkward and underdeveloped. A friend who would make sure I never felt out of place no matter where or with whom I was. Someone to just like me for the me I was. Maya was one of the first to give me confidence in my relationships, and that even took awhile seeing how even in college I was so scared of having all my new friends disappear that when I returned to Brown my sophomore year, I made my mom come with me. She came to support me and I then proceeded to fight with her so bitterly on the way there, venting my fear and treating her as if she were every person who wronged me, that Mom almost left me by the side of I-95. For so long I waited for a girl like Maya. Now, she was to be a permanent-plus-one while I was lucky if I got a loaner for an evening. What gives?

See, I was supposed to be first, the first one balled and chained. For some silly reason, my chums in college all decided that my hyperobsession with boys would translate into finding my beau super quickly, marrying, and walking around barefoot and pregnant shortly after I graduated. It was supposed to happen to me before it happened to all of them. I would protest every time they brought up this little witticism for it is so not "women's lib" to want a baby and a boy, but what's the expression? "Thou dost protest too much?" I deep down wanted to become a happily-ever-after, and I wanted to be the experiment not the control group. If I were the first, then that would mean that I would have found "him." The all-encompassing

him who is so far from me now he is probably an astro-
naut on the Muir space station losing bone density and
viable sperm. How are we going to make babies without
gravity? I have to admit that the whole "happy home"
concept is my ultimate goal. Sorry Gloria and Betty and
any other wonderful feminist, but I just can't imagine
something better than finding a partner and reveling in
that support while watching my tykes toddle in the yard
with fists full of Oreos.

I wonder, though, why I am freaking out so much.
This response seems so irrational, so melodramatic that
it might win me a *Soap Opera Digest* award if I was an actress
on daytime TV. Who knew I was such a ham? Hello, earth
to Lilly, I am only twenty-fucking-four! Until this very
minute, marriage has been on the back burner of a stove
I have not yet even bought! A beautiful meal I am excited
to eat, but not yet ready to be served. I do desperately
want what Maya has, but I am surprised by this reaction.
Maybe what I am really afraid of is that everything is about
to change with us. I am not so sure that's a good idea right
now. I'm finally on course, on the right track, and getting
somewhere, even if I don't have a clue as to where that is.
Maya's getting married is a big bump on this steady but off
center course. I just don't know if I can handle this. My
twenty-four-seven girl, available to me every hour of every
day, seven days a week, is going to be someone else's, and
I was never very good at sharing. What am I going to do
now that she has this permanent other priority?

"What is wrong with you, Lilly?"

"What?" Ignoring myself.

**"Why are you making this great, glorious event happen-
ing to your best friend all about you?"**

"Because it is making me freak the fuck out!"

"But it isn't about you."

"I know." Quietly agreeing. **"I definitely would have been a target for the serial killer in *Seven.*"**

Am I so selfish? So lame? So human? I'm going to side with so human because I know I'm not a bad person and cannot be the only one to feel shattered by someone else's good news. I mean, people out yonder get off on celebrity breakups or hang-ups, so I know I'm not alone. It's just that this major proclamation of coupledom reminds me of how uncoupled I am. Like nine-year-old Maya was right in front of me in line for the new Cabbage Patch Kids, you know the ones that actually burped, and she got the last one in the store, maybe even the whole state. I want what she has, and as evidenced by last night, I had no shot of finding true love when the sea was bobbing with better boobs.

Damn . . . there's the phone. It's probably Emily to dish about Maya's news.

So, I just got off the phone with Emily, then Jack, then Danielle, then Josh, and then, finally, I got a respite and was permitted to stop being so chipper. My mom broke the chain with her call. Our conversation went something like this.

"Hi Mom."

"Hi sweetie, what's new?"

"Oh, just that Maya is engaged."

"Wow. That's terrific." Gushing. "Send her my love."

"Yeah, it is, and I will, but why do I feel like the wicked witch of the west after Dorothy's house landed on her?" Starting to cry. "Why the hell am I crying?"

"You are being a little melodramatic, Lilly."

"Thanks a lot, Mom. You're so understanding." Getting pissed. "I tell you I feel like a house got dropped on my head, and you tell me I am melodramatic!"

"I'm sorry. What do you think is going on with you?" Trying to make up. "What are you thinking?"

"I don't know. It's just that when she told me, it was like all the air was sucked from my chest. Nothing is going to be the same."

"That's what growing up is about."

"Nice cliché, Mom. You'd better have something else in your advice book or I'm hanging up."

"Easy there kid. Give a mom a break. You want to know what I really think?"

"Yes, but only if it will make me feel better."

"That I can't guarantee, but here goes." Taking a deep breath. "Does your getting upset have anything to do with the fact that you're a hopeless romantic and don't have a boyfriend, and always thought you were going to get married first?"

"Did you just read my journal or something?" Starting to laugh. "Mom, have I become an open book? I feel naked."

"I'm your mother, I know you. I remember all the drawings of wedding dresses you used to do when you were ten. You will find him, I promise."

"Yeah I know, it's just that now I have a friggin' time limit. I refuse to go dateless to her wedding."

"But weddings are the best places to meet men."

"Her wedding is months from now, if I am alone for another year I will die."

24   "No you won't." Chuckling at me. "You just might get sex starved."

"It's already reaching famine levels, so I think death, yes, death, for sure."

"Feel better?"

"Sort of, oh, call waiting. We're all swapping calls right now. Love ya."

"Bye sweetheart."

Leave it to mom to tell it like it is and make me giggle a bit. That's really how my whole family works. We tell each other the truth despite how it might sting and then try to flip the given scenario into a positive. We know each other so well, know the buttons to push and how to push them, and then, how to love and support one another unconditionally when the buttons need some grease and get stuck in the "on" position.

Again the phone. Who the hell knew I was so popular? Maybe my friends should get married more often and I could live in a delusion where people actually want to talk to me.

"Hey Lilly." It's Max. "You hungry?"

"Why are you up? It's only ten-thirty. I thought for sure I wouldn't hear from you until way past noon."

"Not the late night I had hoped for." Yawning into the receiver.

"Struck out?"

"At every at-bat."

"Things looked so promising." Grinning over the phone cord. "I imagined there would be a boob kerchief balled up on your floor this morning."

"Well, what can I say? Not being able to seal the deal must be a shared genetic thing."

"Thanks a lot, ass breath."

"Stinky hole."

"Poo face."

Max and I have this new thing where we try to come up with the best bad names to call each other. I think it's sort of endearing, but you should see the reactions we get when strangers overhear us!

"Poo face?" Max laughs. "Not one of your best."

"I know. It's early." Laughing with him. "Food?"

"Burger, fries, chili?"

"Perfect."

"I can meet you in an hour. I want to jump in the shower and drop Winnie off to get washed."

"Nope, too long. I have to help Danielle paint her bathroom this afternoon because that family outing tomorrow could potentially suck up the entire day. She will kill me if I push it to another weekend. We have to go now or I am out."

"What color?"

"I don't know. She's getting the paint now. Also, I still have not finished the 'How Does Your Chapstick Rate' for the February issue." Catching him up. "I have enough Blistex to keep this pucker perfect for the next year."

"Just think when you finally kiss someone, your lips will be smooth like a baby's butt."

"Exactly."

"It's the little things that keep you happy." Teasing me.

"You know it. Free products are always a good thing."

"Meet you in twenty. I'll deal with the dog after."

"By the way, I have crazy news."

"What?"

"Maya's engaged."

"Why is that crazy?" Asking in that confused guy way.

"Because it is making me crazy."

"Oh, I see. It's one of those meals." Understanding my shorthand.

"Yep."

"I'll be ready." Hanging up.

Small things usually do make me happy and right now a big wedge of beef with a side of some greasy potatoes and my brother's sympathetic ear could be just what the best-friend-is-getting-married-and-I-am-not doctor ordered. As I drove to meet Max, I got to thinking again about Maya and her good luck. Maybe I should get her to let me rub her belly à la Buddha the next time I see her. Hopefully some trace of magic will remain on my fingertips like those invisible stamps they give you when you leave Disneyland. My luck will then at least glow in special amusement-park lights, and possibly prevent, as illustrated before, the constant jinxing I submit myself to whenever I interact with men. Well, maybe not jinx myself. I just seem to get myself into ridiculous escapades that never lead me down the path of true love. I always wind up on the wrong course, or like the other night, taking myself off the course entirely.

There was the time I asked a guy to coffee, and he says, "I don't do coffee," and I still pursue him for a few more weeks hoping I can convince him to "do" tea or something. Then there was the time I saw this agent at a party whom I had kissed in an alley on a blind date after downing too many gin and tonics a few nights earlier. He was wrapped around this other girl who Max happened to know was a girl who knew everyone, if you know what I mean. And then there was this beautiful Brazilian model whom on our first date went on to describe the beauty and joy that two men could have enjoying each other. Not my scene. Let's just say I have never been that lucky in love, and that was going to have to change real soon because now I have a wedding to get to.

Here's the dilemma, though. How do you change a lifetime of disaster in a short time? I know I am blessed with so much that dating or not dating shitty men is my token burden. And, I have to admit that deep down I enjoy the silliness of it all. In my humble opinion, even with the possibility for utter emotional destruction, having a crush makes everything a little more interesting. Liking someone makes the day glitter and shine in the best way. So, I am one hundred percent devoted to being boy crazy. I just can't get guys off my mind. They are too sexy to ignore. Even after getting dissed or dumped, I am always hopeful someone else will come along for me to fantasize about. The problem is that no one better has come along yet. How cool could bar-code boy really have been without beer goggles? Or champagne goggles in my case. I think I am going to have to supercharge my optimism to arm myself for the battle ahead. Trust me, it is going to be a battle.

WHEN I MET up with Max, we chatted, ate, and the grease feast made me feel a little better about being alone. By the way, the French fry cure is a marvelous thing. If there's one person in the whole world who does not perk

28 up when their mouths are bathed in hot potatoes and ketchup, I would be extremely surprised. I managed to shake off my self-consciousness and began building myself up for the long war ahead. I would find someone great, even if I had to look in the yellow pages for an escort! After lunch I went over to Danielle's and we inhaled way too many fumes while artfully washing her bathroom in periwinkle blue. Paint thinner is a wicked high! Then we ordered pizzas and watched *Sixteen Candles*. Sunday, I had a typical deli lunch with my family and then spent the afternoon and evening working. I brushed, chewed, and scraped away, so by Monday morning, I had given myself about five raspberries and my mouth ached. By Thursday, the sores were still there, and I certainly was not ready to be social. Then I got a call from Danielle.

Like Maya, Danielle was my girl and I would do just about anything for her since she was the only friend to survive fluorescent everything, lace half gloves, off-the-shoulder sweatshirts, and puff paints. Sure, we were only eight years old, but we had the *Flashdance*/Madonna look down pat. Years past and then came delayed puberty, the early nineties, and high school. She was my one solid friend when I was fifteen and filled with braces and loneliness. As we got older, no matter where we went, how we evolved, or how long it had been since we had spoken, everything was always the same with us. Our friendship was beyond the bounds of daily ego massaging and phone call returning. We were soul mates. Giving her a helping hand was as natural as shaving my legs or checking my voice mail every ten minutes. And, we have already agreed that if things don't pan out with men, we'll buy a big

house with a huge porch swing. We'll hang together 29
smoking joints and eating Raisinets as the sun sets on our
wrinkly old bodies.

There was something about her daily five P.M. almost-
done-with-work-let's-gossip phone call that evening that
told me there was something amiss. Usually, Danielle has
this nonchalant, I'm-making-my-own-private-calls-
from-my-small-cubicle-on-your-dime-and-I-don't-
give-a-fuck tone to her voice. She is always fearless, full
of confidence and purpose. I, usually skittish on the
other end of the line, tended to whisper or half grunt
replies to her jabbering—always fearful the battle-ax at
the new office would overhear and take her pent-up
sexual aggression out on my sorry ass.

Anyway, Danielle called with a panicky words-
jumping-into-my-headset kind of voice. I could only
pick up every third syllable, but I gathered she was freaking out about something or another. Right then and
there, I knew it wasn't Chinese food and Must See TV for
me. I was a little disappointed, seeing how Dr. Green was
going to get busted for his extracurricular medical activities tonight. The scenes even showed Carter finally getting it on with that other blond doctor woman, and now
I was going to have to hear about it from Josh second-
hand at lunch tomorrow. In my old age (smirk), I seem
to have become a creature of habit. I have order, sched-
ules, quirky little activities I dig that fill up my days. Even
though I hang alone, I hang alone well.

In the two years since I got back from my seven-month
postcollegiate sojourn in gay Paris, I have gotten used to
spending most of my time alone, playing inside my head.

30   All those solo walks along the Seine, nights spent reading
in my apartment, and weekends lurking in dark cafés
conditioned me to like my own company. Sure, I was
lonely not having anyone to gab with or laugh with, but
somehow I found serenity in solitude. Now, even with
friends around, I like being able to tune everything and
everyone out. I have become selfish with my freedom,
filling it with things I deem fit. This is how I deal with
loneliness in my life: I learn to love it, and then it isn't
loneliness, it's just lovely.

Now I would have to dress, make up, primp, and hus-
tle my haven't-been-to-the-gym-in-a-month butt down
to the China Club to meet Danielle for a martini.

"Ooh, tough life."

**"Please, not now. My mouth hurts and I have a
headache."**

"You can be such a whiny snot!"

"Umm, that's not a very nice thing to call yourself."

"Well, you just sound like such a diva."

**"Everyone else gets to bitch about their days and
extra pounds. Why can't I?"**

"Because we have to be above such things."

"You have such high hopes for me."

*"Stick with me and I will bring you to a higher conscious-
ness."*

"Really profound, idiot. You are me." Laughing at
myself.

"Whatever."

When I got to the bar, Danielle was already on her second shot of whiskey. I could tell the first one went down
quickly and had yet to take any effect.

"Hey, honey. Sorry I started without you. Time to catch up." Turning to the bartender, "Eric, can you please bring Lilly . . . dirty martini, right?" Asking me, I nod. "A dirty martini on the rocks with extra olives?"

Danielle took a cigarette out of her bag and lit up, taking a long drag as Eric set my drink in front of me.

"Thanks . . . so what is the big drama, Daniel? You know it is my house call night."

Danielle downed her second shot and grimaced loudly.

"Tom is getting married. He's engaged. I just found out today."

"What the fuck? Is this getting married thing a friggin' epidemic?! Everyone is getting married except for me!" Saying a little too loudly. "I can't take it!"

"You cannot still be on a tear about Maya?"

"I am a little. I suck, but I can't help it." Hanging my head. "Let's try this one again. Go ahead."

"Tom is getting married. He's engaged. I just found out today."

"Oh, shit. I'm so sorry!" Guessing now would be a good time to ditch the sarcasm. "Who told you? How did you find out?"

"He told me . . . just after I got dressed this morning . . ." The last part of her sentence tapered into a small silence.

"Excuse me? Rewind. What did you just say? Did I just hear something about dressing and morning and Tom?"

"He told me just after I got dressed." Pausing, swallowing, and then exploding. "Just after we had sex all night and all morning before work!"

"You're sleeping with *Tom*! What the fuck are you thinking, Danielle? That prick was so rude to you, rude to you, I might add, *six months ago*!" Yelling a bit too loudly. "How long has this been going on?"

SHE WAS FUCKING Tom again? What was this world coming to? Was it Groundhog Day? Did I wake up on the wrong side of the bed? Danielle met Tom a year ago at a work party. He was a commercial director doing a shoot for some product Danielle's company represented. He was new to LA, just in from New York. He didn't know anyone, and didn't know where to get a good drink or burger at two in the morning. All the things only a local would know. Somehow they got to talking, and Danielle agreed to help him find some groovy furniture for his rental. They made a date, and that date turned into a weekend date which turned into she-didn't-surface-for-about-three-weeks date.

When I met him over drinks at Super 8, my first thought was, what a hottie. Tall, skinny, dressed in Helmut Lang, big shiny brown eyes and this slightly devilish smile. I knew why Danielle was glowing, and I was so fucking jealous I thought everyone could see the green rising in my cheeks. It had been too long since a designer guy had eyes only for me. I wanted my own version of this man to spend days in bed with. Well, as it turned out, my face actually became green, but I think it was a nauseated reaction to this slimy piece of shit. Looks can be oh-so-deceiving! The minute Danielle went to the bathroom, he began totally Don Juaning me! Leaning in, smelling the perfume on my neck, telling me how if he had known Danielle had such a cute friend, he would have wanted to meet me sooner. I was shocked, embarrassed really. When Danielle sat down he returned to her side and pretended we had been talking about my work. I knew I couldn't tell her what had happened by the way she gazed into his eyes, that I-am-making-love-to-the-sexiest-man-and-he's-all-mine look.

Well, that little interlude was just the beginning. Once Tom had really settled into the LA swing of things and used Danielle to make all these great connections, I began hearing the stories. Tom and the hot young actress from his first feature. Tom and his friend Andrew with three Hawaiian Tropic fake-boob girls in Cannes. Tom and Channing, a rising new Jewel whose video he shot. There was even a story that Josh heard from his gay friend Tony about Tom and a male hustler at some Hollywood Hills fete. Josh and I tried to filter out the really ugly stories from Danielle, but in the beginning, no matter what she heard, she just didn't seem to care, because to her, Tom was the most charming, interesting, and kindest guy she had ever met. I will have to concede that he was really respectful of her when I saw them together, as if she were a piece of fine china he didn't want to break. Maybe it was just for show, but at those times, I could see why she fell for him. My friend does usually have good taste, so there had to be something there to make her stay.

The stories kept surfacing, and she eventually entered into this cycle of confrontation with him. He would deny every single accusation, then seduce her with his sneaky

34 charm, and finally fuck the anger out of her. This went on for a few months. Danielle convinced herself he loved only her, he had changed, and that she was truly happy with this guy we all knew was a pathetic loser. Danielle stayed the doting girlfriend until she caught him in her bed, wrapped in her favorite promotion-treat-to-herself Frette sheets, with her assistant, Mary. Tom didn't even try to apologize. I guess he figured there were greener pastures to fertilize, and it was time to enjoy them. This must sound like a bad version of *Melrose Place*, but hey, it happened, and I was there to pick up the pieces. And let's just say she was not an easy puzzle to put back together. Many hours of cheesy movies, indulgent, superfattening food, girl trips to Palm Springs and Napa, wild partying with our college buddies up in San Fran, flirtations with two handsomely stupid twenty-something actors I cajoled into freelance interviews. . . . Tiring, but it worked, and eventually the old Danielle was back. How could she, after everything that happened, have gone back there? After all that friend therapy? What was she thinking?

"CHILL A LITTLE, Lilly. Everyone is staring. Shit, if I had known you were going to act like this, I would have called someone else." Anxiously twirling a strand of her shoulder-length auburn hair. "Can't you just listen to me? This is not what I need right now."

"I just don't understand, Danielle. This guy was wrong for you. He's even too sleazy for a random night of sex with your ex. . . . How long have you been sleeping with him?" Swallowing the last of my drink. "Eric, one

more martini and another of whatever she's having when   35
you get a chance."

"I know Tom sucked. You think I have forgotten Mary
and how it felt to burn my favorite sheets? It's just that,
well, I was lonely and I missed him, missed being with
someone. It happened a few weeks ago after a really bad
blind date with that agent Josh fixed me up with. Anyway,
I bailed early from drinks, faked a headache, and decided
to go to this party Sandra from work told me about."

I shot her a look of contempt. Party, what party?

"Oh, Lilly! Stop with the left-out leper look! You
were at that movie thing with Max. . . Anyway, I was feeling a bit low, having been on yet another dead-end date,
with yet another dead-end guy, so when I walked in and
saw Tom my head just started swimming. Soon we were
talking like old times. He looked so good dressed in this
Prada suit we had bought on our trip to New York, and
we were just clicking like we used to. One thing led to
another, and he came home with me. It was so fantastic,
sort of like that final scene in *Like Water for Chocolate,* only
we didn't spontaneously burst into flames. It had been so
long since I had been with him or really anyone, and
Tom always knew just how to touch me."

"Okay, enough. You are sounding like some textbook
cliché on what happens when we run into exes when we
feel lonely. The rules girls would be very disappointed. I
do get it. I mean, I have no right to criticize you. I've
done it myself. It just doesn't sound like you're thinking
this is a fling. It sounds like you are falling for him again
and hoping to rekindle. From what you said, he obviously doesn't intend to let himself feel the same."

36   "Yeah . . . I know . . . but we have been spending pretty much every night together. He keeps telling me he loves me and that he wants us to get back together, that no one has affected him like me."

"Affected him? What does that mean? He can actually have an intelligent conversation with you?"

"We haven't really had many of those."

"No conversations? So basically what you are saying is, he whispers a few sweet things after he gets off and all of a sudden you can just forget all the shit he put you through? And, by the way, where the hell is this other girl if he's been with you so much?"

"I asked him the same thing this morning after I remembered how to speak, and apparently, Kira is a model off in Paris for the collections. They have been engaged for a few months." Taking a big chug of her drink. "Of course it had to be some beautiful model. That makes it all worse."

"Of course it would be. Tom is one of those guys who needs lots of pretty things around him. Don't you see what a stereotype he is? I didn't think guys like him really existed. They were only supposed to be stars on bad daytime."

"But, Lil, he was my cliché." Starting to whine.

"I know, but you have to be somewhat glad you aren't that poor girl, what was her name? Kira? Off in Paris getting cheated on the minute she leaves the country. Doesn't this just show you how much he really hasn't changed?"

"No. I mean, well, probably yes. Of course yes. That doesn't make it any easier. Right now I'm just bummed. I wish I was that girl." Pouting like Betty Boop.

"Well, so do I. What twenty-something woman wouldn't? Pretty, young, rich, anorexic. What can top that amazing combination?"

"Miss sarcasm, stop. Lilly this really sucks . . ." Getting quiet and sullen. "I still love him."

Danielle got real subdued and somber, and I realized there was no way to cheer her up. Eventually she would be okay. We all get up on the saddle again. Sometime.

"Okay, okay. I was hoping it wouldn't come to this, but now I am just going to have to get shitfaced with you and start dancing on the bar while reciting volumes of my bad poetry." Gesturing to the bartender. "Eric, another round and keep them coming. I plan on not seeing the bottom of my glass. And, Danielle, if you want to wallow and cry in your beer, I'll get some Kleenex and tell anyone who comments you got glitter in your eye."

"Thanks Lilly. Cheers . . ." Raising her drink. "To shitheads and models and best friends who are cool."

"We are cool." Clinking glasses with her.

"Too cool." Sighing as her face turned into the beginning of a smile.

Thank goodness I got her grinning. I was a little worried it would take a year and a day to get her to start feeling better. Poor thing. This was going to be one of those life-changing experiences. One that would tear her down, force her to reexamine herself, swallow a good helping of chicken soup for the soul, and rebuild herself into someone new and improved. I was glad to be there to listen and comfort her. Sometimes life isn't about being the star of the new disaster flick. Sometimes life lessons happen to those around you. That's why we have friends

38 in the first place. All of us have a duty to experience different things and report back. This way, we all don't get demolished at the same time doing the same things. We are each other's guinea pigs, testing out dating hypotheses for one another, and seeing which approach is the most effective. Who needs self-help books when you got buddies out there living life? Watching how your friends handle themselves in various situations arms you better for battle, and life can sometimes feel like a war. Everyone is screaming and shouting for attention, praying the bombs miss them, and hoping for peace, love, and understanding. And, sometimes, life is about picking up your buddy's purse, leaning down and listening to her heart to see if it's still ticking, leading her by the arm into the nearest toilet to puke and cry and get on with things, and then making sure she gets safely into a cab. Learning how to be a cheerleader is a wonderful academic challenge. Plus, I know that now, if any of my exes come slithering back, I will most certainly check their wallets for engagement ring receipts before dropping trou.

pink flamingos

After I managed to get Danielle and me
home, and after the room did ten spinning revolutions, I was surprised to find I
couldn't fall asleep. Drunk and drooling
is so not how I needed to be at three in
the morning on a school night. So, what
do you do when focus is blurred but bed
is impossible? Flick on the tube and pray
for a Shannon Tweed sexy psychiatrist
movie. I surfed until I landed on the
Independent Film Channel and a late-
night tribute to John Waters. It took me
about five minutes to realize what I was
watching, and I got queasy. Actually, I
ran, puked my brains out, and skulked
back to bed hoping I could get off my
personal teacup ride. The glorious *Pink
Flamingos*. Didn't think I would ever see
that one again or at least not for about
ten years. The film was a snapshot of my
most recent heartache. Its frames

40   reminded me of what I thought I had forgotten. Danielle had her Tom and I had my Jonah. Oh, boy.

I should have known our relationship was doomed when Jonah took me to see *Pink Flamingos* on our first date. I knew nothing of John Waters's earlier work featuring the lovely, if not vulgar, Divine. I had only seen that Johnny Depp flick, *Cry-Baby,* and Ricki Lake's *Hairspray* before she became the cheesy tell-all pulp TV hostess with the mostess. Those films were innocent enough, a lot of hot young things vamping it up, running around dancing and singing. Given the information I had, I was definitely not going to balk at this suggestion of the movie. Besides, in my mind, no movie could ever signal potential disaster because all you were doing was sitting in the dark, watching actors on a screen, and maybe, if you were lucky, touching hands inside the popcorn box. I had waited seven long months for this date, and I was going no matter what. I wanted this date! I wanted Jonah from the very first moment I met him.

I stumbled upon Jonah about three years ago, just after I graduated from college and came back to LA. It was at a random party of some guy who was friends with a guy Josh knew from college. Josh was a new friend at the time as well, but was slowly moving into that best-friend role of spending every minute together doing every single thing together. At this party, when I walked into the kitchen to get a beer, there was Jonah. Gorgeous. Tall, thin with "the hair." "The hair" being my ultimate turn-on and catch phrase. It fell to his shoulders and was wavy, thick, and black. Sam, my first love, had "the hair," and I let him have my virginity. So let's just say it worked for me. Jonah had the goods, and he had 'em good. I got the introduction and then a little 411 when Jonah left the room to go to the bathroom. Josh didn't know much except that he was from New York and sang. Ahhh, one more enticement for me to dig this guy. He was a musician.

"You get worse every day." Inner Lilly sighing. *"I can't believe what a cliché you are."*

"Stop making fun." Pouting ever so slightly. "You can't tell me that you have not had a fantasy about dating a rock star."

"Well . . ." Stuttering.

"Ha!" Triumphant. "Even you can't deny the power of hip-hugging leather, tribal tattoos, and luscious Mick Jagger lips."

"I prefer Lenny Kravitz myself." Caving ever so slightly.

"For once you are on my side. It's a miracle!"

"Come on, what chick, or guy for that matter, doesn't lust after disheveled, stubbly, longish-haired, sleepy-eyed lotharios that string words together like the pied piper? It is quite a normal fascination."

"Then why call me a cliché?"

"Because it's my job." Poking fun.

"Not like you weren't grooving right next to me to the Magic Melodies box set featuring Bread, Chris Isaak, and the Isley Brother's best and brightest love songs I just bought."

"That so was not me." Denying everything. *"You have no proof!"*

"Okay, okay. So I should just walk away from the handsome, dark-haired Jakob Dylan in the making, just a few rooms away, who could and would be ours? I can already hear the strains of 'Oh, Lilly.'"

"It will never work out, but how cool would it be to have a song named for us in the rock and roll song hall of fame?" **Getting excited.** *"You go, girl!"*

I had only one glitch in the plan to become Jonah's girlfriend. I met him when I was about to leave the country for my stint in Paris to live and learn the cook's life. Unfortunately, long before I met the man of my dreams, I decided I wanted to be a chef and that meant hopping a transatlantic flight to France. Cooking had been my thing in college, all that nurturing and entertaining made me happy-go-lucky. It was a natural extension of this passion to learn the basics of master technique in the heartland of three-star food. After staring at another form of passion, a more visceral one at that, food just didn't seem as important. When I met Jonah, I think I had only a few weeks left in the United States, and according to my parents, my ticket was definitely nonrefundable. All I could do was put my best foot forward and flirt my ass off while I still had time to make an impression. I managed to wheel and deal my way next to him, and we began talking. I don't remember a damn thing we talked about, but I am sure it was really important . . .

"This is very strange. When I met your sister recently, she told me that she wanted to introduce us. Here we are meeting totally randomly."

"Yeah . . . Maybe it's fate or something. . . . What was your name again?" Jonah, asking politely.

"Really great way to make an impression, Lilly."

"Lilly." Shutting down some of my smile wattage. "Jonah, right?"

"Yeah. So you want to get high?"

"Sure."

Now, if this wasn't the beginning of a love affair, I don't know what would be. I followed him into one of the bedrooms. It was painted this bright yellow color, almost like a school bus.

"I could never sleep in this room. I'd feel like I'm trapped inside a banana." Me, saying quietly.

"Me neither. It's draining. Isn't there some theory about colors and how they are attached to different emotions?" Asking me, while packing a small glass bowl with pot.

"I read that somewhere too. I think yellow's supposed to make people agitated and jumpy. They did this study and found that most household arguments take place in the kitchen and yellow is the most common color in kitchens."

"What about the other colors?" Sparking up the bud.

"I don't know that much, but red is supposed to keep you alert and awake, so it's bad for bedrooms, and purple is soothing and calming, so a lot of spas paint their walls lavender to boost their Zen quality." Taking the pipe from him.

"Lilly, you're rambling about what exactly?"

"Zen and color therapy." **Saying matter-of-factly.**

"Like that's normal? You sound like an idiot. What the hell kind of pot are you smoking?"

"I just started a book about Zen and spirituality. It's so cool that you mentioned it. It's called the *I Ching*. I haven't read that much of it, but when I finish, I'll tell you about it."

"Score one for the Lilman."

"Touché."

"That would be cool." Responding. "Josh told me that you sing. How's it working out?" Changing the subject.

"Okay. I'm just starting to get it going. Besides, I'm beginning my second year in law school right now. That takes up a lot of my time."

"Interesting combo." (And he's smart!!!!) "How do they all fit together?"

"Well, music is my real passion, but I'm fascinated by law and logic. It is hard, though, to do both. They originate from such different parts of my brain. I'll be psyched when I'm done with school and can focus on the music alone."

"Not planning on practicing?"

"Can you imagine me with short hair and a suit?"

"I don't know about the hair." Smiling. (NO WAY was I going to let him cut it.) "But I bet you'd look pretty good in a suit."

He laughed, and then, just when I was getting somewhere, his friend came in and sat down with us. That was essentially the end of our conversation. I got up to go find Josh, and when I stood up, I realized I was slightly woozy, more buzzed than I thought. The minute Josh saw me, he could not resist rubbing it in.

"Eyes are looking a little red there, missy. Where have you been for the last half hour?"

"What do you mean? It's been a half hour?" Playing dumb.

"Hummm, yeah. I'm ready to go, are you?" Pronouncing in that tone where I knew he wasn't asking but telling while still trying to appear nice.

"I guess. Where to?"

"Why don't you guys come with us? We're going to this
after-hours bar in Hollywood, Vigo's." A voice says from
behind me.

"Where is it, Jonah?" Josh, asking.

"It's on Sunset. You know where it runs into Hollywood. It doesn't have a sign, but there are usually motor-
cycles in front and some biker dudes."

"Sounds appealing . . ." Josh, trying to hide his sarcasm. "Lilly, what do you want to do?"

"Whatever." Trying hard not to give away my total and
complete desire to go anywhere with this guy. I probably
would have agreed to a walking tour of the city dump after
a rainstorm if asked.

"You're coming then. I'm deciding for you. We'll see
you there." Jonah, stating with authority while turning
toward the door.

And we were off. The minute I got in the car, Josh began
ribbing me, the way only a friend does. I didn't think I
had been that obvious, but a good friend has a way of seeing through you with Superman's X-ray vision or something. He seems to know even the secrets you keep from
yourself. The entire ride there, all I heard was, "Lilly's
got a crush," "Your new boyfriend is cute," "Maybe he'll
sing a song for you." On and on and on he went, but I
had to smile because it was true, all true.

Vigo's ended up being a very, very scary place. Not our
scene at all. I knew when we walked in, and the sixty-year-
old Hell's Angel biker at the door gave me the once-over,
that this was just not our cup of tea. The fact that I was
dressed all prim and proper in my cat-eye glasses and
black-and-white houndstooth pants didn't help in mak-

46 ing me feel at ease. As it turned out, Vigo's was also a strip bar; we just were too early for the show. Oh, too bad. . .

"What do you think, Lilly?" Jonah asking, handing me a beer.

"Well, this isn't like any other place I've been." Taking a very big gulp trying to wash down the taste of my nerves.

"Should I interpret that in a positive or negative light?"

"To be honest, I'm not real sure. I'd have to get back to you." Swallowing another big gulp. Those nerves would just not stay down!

Idle bullshit went on for about twenty minutes, and then I got the eye from Josh. Quite frankly, I was glad to see that eye, because the place was starting to irritate me as more and more been-drinking-all-night-with-my-buddies-want-to-see-some-titties type boys filtered in.

"Jonah, we're out of here. See you later." Josh saying while standing up.

"Bye, Jonah. It was nice meeting you." Extending my hand toward him. "Maybe we'll get to talk about that book sometime."

"Sure." Taking my hand. "Lilly, I'll see you soon."

I could swear Jonah gave me a little hand squeeze, but it was three in the morning, so it could have been a tired muscle twitch or more simply an overeager hallucination on my part. As Josh and I walked out through biker heaven, I knew I was gone head-over-heels-over-a-fucking-steep-cliff for this guy. The chemical reaction known as lust was slowly beginning to ignite in my blood-stream. Things were popping, and I felt a million little butterflies fluttering. Funny, though, every opportunity I had to work my mojo on him before I left for Paris failed miserably. There was one dinner at Diva with a group of us that was full of bad service and bad table placement. (He was all the way at the other end.) Then there was the Halloween fiasco.

My brother and a bunch of his friends were throwing a huge bash in the Hills to which I had invited Jonah. There were crazy costumes, invited cops, and loud techno beats blaring from the DJ. Five hundred people milled about drinking and laughing on a lawn decorated with twinkling lights, twenty hand-carved jack-o'-lanterns, and enough fake spiderwebs to give an exterminator arachnophobia. I decided, along with a few other idiots, that this was the perfect place to trip on some God-forsaken illegal substance. Not a good move, because when my Romeo made his way to the party, I was off on some back terrace reciting Juliet's balcony scene with a tree. There was no hurried tryst after that, just me on a plane, alone, bound for France.

Months passed, I chilled in Paris, and I forgot about him.

"Yeah, right, you forgot about him, Miss Fantasizer."

"Excuse me? You know, you are starting to get on my nerves. I do not fantasize about guys I barely know." Answering my inner voice. **"Besides you were all for the 'fall for the rocker fantasy' not too long ago."**

"True, but that was just a moment of weakness. Lenny Kravitz's **Behind the Music** *had been on repeat all weekend."* Explaining. *"This is reality now. You are going a little over the edge."*

"Edge, what edge? I am already talking to myself, how much worse can it get?"

"Much. Listen, I'm just speaking the truth and you know it. You can't hide from me. I know everything."

"What do you mean, hide from you? I am me and you are some whacked out, sarcastic figment of my imagination who gets more punchy every day."

"Hummm, whacked out, sarcastic figment, you have such high regard for yourself. Personally, I would have hoped for wise, truthful babe."

"Shut up already. You don't even exist. Besides, if I knew yet what was going to happen with Jonah or any guy for that matter, you'd never get material for developing this wry banter you are so fond of."

"How sweet. You fuck up for me. I'll remember that. Tootles." Fading into a hushed hum.

Where was I? Oh yeah, I tried not to spend a really long time thinking about Jonah in Paris. There was school to worry about and flings with French men to consider, but somewhere along the line, he got the best of me and I decided to write him a letter. It was all about music and my trip to London, the drum-and-base capital of the world. Maybe he'd write back, maybe not, but I needed to plant a little reminder seed that I hoped would sprout into a full-blown Lilly tree as soon as I returned to the good ol' US of A.

You probably think that I have forgotten all about *Pink Flamingos* and the start of this little anecdote but, hey, what's a love story without a long preamble? All this time, before the actual date, was when I built Jonah into Adonis. Jonah was cute and all before I left, but in Paris he became a God. It was a rather simple equation: loneliness + silly crush — reality check = full-blown obsession. I probably just had a lot of time on my hands, but there is something about not seeing someone, not talking to someone, nor hearing about someone for a long time that makes him hot, smart, funny, charming, witty, honest, respectful, interesting, and passionate. Sure, we never exchanged new words, but what does that matter? I loved my image of him, and I knew it was all true. . . . Well, it was going to be true.

Jonah became perfect and perfectly in love with me when I actually got a letter back. I remember the exact moment I got it. Danielle took a week off her job and decided to spend her vacation in Paris visiting me. It was her first night there, and we were on the way out to dinner when my concierge placed the sacred missive in my hands. Immediately, I ripped into the paper and read the black scrawl as we walked down Boulevard Saint-Germain toward the restaurant.

"What does it say?" Danielle asking, leaning in.

"Nothing, really, but he signed it, 'Love, Jonah'! I'll read it to you when we get to Cosi." Folding the letter, putting it in my purse.

"Promise?"

"Of course, let's hurry." Quickening the pace.

We ordered some sandwiches and wine and spent the next three hours pouring over his handwriting, his words, the little "love" he signed before his name. We read into every single nuance. By the time we got home, Danielle and I were convinced this guy had spent months pining for me. He must have dug me since he wrote. It was hard enough getting my dad to write me a letter much less a stud boy who thought he was really cool.

50   **"Psst. Hey you. Have you read that letter recently?"**
Inner Lilly, questioning.

     "Speak up, I can't hear you." Feigning deafness.

     "I asked if you have reread that letter recently."

     "No, not since then. Why?" Trying to ignore her.

     "Well, just thought you might want to."

     "And why is that?"

     "Because you would blatantly see that nothing was said in that letter, nothing at all. You created your own little interpretation full of love and possibility from basically something that said, 'Hi, Lilly, what's up? My music is going well. Wrote some new songs. See ya soon, Bye. Love, Jonah.'"

     "Yeah . . . so what's your point? It said 'love.'"

     "God, you are desperate. If you had just been a little more based in the real world you would have seen nothing was there from the beginning."

     "Maybe I didn't want to see. Why do you constantly have to remind me of my failures? Don't you think I know that I fuck myself over with my imagination?"
Whining.

     "I'm not trying to make you feel bad, just avoid lame-ass situations like the one you're in store for." Replying wisely.

     "Well, if I avoid them, how do you get to be so smart and experienced? I toil in the fields so you can grow bright and strong."

     "YUCK! What kind of strawberry shortcake saccharine-sweet metaphor is that? 'I toil in the fields so you grow bright and strong'? Where did you get that? Hallmark Hall of Fame? I thought you were a poet?"

     "I hate you."

     "Love you."

Unfortunately, I somehow have created this one rule for myself that I have yet to break. Jump first, look after. No matter how many scars I get, nor words of prevention my inner voice tries to spout, I still can't convince myself to really listen to myself. Why is that? Because, if I for once unclogged my gut reaction channel, I would have assuredly avoided seeing what was essentially a satirical porno flick on my first date with a guy I so wanted to kiss.

When I returned home from Paris, I called, he answered, and we made plans. Apparently, there was a little Lilly sapling slowly growing somewhere in the back of his mind. However, I should have paid more attention to her nurturing and development. Maybe gone for a simple coffee, slice of pizza, or a beer instead of that film. *Pink Flamingos* was filled with penises, dog shit as a food group, strippers, flashers, and just about every sexual abomination you could think of and then some you never could have imagined. I think I was the color of a very ripe tomato the entire time I sat in the threadbare theater seat. Who said movies were harmless? Oh yeah, me. It was about the time when some guy's ass in full close-up was taking a dump that I had to flee to the bathroom. Sure, I was a somewhat mature girl, but that was too much. I fell into this hysterical giggle fit in there as I stared at myself in the mirror. How was I ever going to look this guy in the face? Did I have to go back in and sit down? Help!

It took me about five minutes to calm myself down, and I reluctantly returned to my seat. When the movie ended, there was the issue of how did I handle myself when my skin had crawled off my body and hidden inside my purse? Was I supposed to be appalled, embarrassed, intellectual? Talk about the film and its cinematic importance or pretend that we were never there and just ignore the last two hours? Why did this have to happen to me?

"Well, that was interesting." Saying, somewhat blushing, as we walked to his car.

"Yeah." Clearing his throat as his face too began getting a little red.

Jonah then fumbled for the keys not really knowing what else to say.

"Jonah, how about next time I choose the movie?"

"That seems fair."

"How about the time after that and the time after that?" Giving him a little flirty nudge.

"Hey, let's not get ahead of ourselves. One bad pick on my part grants you one movie selection, not three." Nudging me back.

"One bad pick? This is not what I call a bad pick. This is beyond that. A bad pick is like a Kung Fu dubbed action movie, or *Species III*."

"I like action movies."

"So do I, but that's not the point. It was just an example."

"What are we talking about anyway, Lilly?" Starting to laugh.

"Nothing really, just bullshit. Personally, I'm just trying to avoid talking about the movie we just saw. Pretty much anything would do."

"I guess I am too. I'm sorry, I didn't know it was going to be like that."

"It's cool, I just get to pick the next few movies we see." Grinning.

"Okay . . . I can deal with that. Let's get out of here."

Although there were other movies and other dates, I think that film haunted everything else. The foundation was all screwed up. That's probably why we never got to sleep together. Fear of flying chickens or something. Who knows? When I told my brother what we did on our date, he just cracked up. Apparently, it was so humorous that Max went on to tell every one of his friends, every single opportunity he had. Had Jonah and I got married, Max would have found a way to work it into a very funny embarrassing roast . . . I mean toast.

Pink Flamingos was only the beginning of a long line of strange movies and stranger conversations in the strangest of places. We'd talk about history and politics in alleys behind bars, art and music in a small booth at Damiano's surrounded by darkness and Italian wine, and foreign films in the back bathroom at his friend's house. The more we talked, the harder I fell. When he did lay the first kiss on me, I melted into the tiles beneath my feet. I felt like I was floating. For about three weeks, we kissed and joked and hung out, and then we had a fateful discussion about him and his music and focus, and I was relegated to the role of friend. Yes, it only took a measly few weeks.

"Lilly, I can't do this." Whispering in my ear over the loud music.

"Do what? Dance?" Oblivious to what was coming.

"This. Us." Pulling me over to the bar. "You are too distracting."

"What does that mean?" Looking him in the eyes. "Distracting good or bad?"

"Distracting bad because it's good."

"Huh?"

"I just don't want any responsibility. No ties with any-one."

"But what then has been going on with us? Am I crazy to think that maybe we were starting something here?" Getting a little upset. "I thought that things were going great."

"No, you're not crazy, and they are. But I just can't do it. Like yesterday, when we were supposed to hang out and I was in the studio. All I could think about was how mad you might get with me because I was flaking on you. My head wasn't on my music, it was on the fact that I had to find a phone and find you and deal."

"You are making a bigger thing out of all this than you have to. I like that you have all this passion and love for music. It's why I like you. I don't want to fuck that up." Trying to talk him back into liking me.

"I know, but I just can't be involved. The whole girl-friend thing isn't what I want right now, and that's where this looks like it is going. I like you too much to continue."

"That really does not make sense."

"Maybe not, but I know it just won't work. I'll become a dick and do everything wrong, and then you'll refuse to even talk to me."

"So, that's it?" Looking at him.

"I guess so. Friends?"

"It's not like I have a choice." Smiling a weak, sad smile.

As quickly as that conversational exchange occurred, I became his friend. By agreeing to something I did not want, I managed to keep him in my life. It was the only way I could get to be around him at all. I needed my fix.

The "just friends" thing was only a small percentage of what I wanted from him. It would make me cry and complain to my friends, but time went on, and I started to realize that maybe being around him wasn't the best idea. Spending every moment focused on him was probably not so healthy for me. Gradually we parted and I faded away.

We would still talk and see each other sometimes, but it got to be less often and less necessary on my part. Thinking about it now, it's been awhile since all this happened. Furthermore, besides Jonah, lots of things that I had planned didn't work out. I didn't last long as a chef: the whole nurturing, feeding, and enjoying food went south as soon as I was relegated to pitting flats of cherries, kneading dough, and cleaning lettuce leaves. Food stopped being about the enjoyment of someone else's pleasure in eating something I made, and became a tedious rush to produce a small part of a meal that no one would ever know I had a hand in at all. I started writing instead, and as mentioned before, began writing for magazines and then started working for *Chick*. Everything changed and here I am all grown up. Time passes and lives evolve. My plate became full of so much more than him and food. In reality, you can only go so far into the I-want-more-and-he-wants-to-be-friends scenario, because soon you start to hurt yourself more than he ever did and then it is totally your own fault for sticking around too long. It took some doing, but I thought I finally let go.

THAT'S WHY THIS resurgence of Jonah images tonight threw me for a small loop. By the time I fell asleep and

56 tried to deal with all the memories of Jonah that resurfaced, it was well into early morning. When I showed up at my parents' house the next evening, the lack of zzz's was pretty obvious. My face hurt I was so tired, and my mom could not resist.

"Lilly, you look like hell." Hugging me. "Long day at work?"

"Yeah, but more like long night without sleep." Throwing my keys and purse onto the waxed wooden breakfront. "Is there anything good in the fridge?" Walking into the kitchen.

"I made some hummus and there is pita in the pantry. Were you out last night?" Following me.

"Sort of. I went out with Danielle. Her old boyfriend is getting married to some waif."

"Ouch. Is she okay?" Getting some plates down.

"Yeah, probably hungover though."

"So, you were drinking?"

"Yeah, but it was more like I laid in bed for hours thinking about things." Pulling the container out of the fridge.

I walked to the silverware drawer and grabbed a spoon.

"Maya?" Grabbing some glasses.

"That, and for some reason I got on this whole Jonah vibe."

"Jonah? Oh, Lilly." Shaking her head at me.

"Please, I am done with that. Don't worry."

"I do. You were a disaster."

"Don't." Cutting her off. "Look, never mind. Where are the books for our trip?"

I slowly scooped hummus methodically onto my plate.

If I stared hard enough at the cement-colored mixture, placed it in perfect globs, and didn't say a word, maybe my mother would get a clue and drop the subject. I was on my fifth scoop when I realized she was not seeing my silent signs. Not like they were that obvious, but mothers are supposed to have KSP: kid sensory powers.

"Lilly, that boy wasn't one of your better picks. You think I don't know how many times you cried yourself to sleep?" Pushing on. "You created this intense fantasy of a boyfriend practically before you knew his last name."

"Mom!" Eyeing her. "Let's start planning this American adventure of ours." Trying to fully get Mom off the subject.

"Okay, okay, but Lilly, you really have to get that guy out of your head."

My sixth scoop. No way could I endeavor to eat this much Middle Eastern fare. I would be in the bathroom for years! Another vocal prompt.

"I know, Mom. I know." Getting annoyed. "Just drop it."

"Fine. The books are on the table and I got a few maps from Triple A today."

"I am getting more and more excited for this minivacation every day." Sitting down.

"Me too." Sitting down next to me and kissing my cheek. "Let's start with this one."

As Mom talked and plotted points all along the Southwest, I kept flashing to her face when I mentioned Jonah. It was like she had eaten a kumquat. I hate that face, the disapproving-yet-trying-to-be-caring face. Man, parents have this knack for reminding you about all the stupid things you did, how stupid the guy was, and how you are supposed to be this evolved chick who is way past all that. And I guess so do best friends, since I did this exact thing to Danielle. I am such a hypocrite. It seems to be easier to pontificate on the virtues of being a tough chica than to actually whip yourself into Wonder Woman shape.

My mom was right about the whole imaginary, day-dreamy fantasy thing. When I think back to what really went down between Jonah and me, it really wasn't all his fault that things didn't work out. Sure, he kissed me and strung me along a bit, making me think we could be more, but I was the one that brought drama to the situation. I forgot that there were two people in the relationship. I pushed and tried to get what I wanted without listening to him. I had all these expectations and ideals that weighed down the situation and put it into this impossible reality. He let me down as easy as he could when we had that friend talk; I just couldn't let go. That was my fault. I seem to do that a lot. I fall for men so quickly that I forget they are even there and that they might have needs and opinions too. Soon they don't even exist as a living, breathing entity—they are trans-formed into a model of what I think they should be. That can't work. Maybe I do pick the wrong guys for myself, guys that aren't ready for or capable of handling my emotional nakedness, but I undress my own feelings. Today, though, I just wasn't in the mood for outsiders, even loving mothers, to judge and comment on my behavior.

reunited and it feels so good

Why was Jonah entering my thoughts?
Too much time has passed since he was in
my life for him to resurface fully. I know
he still lingers just in the back of my
head. All past loves have to inhabit some
part of me, or why bother liking and loving in the first place? I have this theory
that if you forget about them completely,
then you never really had a connection to
them in the first place. The ones that
stick are those that you will tell your
daughter all about when she is utterly
convinced that you have absolutely no
clue about boys. However, that's just it,
they are supposed to be little treats to pull
out when you are old, sagging, gray, and
need to be reminded of what it was like to
be foolish. Jonah is one of my locked in
the attic guys (I don't mean that in a
serial killer way), but he is not supposed
to come out to play anymore.

60   I admit that sometimes he's close enough that I still have fantasies of things working out, but I try to suffocate that notion. I know that even though I'm a hopeless romantic, he's never going to be "the one." I just accept that Jonah imprinted himself onto me in a way. I just can't seem to lose him, like those last five pounds when you are dieting. The ones that attach to your inner thighs and warble "Hot Lunch" every time you take a step. I try to keep moving forward. Until someone else rides up on a white horse (at this point, I'd even settle for a brown donkey), I have him there, and for now that's okay. We all have memories of those intense crushes we don't want to shake permanently, since those infatuations remind us how to fall and get flustered. I kind of don't want to lose his shadow, not just yet anyway. I like the company.

It did take me a few days to shake off the cloud of alcohol and memory lameness, but that's to be expected. When Jonah pops up, he tends to languish for a little while. He knocks me back, I flounder, and then I rise like a postmodern phoenix, still okay, still me. The only problem is that I'm not sleeping. This flashback of losing the man I thought was the man of my dreams, combined with the constant nudge of Maya's good fortune, have totally rattled me. I have never been so stressed. She's marrying her one and only, and I just have foolish memories of an obsession long past. Maya and I are on such different pages and that really bothers me. Every phone call I get from Maya detailing her wedding planning adventures peels away another layer of my confidence. I am an onion girl, slowly being revealed by an overeager cook. I try to be happy and bouncy and better, and I know I am convincing enough for her not to notice, but

I just can't convince myself that everything is okay again. 61
Rationally, nothing has really happened to me. My days
are spent as they always have been, but when I am lying
alone at night in my big bed I'm lying on a bed of pins. I
can't sleep anymore.

"MOM, I CAN'T sleep again." Telling her one morning.
"It's five before I get shut-eye."

"Why not?" Huffing a bit, seeing how I caught her on
the treadmill. "Still thinking about Jonah?"

"No, I don't know. Maybe." Giving in. "It's everything.
The minute my head hits the pillow, my mind races and
soon birds are chirping."

"Did you try warm milk?" Asking through a pant.

"What? Warm milk?" Laughing at her. "Who are you?"

"Your mother."

"Duh. Seriously, Mom, what am I going to do? I have
bags stretching down my face!"

"Why don't you try meditating or yoga? Something
that will calm you and focus you."

"Maybe."

"I have to go, Lilly. I will call you later."

Okay, meditation. I can do that. It's Saturday. Lay
down, breathe steady, focus on that pond with the dripping waterfall and cool breeze, and calm my mind.
Breathe. In and out. Long breaths. I can feel the sun on
my skin. I can hear the rush of water. I can see the sand.
I can see . . . Wait a minute . . . Who the hell is that?
Oh no . . . I am not alone. I hear laughter and cheers.
People are everywhere. I'm naked. They are laughing at
me. They are pointing. I am not calm. I am not happy. I

62   have no peace. So much for fucking meditation. I can't relax.

"Mom, it did not work." Calling her back.

"Lilly, I told you I was exercising."

"But it didn't work and I'm so tired." Whining.

"Right now, I'm tired of this." Huffing into the receiver. "Did you already have coffee?"

"Yes."

"Well, there you go." Breathing hard through her mouth. "Try it tonight. I'm hanging up."

That night I put on my flannel cloud pajamas, made some warm milk, and snuggled into my flannel sheets. I shut the light off and tried to focus. Breathe, focus, breathe, concentrate, and count to ten. There's sunshine, an island breeze, nice Rasta music coming from the trees. It all sparkles and glows, wrapping around me like a smile. I walk along the sand. I stare at the horizon. I don't watch where I am walking. I step on a jellyfish. It stings me. It hurts like a motherfucker. A hand reaches for me. I get pushed down. I get peed on. I am soaked with some stranger's urine. I'm awake. I'm awake all night.

"Lilly, what are you doing to yourself?"

"I don't know. I just feel off."

"You are becoming this masochistic monster. Stop ramming yourself into walls. I am exhausted, and you know how easily we bruise!"

"Like I am doing all this on purpose?"

"It is just hard for me to watch how over the last few weeks your newly achieved and highly appreciated sense of self has taking skydiving lessons." Lecturing me. *"Somehow, Maya's blessed union has started you questioning all over again who you are and what you have to offer anyone."*

"No kidding. The fact that she's becoming a forever while I am stuck in this limbo of forget-me-nots is shattering all the proud-to-be-me work I have done." Agreeing with the lecture. **"So much for the 'I love myself,' 'I love my body,' 'I am funny,' 'I am charming,' 'I kick ass,' 'I am brilliant,' 'I can be anything I want to be,' and 'Girl Power' yellow stickies I pasted by my bathroom mirror."**

"Just go to the loo and look at them again. Try to assimilate."

"Yes, ma'am."

My third night without sleep and another failed attempt at meditation went something like this: I'm in bed. Snuggled. I breathe, in and out. Relax. Be calm. Feel the warm sun on my face. I'm in a park. The grass has just been cut and it smells like spring. In the distance, a Frisbee flies through the sky. Birds chirp and squirrels dart along my footprints looking for acorns. I see a group of children playing duck duck goose. Somehow, I'm in the circle. I'm part of the game. I close my eyes waiting for the tap. I feel a pat on my head and a loud yell. *Goose!* I pop up and run, but there's no one to catch. Everyone has vanished. All I hear are the echoes of children's laughter. I am alone again.

As I sat with my umpteenth cup of steamed milk and watched the sun rise, I tried to figure out what was going on with me. What was going on in my head? Every time I tried to rest, I tapped into a pool of insecurity that seemed to prevent me from the contentment of a good night's sleep. Lucky for me, I think I might have found some answers. I could just be delusional, but whatever works. Maybe the game in that last meditation was a representation of Maya's wedding. I know that sounds a

64   little too Freudian, but I really think it might be so. Like I was picked to play and everyone knew I haven't been playing with my heart, so my friends just bailed.

Somehow they knew I wasn't being a team player. I was being a me-me-me all-star girl. Maya is my best friend, and I owe it to her to participate and give my all. She's always been there for me. I need to step out of my selfishness. Conveniently, I'm supposed to go up to San Fran to see her and go dress shopping with her and her mom next month. I figure resolving some of my issues before I go would be a great move, or I'll end up a puddle in the Happy Bride shop. After finally getting a few relatively restful hours of shut-eye, I woke up with one thing on my mind. It was time to come clean with my girl. I called her from work, and let it all spill out.

"Hi, it's me."

"Hi. I was just going to call you to see what time your plane is getting in so I can meet you at the airport."

"It's still over a month away." Looking at my computer. "I don't have a clue."

"I know, but I'm so crazy lately that things have to get in my calendar quickly or I space."

"This planning is nuts, huh?"

"You have no idea." Sighing. "I'm beat."

"Sorry to hear that. Hold on while I check the time." Grabbing my purse and pulling out my date book. "Okay, I arrive at eleven-ten. USAir flight 221."

"Great. My mom has called every day and sent every bride magazine to me. By the time she gets here, I am going to know absolutely everything about china and registering."

"She's just excited."

"Chomping at the bit is more like it. She made tons of appointments at all the stores."

"Why do you not sound excited?"

"I'm just tired. I'm so glad you will be here to help." Saying sweetly. "You're my respite."

"Me too, and thanks."

"By the way, I made a reservation at that restaurant you like and everyone is coming to meet us so they can see you. Jack, Emily, everyone." (Most of our college friends all live up north; I am the lone LA chick basking in my smog and smoothie culture.)

"That sounds terrific. Thanks for setting it up so I can see everyone."

"No problem. I'm just glad you can come up and deal with the dress thing. I want your opinion." Gushing more. "We can also start looking for the bridesmaid outfits."

"Listen, Maya. I have to tell you something." Broaching the subject. "I don't really know how to start."

"What is it? What's wrong?"

"I just . . . I don't know." Hedging. "I just have reacted very badly to this wedding business and feel I should apologize."

"What do you mean? You have been great. I mean, you sent cards and flowers and are coming up to help. If anyone should be apologizing it should be me because everything has become wedding this and wedding that. I'm Martha Stewart on speed."

"No, you are perfect. I have just been thinking all these evil thoughts."

"Evil thoughts?"

"Not evil thoughts about you, just about how all this changes everything for us. I have been in a panic that you and I will no longer be a you and I now that you have him."

"That is so silly. I have been with him for years now and nothing has changed."

"I know, but wedding and marriage just equaled me losing you."

"That's not going to happen."

"I've been so selfish." Trying to explain. "I have been a flaming jealous hag."

"Well, I would be acting the same way if the roles were reversed."

"Really?"

"Of course. I think all those envious feelings and shit are so normal."

"You are making this very easy on me."

"Of course I am. I need you to be okay with all this. Besides, without you, I would have to depend on Emily to be my ear and helper, and you know how disinterested she is in shopping and primping."

"That's true. So."

"So, I will see you soon."

"With bells on."

That went really well, and surprisingly enough, she's still the same. No wedding beast has taken her over like in *Invasion of the Body Snatchers.* I love my friend. Unfortunately, though, all my problems are not solved. I was naive to think that telling Maya what was lurking in my head would fix everything. I still have work to do on remedying all this insecurity. Something tells me it is just the tip of the iceberg. The good vibes associated with Maya only lasted for about three hours. Things crashed again when I stupidly decided to take the new made-peace-with-my-friend relaxed version of me shopping after work.

I love shopping. There is a little bit of magic found in buying something new. It is instant gratification, a quick fix. The shelves lined with pastel cashmere sweaters, the racks with neatly pressed pants, tables strewn with baubles and bangles sparkling in the afternoon light, the trendy music grooving behind the walls, and the array of flowery or functional bias-cut skirts flowing in the doorway entice me. They seduce me with their potential, with their newness. They are not tainted by bad outfit memories or stains of even worse dates; they are pure. They greet me like a new lover, full of possibility and excitement. But, hello, reality check. No way in hell did I need four new pairs of shoes! It wasn't like I planned to buy them, but the shopping trip turned into a really ugly self-confidence-busting disaster. The store lost its charm and became evil, scoffing at me like a controlling, overcritical, high-maintenance boyfriend.

I went out under the guise that I was in search of a new pair of dark blue jeans because I had just spilled half a bottle of bleach on my favorite Earls and the acid wash look is just so 1983. That was all I was going to buy (wink, wink). So, jeans, easy enough, right? Wrong. I went to the jeans department at Fred's and with the help of a muffin with dreads, I tried to find a replacement. Well, I must have started eating like a pig since Maya's announcement because every fucking pair did not fit at

68 all. With each yank and pull of a fly, I got more and more depressed. Watching the cellulite bulge from above the waistband or hinder the closing of buttons smashed my already faltering ego. Jeans are the all-American staple, and I couldn't find one style to minimize my ass and enhance my cowboy girl chic. What is a girl to do when she can't even fit into the American jean dream?

First, she puts one pair on hold, so her sales guy doesn't know that she has gained ten pounds and has become a girl that a guy with delicious looks would never want to touch. Second, she heads off to the trendy skirt, sweater, and miscellaneous section of the store to redeem herself and find something to hide her flaws. Third, she tries on another slew of merchandise that was obviously all cut poorly and made for wee lassies because again, nothing fits. By now, the girl is beaten, bleeding, and utterly bruised from this vicious attack of the too-small-for-normal-people clothes. She gets in the car, but not before buying a chocolate chip cookie and stuffing it in her angry mouth as she peels out of the parking lot. Somehow, the car drives her to a big department store with an even bigger shoe department. She parks and retreats into the cool white marble Mecca.

She is on a mission. At the Prada section, she runs her hands over the platform heels and Velcros and un-Velcros the tiny straps, listening to the crisp crackle of man-made materials. She smells the leather and pulls out three pairs to try on. Then she heads for the Gucci section. These picks are way out of her league since each shoe costs half her salary, but the candy-colored beaded heels are beckoning her, calling her name like a hot fudge sundae. She can't resist their shine, and she

blindly tosses two pairs to the awaiting salesgirl. Manolos
come next. Their siren call is even more detrimental to
her budget. There is no way she can afford the spindly
stilettos, or actually be able to walk in them, but they look
at her lovingly, standing squarely on the shelf, defining
female power. She picks up a black three-strap heel with
one red rose at the ankle and rubs the shoe across her
cheek, tickling herself with the suede. The salesgirl is ready
to catch it as she moves on. At every table she stops and
admires the careful craftsmanship, the high-performance
spongy soles, the delicate sequins, and the artful contrast
of colors. She amasses four more pairs to slip her peds
into, and she finally sits down before her igloo of shoes.

A half hour and major debt later, she walks out of the
building holding the much sought after shopping bags,
but she doesn't feel like she should. Shopping only made
her feel worse and more empty. She should have known
better. She heads home, strips, and stands naked in her
new heels in front of the mirror. Even though her feet
look divine, she feels rotten. The phone rings, she bolts
for it, trips on the shoes, stubs her toe, and breaks a nail
as she answers. She has no luck.

"Lilly, I need to go out." Danielle, saying desperately.
"It's been a shit day."

"No kidding." Sobbing loudly, venting all frustration.
"I just spent too much money on shoes I didn't need,
realized that I'm a fat cow and have to lose ten pounds
asap, and just broke my toe running to get the goddamn
phone."

"Are you okay? Take a deep breath." Calming me. "Is
it swelling?"

"No." Sniffling. "I'm okay. What crushed you today?"

"I saw a picture of Tom and his waif in a magazine kissing their mouths off."

"Oh, sorry sweetie, you win. Where are we going?"

"The usual place, I'm not in the mood for something new and improved."

"Meet you at your place at ten, then we will go together."

"Wear the new shoes, I want to see them."

"If I can walk." Hanging up.

We met, greeted each other, headed to the bar, and ordered tequila shots right off the bat. Danielle looked like she was in mourning, her face pale and puffy. I looked like I was in mourning too, head-to-toe black clothing to hide the extra you-know-what. We made quite a couple. At least we had each other. After we had downed the third shot of the evening, two handsome strangers asked to join us at our table. Well, I think they were handsome. Anyway, things began to spin, rattle, and run off our normal course. Women on the verge and horny wanna-be musicians with wallet chains and perfectly worn vintage Atari tees are a dangerous mix. I will call them Robert and Shane, seeing how introductions were a little vague. They ordered more shots, we drank eagerly, looking to drown our sorrows in the mind-numbing amber liquid. Danielle gravitated to Robert after he made some comment about hating models, and I got attached to my cowboy, Shane, or maybe it was Ethan? Damn it!

We closed the bar down and wandered out into the cool night. Danielle and I had cabbed it, so I searched for my cell to call our yellow knight. Before I could dial,

Robert had a car, he and Shane had beers at their place, the night was still young, and we were playing dumb. Besides, the whole psychokiller boy throwing you into a trunk, torturing you, and then leaving you in the Mojave Desert to wander scenario loses some of its intensity when you are with your best friend and are armed with a sharp pair of stilettos. Not like that has any real logic behind it, but it did quiet my inner voice for the moment.

Somewhere in Silver Lake, Danielle and I walked into a big green house with fluorescent pink bougainvillea wrapped around the sides. Inside, it smelled like sweat-socks and incense. The pungent odor tweaked my nose as soon as I entered. While the guys went to get the aforementioned beers, we sat down on a brown velvet couch dotted with Indian batik pillows and old Mexican blankets. Concert posters lined the walls, and a mountain of records and CDs lay jumbled in a heap next to a large stereo system. A guitar leaned against the doorjamb like a wallflower, and half-melted candles sat stuck to a three-legged wooden coffee table. Danielle offered me a cigarette, and we puffed away. Robert yelled from the other room.

"D, put on some music. Whatever you want."

"Sure." She called back. "D"?

"How endearing. He is already using nicknames."

"It must be love." Getting up and moving toward the mess. "Let's see what we have here."

"Well?" Asking her as I sucked down my smoke.

"Not like I can tell, nothing is in the cases." Reaching for another CD. "I hate when people do that. It is so

irritating to open up a case and find nothing or something you weren't looking for."

"Just play anything. Who cares?" Ashing my cigarette
in a candle on the table.

"How about *Buena Vista Social Club*?"

"Fine. How cultured of them."

"They are musicians."

"But who the fuck are they in the first place?" Starting
to laugh as I reached inside my purse for some gloss.

"No shit! Lil, where the fuck are we?"

"Got me, but it looks vaguely like college." Looking
around again.

"I haven't seen tapestry like this since junior year."

"Are you drunk?"

"Totally. You?"

"Enough." Assessing her balance quotient.

"Are you horny?"

"Too much."

"Should we bail?"

"Are they cute?"

"Think so."

"Then I think I'm into that drunken horny thing
right now."

"Me too." Danielle, laughing a little to loudly.

"What's so funny, ladies?" Robert, asking as he
returned to the room. "Nice pick." Gesturing to the
stereo.

"Oh, nothing at all." Danielle, responding. "Is that
beer for me?" Batting her eyes.

"Of course. Wanna drink it upstairs on the balcony?"
Robert, wasting no time. "There is a really great view."

"Lead the way."

Danielle followed him out of the room and winked just before turning the corner. Shane came in and handed me a beer as he sat down on the couch. It was only a few minutes later when his tongue was licking my teeth in search of a cavity, and we were groping like teenagers on the sofa. My head was mashed somewhere between two cushions.

"Do you want to go upstairs?" Shane, panting like a hot dog.

"I think so."

"Think so, or know so?" Kissing my neck and running his hand down the length of my torso.

"Know so." Kissing him back. "Definitely know so."

We clambered off each other and rushed up the stairs into his bedroom.

"Lilly."

"Lilly."

"LILLY!"

I knew she would not remain unruffled for long.

"What?"

"Hello."

"May I help you?"

"What . . ."

"Shut up!" Interrupting before any alarms could go off.

He fumbled for the doorknob, and I fumbled with his wallet chain. We fell onto the bed and had a bacchanalian orgy. Clothing came off, hands went everywhere, a condom went on, and well, you know the rest. After a second round, Shane fell asleep in twenty seconds with his arms wrapped around me, and I heard a quiet rapping on the door. I gently disentangled, crawled to the door, and opened it a crack. Danielle stood there disheveled and flushed.

"Is he asleep?" Asking me.

"Like a baby."

"Then get dressed little lady. I called a cab."

"You rock."

I shut the door and found all of my clothes except my underwear. Oh well. I quietly slipped out of the room, and Danielle and I walked stealthily down the stairs holding our shoes so as not to make any noise.

"Nice shoes, Lilly." Pausing to admire my heels.

"Thanks." Looking at them with her. "They're pretty, huh?"

"Gorgeous."

"Should we leave our names or number or something for the sleeping beauties?"

"No, let's just leave this all here."

"But he was cute."

"Trust me, I know you, and you won't feel that way in the morning. Leaving quick without a trace like a fighter plane is the only way."

"Do we really have to *Top Gun* it?"

"Definitely."

"Okay, fine. I do want to go home."

"Your chariot awaits, my dear . . ." Danielle answering as she opened the front door to reveal a shiny yellow taxi.

Danielle was right as usual. The minute we got in the cab and stopped chatting, I began getting ill. Although it may seem as if this meet-then-have-sex thing is a practiced ritual, it is not. Never intermingle weight depres-

sion, marriage, and alcohol, because it makes you come   75
out of your skin and act like someone you are not. The
only other time I had done this was back in Paris, and it
pretty much was the same lethal combo minus the marriage. Even though all I thought about was Jonah when I
was abroad, that didn't stop me from wanting something
French. As much as I fantasized about my musician boy, I
also dreamed of that romantic European relationship
filled with walks along the Seine, picnics in the Tuil-
lieres, and steamy conversations in dark-cornered cafés.
Basically, all I did outside my school hours was daydream
and write about boys. I think that is what usually happens
in the City of Light when you barely speak French and
can't make friends . . .

MY PARISIAN PLACE was located smack-dab in the middle
of the Left Bank in Paris's seventh arrondissement. I
submitted to my parents' desires and let them rent me a
sweet apartment on the top floor of a beautiful old
building on Boulevard Saint-Germain. Please, I had to
cave in, they twisted my arm! (Smirk!) It was decorated in
this Turkish/Chinese/Philippe Starck style, and the bedroom had this dark brown, me Tarzan, you Jane, suede
bedspread. I of course immediately ripped it from the
bed and replaced it with a lovely blue duvet with lemons I
had bought around the corner in the cutest French linen
shop. The apartment didn't need any help presenting
itself as a chic swinging bachelor pad, and the suede was
just a little too much for this still sleeping with her teddy
bear kind of girl. Here I was a young and modern miss

76 from LA supplanted into a spanking new culture with new rules, rules that I was clearly never properly taught. My parents did away with any Miss Manners/Emily Post table-setting lessons long before my brother and I even existed. I did make them take me to a cotillion though. There was something about those little white gloves and the fox trot that always did it for me. Actually, it was dancing close with all the thirteen-year-old boys that did it for me.

Some of these French rules seem to have been left-overs from the medieval kitchen. Women were supposed to be elusive, have some mysterious treasure trove of feminine charms, and display their coy power in the artful way they wore their perfect little scarf. The French had this obsession with scarves; you just had to wear one twenty-four-seven. Heaven forbid you pulled out a pair of earmuffs in the dead of winter! This idea that the "woman" was supposed to be an icon of manners, graciousness, and seduction did not really fly with this post-Brown, postfeminist lady. I had thought that in Paris—which I stupidly had assumed would be bustling with new ideas, independent spirits, and artists who walked the streets quoting Simone de Beauvoir—this old idea that the woman was a tool to benefit male egos would be quite dead. Well, I was somewhat wrong.

I wish that I had had an insider friend there to tell me how I was supposed to behave. Little California me kissed whom I wanted without having sex, had no cares about being wild or a cock tease, gave boys my number, asked them on dates, and definitely did not have the first fucking clue as to how to tie a stupid scarf. I just wrapped until the ends were short enough to tuck in. My lack of education and knowledge in the French way became very clear to me on my first French date.

He was someone I had met briefly at cooking school. He worked in the health club at the hotel where my school was located, and he picked me up in the employee cafeteria. Not too romantic, I know, but he was cute and asked me to join him for a cup of coffee. I think what reeled me in was his English; I could understand it. I went home to the States for a few weeks for Chanukah and New Year's, and when I returned a month later, we finally hooked up to get drinks. Simple enough, what can go wrong getting a drink? Anyway, with a café/bar bustling with people on every corner, it was an easy arrangement. A little conversation, a little flirting, and with luck a huge ego boost, which I so desperately needed.

In Paris, I was suffering from an attack of the bad-weight space quite similar to the one that has recently plagued me since Maya's announcement. The French attack was a little different, for it literally originated from eating pig. I was in Paris learning to cook, and what that really meant was I was learning to eat—everything. I was huge. I was dwelling in that bad female place of self-wallowing body obsession. No clothes looked right, and the sight of my naked body made me cringe. Furthermore, it was never easy for me to meet men, even without body distortion. Wait, let me amend that. It was tremendously easy for me to meet men. It was how to convert "Hi, I'm Lilly Abrams, nice to meet you" into a sustainable, loving relationship that always seemed to elude me.

We went for a drink, and the first thing I learned about the French way was that defined personal space was much different here: meaning, there wasn't much of it.

At home, you lounge-singer away from a new guy, lean in a little as you flirt, but keep a good amount of feet and shoes between the two of you while you talk. This gives you a chance to get comfortable, ease into knowing the perfect stranger you are gracing with your attention, and, by starting far apart, there is more meaning when you finally get a little closer. In Paris, when we sat down, he sat next to me on the same side of the table, and he was instantly within five inches from my face while talking to me.

"You have very clever eyes, very beautiful." Twinkling.

"Thank you, but how can my eyes look clever?"

"They have this sparkle in them." Leaning even closer and staring. "I can see it when you smile."

Helllllooooo, just a wee bit uncomfortable to have a guy you do not really know be able to look at your nostril hairs while giving you a compliment. What if my breath was bad or the makeup covering that damn zit was fading away? I had nowhere to run, and he had me immobilized by the cheesy yet seductive lines he was bombing me with. The only thing I could really do was run with it. Besides, what girl can resist a foreign prince (well, maybe not a prince, but give me a break) whispering sweet nothings into her I-have-not-had-sex-in-months ear? So I stayed close, chatted, and tried my best to appear cool, calm, and collected.

"How long have you been working at the health club, Alain?"

"A few years now, but actually I am starting a new job at another hotel. It is pretty top secret."

"Okay . . . Why?"

"The hotel doesn't know yet that I am leaving and I bring in a lot of business for them, models, designers, et cetera."

Of course he trains models. . . . Fuck me!

"It's nice to finally go out," I said, changing the subject.

"Yes, Lilly, I like you. I am glad you called."

"It was kind of strange calling you at work."

"I live with someone so . . ."

"A girlfriend?" Subtly choking on a swig of my drink.

"Yes, but she is leaving soon. She is a model off to Las Vegas to be a showgirl."

"You're joking, right?"

"Why would I be joking?" Looking puzzled. "She works at the Lido right now."

Not only did this guy have a girlfriend but she was also an exotic dancer at the most famous burlesque show in Paris. Do I know how to pick them, or what? The odd thing was that he didn't stop flirting after telling me about the girl-friend. As I kept drinking, I decided I just didn't care.

"Notice a theme here?"

"Are you referring to my imbibing alcohol?"

"Clever girl. Just watch what it makes you do."

"Yes, Obi-Wan."

So that was his issue, not mine. If he felt comfortable being a cheater, I wasn't going to hold it against him. Under normal circumstances, I wouldn't have dared mess around with a player who hooked up behind his girlfriend's back, but fuck it. What's that expression? When in Rome . . . We talked like this for a few hours, bullshitting like you normally do on a first date. We smiled, he held my hand, did the squeeze thing, and things were going well. We liked each other, or at least had that "special" spark stirring.

Then we came back to my apartment (mistake number one) and here was where I clearly bungled up any rules about dating. I should have never brought him home with me. We kissed downstairs by the elevator (mistake number two). I should have never invited him up. By this point, it's obvious that we were coming upstairs to fool around. Fine with me. I was horny, he was hot, and I had not kissed anyone in four months. Sometimes, a girl just needs a little love and affection.

"Alain, can I get you something to drink?" Asking when we got inside. "I'm getting one for myself."

"Like you need another?"

"Some water would be fine, Lilly." Curling the "L."

We went to sit down in the living room, and all I'm thinking is it's a much safer spot than my bedroom. I shortly realized that this time there would pretty much be no safe spots. When, after only about five minutes, he had removed most of my clothes along with his, I knew this innocent fooling around would be a little more than that. What's a girl to do? Do you say no to a gorgeous, half-naked trainer kissing your neck in just the place you like? Do you pull away from a hot, taut bod embracing you? I don't think so (mistake number three). I should have never led him to my bedroom. This was where I think the LA girl, smart, sensible, calm, and somewhat square, decided to leave my body and vacate the premises. She definitely left willingly, but I was on virgin territory, not literally of course, but the first-date fuck was a very new thing for me.

An hour later on the dot, he left after an experience that was crazy and totally not me. We had sex in so many different positions, he put my college boyfriend's vivid bedroom imagination to shame. I think at one point, we were even doing it standing up without the usual wall for support. That trainer strength really came in handy. If I had been just a wee bit more flexible as I imagine his showgirl girlfriend was, we would have been able to try one of those weird tantric pretzel positions I have often read about. He just totally knew what he was doing and how to do it in just the right way. Let's just say it was energetic, sort of like a circus, lots of lights, noises, and big wild accentuated movements culminating in a big animal salute to the ringmaster.

"That was fun. You're sweet." Saying as he leaves. "I'll call you."

It was at this moment that I realized I had just been one hundred percent seduced. Finally, I knew what it meant, and I had to smile. Wow, I mean, yeah, I saw the machinations at work, but I see that a lot. It just never really had worked on me before. I was always too clever, too hard-headed, too much of a prude even to wander into seduction land. This time, I finally felt completely taken by a man in a completely and willing way. Unfortunately, I also realized that I had broken some hugely important unwritten French rule. The one that says never fuck a French guy on the first date, because his whole purpose is only to get the little American girl in the sack. I immediately called long distance to San Francisco. Maya.

"Maya, you'll never believe what I just did!?" Lighting a Gitane cigarette. "I am a freak!"

"What? This has got to be about the date."

"We had sex, I mean we had SEX, crazy shit."

"Is he still there?"

"No, he left. He has a girlfriend." Exhaling. "What was I thinking?"

"Who cares? The girlfriend isn't so great, but, whatever, don't start stressing."

She knew as soon as I told her what had happened, it would sink in for me and make me feel kind of nasty.

"Lilly? Are you still there? Don't start feeling guilty for having fun. You were safe, and come on. Every letter you have written me detailed that French affair you wanted to have. Besides, we've all been in the same situation. You did what any girl would do."

"I know, you're right, but I have never done this before. It's one thing to romanticize a liaison in letters to a friend, and another to go through with it. This is sort of weird. . . . But, God, it was so fun. I am going to be so sore." Rubbing my thighs. "I think I almost OD'd on endorphins."

"So I take it you enjoyed yourself?"

"Fuck, yeah."

"I hate to do this because I want more details, but I gotta go. I'm late to meet Emily. What time is it there anyway?"

"One A.M."

"I'll call you before I go to bed tonight. Just relax and do not, I repeat, do not freak out."

"I won't. Or well, I won't a lot. Bye."

That girl knew me too well, because the minute I hung up, I began tripping. Once you start remembering just what you did and where your hands and mouth had been, it's hard not to get sketched out. Maya knew how my mind worked, and how certain situations affected my balance. The fact that I fucked a French stranger really threw me for a loop. No amount of friendly wisdom was going to let me escape from under the disgust that began swelling the minute it was over. Sure, Maya told me to chill and enjoy the positives, but I soon began to feel a little dirty. Alain had accomplished a major feat, seeing as how no guy before him ever really got me in the sack without long analytic discussions or mood-ruining shy moments on my part.

IF ONLY NATHAN knew. Nathan (my last ex from college) and I had this exact conversation when I went to see him in San Francisco a few months before I left for Paris. We hadn't seen each other since this extremely awkward and lame I-have-no-idea-what-to-say-to-you good-bye after graduation. During the last months of school, we had had an on/off thing that never really asserted itself as being on or off. When we met, it was like a breath of fresh air. Here was a new pair of lips amid a student population of have-kissed-alreadies. It was an instant attraction, and I knew he was going to be a good match since the real force behind our meeting was this cheesy charity-matchmaking Valentine thing. Everyone who wanted to participate filled out this form of questions that was supposed to assert your dating IQ, and for a dollar you could get a computer printout of the most compatible men and women for you at Brown. Of course, being a slightly

84   randy, second-semester senior girl unwanted by most men since they all had predilections for younger girls, I did not hesitate in filling out a form or procuring my list. I had never even heard his name before, but Nathan was number three on my chart, we had an eighty-something percent chance of getting along, and therefore maybe getting together.

When we finally met a few weeks later, as he just happened to be playing a gig with a friend of mine, that list made a great pickup line. From that night on, we were together. Despite having this fatelike connection, everything was always really vague. Since it was the end of school, and college for that matter, neither of us could commit. Underneath all the indecision, we really dug each other, but we never slept together. A few months after graduation, we managed to reconnect via letters, and I wanted to see him before I left the country, for a little closure. I needed to be able to say that we properly addressed (or really undressed) our relationship, one last time. After meeting up for dinner and drinks with Maya, Emily, and a few other friends, we returned to his apartment for some recreational activities. After fooling around for about an hour, up came the sex conversation, which until this point had not yet been broached.

"So, what do you think, Lil?" Nathan, asking softly while nuzzling my neck. "Do you want to?"

"I don't know." Rolling to face him. "I do, but we haven't, and I'm leaving."

"I know, but does all that matter?" Caressing my face.

"Maybe, yes . . . I mean, what would it mean?" Running my fingers over his lips.

"Mean in what sense? Sex can't change our relationship even if we wanted it to." Pulling me closer to him.
"We still don't have the time or place to really be
together. But that isn't to say that it couldn't be really
special. I'm happy just to be with you now, just kissing
you. I care about you a lot." Kissing me softly.

(I know what you are thinking, too bad we never got it
together. . . . No shit!)

"I know you do, but it's like I have this angel/devil
complex about sex."

For clarification, this complex is one of the many
versions of the "Wannadoer" and "Wishidinter"
dichotomy.

"This haloed fairy in white tells me sex should mean
everything, be special, and be all about love. Then there's
this horny red imp who tells me how great sex feels and to
live in the moment. It's like I'm a master flirt and can
comfortably get a guy to the door, but once inside, I get
all shy and nervous. Sometimes I feel like I'm all talk."
Kissing him back.

"Personally, I like that combo in you." Kissing small
circles on my neck. "It's sexy, and it always makes me
smile."

"I bet I'm probably bright red right now." Blushing at
all his sweet words. "My cheeks are burning."

"It's cute. So do the angel and devil usually talk to each
other calmly and rationally or do they duke it out like
prizefighters?"

"They're like fucking Jerry Springer!" Laughing at
myself. "Sometimes they even throw chairs. Especially in
moments like these."

"You better duck. Would hate for them to bruise your cute face." Pulling me tighter. "Seriously, we can do whatever you want."

"You are so great." Kissing him again. "I miss you."

"I miss you too. Hey, by the way, what the hell is going to happen to you in Paris? How are you going to explain all this to some guy that doesn't even speak English?" Smiling, beginning to giggle.

"Why are you smiling about this? I'm fucked . . . *oops, wrong word*." Starting to laugh myself. "Stop laughing, it's not funny."

"He'll probably smile and nod, all the while thinking 'All my friends told me American girls were supposed to be easy. This girl's a nutcase.'" Chuckling even harder.

"Nathan! Enough already!" Giving him a little shove. "Knowing me, I'll just avoid the situation altogether."

"Wow, seven celibate months. That's a really long time. How will you manage?"

"Is this your way of trying to tell me we should sleep together now? Trying to seduce me?"

"Maybe . . . I do speak English very well."

"Cute, real cute." Falling into another passionate kiss, and then falling into him.

FAST FORWARD TO Paris just after my fast French fuck. Now that I was reexperiencing Nathan and my joke, I wondered if the French guy calls back the American girl after he has had her. Does he go back for more or does he bail, happy to get laid once? There I was trying to change this fling into something I knew it would never be. A one-nighter always stays a one-nighter, even if you convince yourself it was more. I wasn't in love with this man, not by a long shot, but the LA me was feeling used and totally lame for falling prey, but the new no-hang-ups-good-time-girl was lusting for more of this amazing lover. It was a dilemma. I began picturing what I looked like in bed with this guy, or any guy for that matter. I can see why some couples videotape themselves. Not like I really would ever ever ever want to do that myself, because knowing me the tape would go public like Pamela Anderson's. I just wonder what it all looks like. Maybe there's a porn star lurking underneath my schoolgirl sensibilities. . . .

When I did see Alain again, it was before either of us had made any attempt at communication, and I tried to play it cool. It sort of worked, and I held out and managed to wait a few more days to call him. That was a major feat for me since I am usually an overeager beaver. When I did call six days, five hours, and thirty-two minutes later (sufficient time to appear calm), he wasn't even there! I hated that I left a message, because that put the ball totally in his court. I was stuck waiting by the phone hoping he would call so we could fuck again. Why did I wait? Well, honestly, I had nothing better to do. I also would have felt more in sync with the LA me if we did it again. Somehow this was my little rule when my horny side overtook my brain. Twice indicates a different thing than a one-nighter, not that a two-nighter is any better, but let me have my own mind games and rationalizations.

Surprise, surprise! He never called again. Although I saw him a few times walking the hotel halls, we never shared more than a hello. He even tried to get on my friend a few weeks later. Slimeball! The funniest thing

88 happened after I told the story to a few more friends back home. Potential tragedy turned to personal triumph.

"Lilly, what's the name of that trainer you slept with?" Josh, asking during one of our transatlantic phone calls.

"Alain. Alain Devoir, I think. Why?"

"You're going to die. In *W* this month, there's this whole article on trainers and health clubs in Paris. There is a picture of him."

"No way!"

"Yes, way. He is a little hottie. I see why you had sex with him. I would have."

"You have to save the article for me. How funny is that?"

"Only you would end up having a one-night stand with *the* trainer in Paris. You finally got your story."

Yes, I certainly did, but that was just it: I decided then and there that that was going to be my one and only story. My perfect Parisian one-night stand.

"v" day

This time was not quite so perfect, seeing how I wasn't counting on losing my resolve and turning into a floozy for a guy who may or may not have been named Shane and who may or may not have had clean sheets. I looked around my room and had a moment of satisfaction over the fact that I was actually in my room. But that respite soon faded. The light hurt, the covers were hanging sideways off the bed, and knowing that I left my favorite Cosabella lace-trimmed white tap pants on the floor of his room made my stomach turn.

"You have become a harlot!" Scolding myself. *"In no way, shape, or form will you ever do the horizontal one-night mambo again!"*

"I know, I know." Hanging my head. "I held out for nearly two years only to

90 throw it away one insecure, drunken evening. What
the hell?"

"*I'm not impressed by your actions.*"

"My underwear!" Groaning.

"*That is the biggest tragedy of all. I fucking loved those panties.*"

"They were so comfortable."

"*That cotton was so soft it felt like our ass was wrapped in cashmere.*"

"And they didn't ride up." Savoring the memory.

"*Enough!*" Breaking up the reverie. "*You did it. It's done.*"

"I am disgusting! It wasn't even that good."

"*True, but now you have to move on. Don't dwell.*"

"With all the confusion of the past few months, I seem to have jumped out of myself and become a bad version of me."

"*You just need to take a step back and regroup. The trip with Mom will do you some good. Sometimes all you need is to make a break. Then you can truly leave this night of mediocrity behind you.*"

"Why am I doing all those things I said I would never do again?" Asking. "I am spiraling into a tornado of wrong decisions. Something has got to change soon."

"*It's a crazy time. Just keep plugging away. You can do it. I have faith.*"

I had to give myself some simplistic boosting because once I physically moved and tried to get out of bed, an inner-thigh soreness I haven't felt in a long, long time just about killed me. The sight of fingerprint bruises on my right arm and a red scratch on my stomach almost made me pass out. Battle scars from an ill-conceived war.

I felt raw, used, and totally nasty. A meek *"You can do it"* was clearly not going to do it. I slinked into the shower and let the spray steam my body, blasting away any detritus from the night before. Luckily, it was Saturday, so I had nowhere to be. I got dressed, carefully hiding my wounds, and I immediately called Danielle.

"I need French fries." Saying to her. "Lots of them."

"I need coffee and a cigarette." Her voice rolling with sleep. "Come over and get me."

"Why do I always have to get your ass? You're like Max." Getting sassy.

"How so? I don't remember your brother having tits."

"Funny." Answering blandly. "No he doesn't, he just always makes me go get him. I think you both have been to my house a total of five times."

"It's because you live so fucking far up that dumb hill. It's a hassle."

"You're a hassle." Starting to get snippy.

"Don't tell me you've already boarded the shame spiral. I thought we at least had a day or two."

"Started last night in the cab."

"I figured. It's time for a pig out and cheesy movie day."

"Exactly."

"So come over and I'll drive from here." Danielle compromising. "Okay?"

"Okay." Relenting. "Be there in twenty."

I hopped in the car and drove to the Coffee Bean. Bought two overpriced yet frothy nonfat lattes and headed over to Danielle's. During the drive I got to thinking that Hollywood Shane had been my first since Parisian Alain. Wow, could this get worse? Their names rhyme. Anyway, Shane was the first guy I had slept with in

92 almost two years because I was waiting for something more than a fuck. There really haven't been that many sexual escapades in my life, and sex is still a very, very big deal to me. I usually don't troll bars with my buddy, toss back Patron Gold, and hop into the sack, even though it might appear that I am comfortable in such a vampy role.

From the beginning, sex was important and special to me even when I could hear my hormones shouting at me to get busy. It sounds so old-fashioned, and it's not as if I'm so pure, but I just can't fuck someone and not care. With so many sketchy diseases roaming around looking for hosts, I'm frightened about getting intimate with someone I don't know. I don't want to ruin my chances for children on a random fling. I want sex inside a relationship, not as the relationship itself. The guy lying next to me should really want me, Lilly, and not just a sexual partner.

I remember how a lot of things in my early years, like haircuts and outfits, were contingent on sex. Besides getting your period, having sex is an important rite of passage every girl goes through. My trek down this path just happened later than everyone else's. My brother, Max, told me not to cut my long-to-the-butt hair until I did "it." At seventeen, pre–serious boyfriend, precollege, pre–sexual awakening, that seemed a mighty odd thing to say. I hadn't cut my reddish-brown hair more than a quarter-inch since I was ten. Actually, I was still reeling from a flippant comment a stewardess said when I was six and on my way to San Francisco. I had just gotten my haircut really really boy-short and was feeling a little naked. This lady had the nerve to tell my mom (after I

ordered some tea) that it would be too hot for him. *Him!*
Hello!!!!! I am a *her* you twit! Totally humiliated, I was
unable to say anything to her, but I silently vowed, then
and there, that my gender would never be misinterpreted
again.

Even though I was seventeen, a grown girl, and showed
every sign of proper xx anatomy, I still wore my hair like
a shroud. It protected me from potential idiots and
unwanted insults. I guess I also stowed Max's advice away
in my memory bank for future reference. I knew that
one day I would be on a need to know basis about everything and anything to further my sexual vocabulary even
if it was a passing comment regarding the proper hairstyle. I was a very late bloomer. Puberty bypassed me
until very late in the game, so actually having sex seemed
to be an event that would occur light-years away. I mean,
I don't even think I had boobs until I was sixteen! My
classmates used to call me "the Young and the Breast-
less." Nice, huh?

When I finally got to college, I was raring to go. All
those latent teenage hormones began rearing their new-
born heads the minute I walked into my freshman dorm.
At Brown, I was like a little girl let loose in an Atlantic
City boardwalk candy store. Everywhere I turned, there
were all these pretty, shiny, sweet available men artfully
displayed in hallways and doorjambs, waiting to be gob-
bled up. As you could guess, despite an enormous sweet
tooth, I was just too shy to buy. Men still freaked me out.
Most of the time I just looked instead of tasted, examined
instead of bought. In reality, most of them didn't even
know they were being weighed and judged for calorie

content because I never even introduced myself. It was all a lot of wide-eyed, openmouthed staring on my part. I had never seen so many pairs of boxers and abs before in my life! That was a bit intoxicating. Since I was behind the other chicks in the development process, my pre-college interaction with guys was kept at a minimum. High school boys managed to overlook my vacant body and settled their eyes on my girlfriends' curvy waists and ample bustlines. In college, it was time to inhabit my finally fleshed-out form and find a means to make myself part of the conversation. It was about time I started shopping.

By the time November rolled around, I had developed a rudimentary knowledge of how to utilize my feminine charms and even wound up having a handful of flings/boyfriends. There were a few wanna-be musicians, athletes, and various stereotypical college types. One of my favorites was a freshman quarterback named William. He was so beautiful: tall, dark, and handsome with perfect muscles, a six-pack stomach, and the most seductive smile I had ever seen. It lit me up like a Live-Nude-Girls flashing neon sign. I can't even remember where I met him, probably some really bad Delta Phi fraternity party I went to when I didn't know any better. I do remember that the minute we began talking, there was electricity everywhere. I think my flannel shirt was abuzz with static because finally one of "the" guys only had eyes for me. For a week or so we bantered back and forth, meeting up, and standing each other up until the inevitable happened, and we kissed. After a few nights of innocent fooling around, we were in my room, and tangled up in my tiny, less than twin-size bed. At this juncture, I chose to humiliate myself one hundred percent and ensure we would never hook up again.

Penis phobia. I'm not sure if you have heard of it, but in high school Danielle and I had this long-running inside joke (but not ha ha ha joke) about penis phobia. We both were afflicted with an incredibly paralyzing fear of the male member. Any boys I had kissed precollege were left covered in whatever clothing they had on their backs when they walked in the door no matter how much I liked them. Some guys tried to teach me, coax a hand job out of me. Some of my girlfriends even gave me lessons on bananas, but to no avail. This chick was not ready for hand-to-hand combat. Poor William and his penis never really had a chance, even though I was hoping finally to face my fear. (Don't worry, we aren't even talking about blow jobs yet.) I liked him a lot. He was nice, sweet, into me, cute, everything a girl could want. He was a teddy bear in bed, cuddling me, tickling me, making me laugh. I felt I could trust him.

Yeah, right! Everything was going fine. We were fooling around, clothing was coming off, and I was having quite a good time. Then, out of nowhere, terror struck like a shock from newly laid carpet. I somehow managed to freeze completely, à la Hans Solo when Boba Fett froze him and brought him to Jabba. I have no idea why the panic attack decided to drop in, but within one minute it was incapacitating, and I could not get my shit together.

"What's wrong?" William asked. "Are you all right?"

"I don't know." Squirming.

"What's going on?"

"All of a sudden I'm so uncomfortable."

"Why? Did I do something wrong?" Shifting his weight off me.

"No, no. It's me. I'm a freak. I just can't do this."

"Relax. It's okay. It's really okay." Looking me in the eyes. "It's fine."

"You don't understand. It's not that I don't want to. I just can't, I really can't." Getting embarrassed and averting his gaze.

"Okay. It's not important." Disentangling himself from me.

"It is though. Is it hot in here?" Bringing my hands to my face as if covering my eyes would make him unable to see I was naked and blushing.

"I think it's just you. Your face is bright red. This is actually really cute. I've never had a girl flip out like this before."

"I can't believe you think this is cute! I'm so humiliated." Rolling onto my side, totally unnerved. "In my head, I'm all for this, but my body won't cooperate."

"It's really okay. You're really sweet and it's cool." Fumbling for his clothes.

"Sweet is such a sickening word. Ten-year-olds are sweet. Cotton candy is sweet. Don't go." Sitting up and covering myself with the sheet. "I'm sorry, maybe I'll be okay soon."

"I kind of have to. I'm actually really uncomfortable, physically speaking, and I just can't wait around to see if you are going to be into this."

"I'm so ridiculous. I don't get it. What is wrong with me?"

"Really, Lilly, this isn't a big deal. I just have to get out of here." Moving quickly to the door.

"I think I've just doomed our relationship."

"Chill, I'll call you."

"Sure you will." Throwing on a T-shirt and walking to the door. "I really did want to do this."

"I know. It's really okay. Like this is why I hang out with you in the first place? Good night."

He gave me a kiss and left, sort of shuffling down the hall with his shirt pulled down real low.

Penis phobia had reared its ugly little head, no pun intended, and left me all alone. William did call, but, as you can gather, he never did want to tuck into my loving embrace again. If you jinx something too early, it just falls by the wayside. At least there were no other catastrophes like that one. After losing one potential boyfriend, I decided it was best to just avoid the situation entirely. The one problem was, despite being so nervous and uptight about anything more than a double, I had developed this sick obsession with finally wanting to have sex. I'm confident no other normal girl would think, "Hey, I can't even deal with foreplay but sex sure sounds good," but I did. No one was making me feel like an outcast from a carnival sideshow for being a virgin or pressuring me to do it, I just couldn't participate in so many of the conversations my friends had. It was like playing "I Never" and being the only one sober . . . four hours later. I wanted to know what all the fuss was about. What did it feel like? Did it change you? Change the way you thought? Acted? Would I look different after? Would I bleed? Would I be good? Would it be something I'd want to do all the time? Can legs really bend up over your head and not cramp?

I remember now that I even tried to get Jack, a good

98   friend with whom I also happened to think I was in love,
to be my first. Who knew I was so brave to actually broach
the subject with him on the train back to school after a
Celtics/Lakers game. Maybe brave is the wrong word—
how about a little insane! We went to the game, had some
dogs and some beers, watched the Lakers win, and then
headed home. Maybe it was the beer and the meat products that loosened my tongue. I just let it all spill.

"Jack, what do you think about us?"

"What do you mean?" Squirreling slightly away from
me.

"Well, like if I said that I was thinking that it was time
for me to have sex, and in theory I was thinking that it
would be fun to do it with a friend, a friend like you,
what would you say?"

"Hummm, not too sure about that." Blushing slightly.
"First times are kind of important."

"Yeah, and?"

"And, maybe, Lilly, you should wait to have sex with
someone special."

"Jack, you sound like such a romantically challenged
girl."

"I'm flattered by the offer, but, you, my friend, even
though you are putting on a good show right now, are
exactly such a girl."

"You're probably right. I'm just so sick of it being a
thing."

"But you've made it a thing all by yourself, and now
that you have, you have to stick with the big plan you
imagine in your head."

"Who knew you could be so wise?" Hitting him playfully on the arm. "I did freak you out slightly though, didn't I?" Winking.

"Uh, yeah." Looking at me. "I mean, I am a guy and having sex with you would be fun, no doubt. I am just the wrong guy for the job." Kissing my cheek. "You'll find him."

A few weeks later, Jack started dating my friend. Oh, well.

AFTER THE EXCHANGE with Jack, even though he was kind enough not to share it with anyone, a little joke that cute Lilly was obsessed with having sex was born. I truly had sex on the brain. Wonder why they never made that a cocktail: Sex on the Brain instead of Sex on the Beach? My friends knew I thought about it constantly and joked about it frequently. They also knew how innocent I really was, and definitely watched out for phobic girl. That's why I gave Maya quite a scare when I got back from winter break.

"Hey, sweetie, how was home?" I asked, dropping into her room down the hall in our shared dorm. "I missed you."

"Mellow. Really didn't do that much." Giving me a hug. "I like the new hair color."

"Thanks. I almost decided to cut it all off."

"Excuse me? Cut your hair?"

"Yeah. I was all into doing it, but the guy who was going to lop it off didn't have any appointments available before I had to come back here." Responding calmly. "I was really bummed."

"Wait a minute, am I missing something? You did just say you were going to cut your hair, right?" Prodding, looking a bit startled. "Anything you want to share, Lilly?"

"What's up? What's with the face?"

"Because I thought you made a deal with Max about your hair and cutting it was some sign about . . ."

"Oh, NO! No, no, no! I didn't have sex! Please, like that wouldn't be the first thing out of my mouth?"

"Thank goodness. Man, you scared me a little there." Breathing a sigh of relief. "Especially since I know you had no romantic prospects at home, and I wouldn't want my girl to give it up to just anyone."

"How sweet that you're so protective. Don't worry. As much as I want to get it over with, it sure as hell isn't going to be with a total random unless he is Keanu or something."

As you can see, Maya knew the haircut challenge, and it became etched into our friendship ledger. As second semester rolled around, I continued my search for an enlightened soul to take me to that next level, and as luck would have it, I did end up meeting him. Before college, I had this preconceived notion of how my guy was going to look, and it was all based on his hairstyle. Maybe a little shallow, but other girls go for eyes, or lips, or hands. Like I mentioned before in regards to Jonah, I go for wavy, thick, and to-the-shoulders black hair. My girlfriends would all tease me because I was so predictable. They could pick out the guy I would think was hot within one minute. Walking into every party, they would see who had the hair, and then know where to find me when they wanted to leave. So it was a very big deal when, on my eighteenth birthday, I went to this off-campus kegger with a few friends and saw him. Sure, I was a little trashed, but it was clear from the get-go he at least looked the part.

Sam and I were introduced and proceeded to spend the rest of the night talking only to each other. No matter who else came to say hello or happy birthday, we couldn't tear ourselves away from each other. There was an instant, immediate, intense connection. The line between friendly chatting and heavy flirting began to blur as hours passed and our smiles got bigger and more earnest. You would think this was a great thing, when finally I met a guy with whom I immediately clicked, but it was far more complicated than a simple meet-the-man-of-your-dreams scenario. Unfortunately, I had a sort-of boyfriend at the time who happened to be one of his best friends. Did that matter? Nope. Boyfriend or not, there was no way in hell I was going to walk away from Sam. You just can't bail from a one-in-a-million chance at everything you think you want. And yes, after only a very short time, despite its being totally unrealistic and unhealthy, I knew he was everything I wanted.

"Lilly, you know we've met before."

"We have? I don't think so." Batting my eyes in a very cheesy fashion. "I definitely would have remembered."

"You were playing pool at my friend's house with a blond girl a couple of weeks ago."

"Okay. Yeah, I was. My friend Maya and I thought we were kick-ass pool players, that is until we tanked every game. You were there?"

"Yep. You sucked."

"Thanks a lot!" Nervously guffawing. "Make me feel bad on my birthday."

"Sorry. Just speaking the truth." Ribbing me.

"We did talk such trash. I guess big mouths never win."

"Well . . . that is not entirely true." Winking.

"What?" Not getting the joke. "Oh . . . ha, ha. You've got a dirty mind."

"Thanks." Starting to blush. "You guys did look pretty cute losing."

"How sweet, Sam." Smiling bigger because he was blushing. "Is that your idea of an apology?"

"I think so."

"Well, it worked. Flattery will get you everywhere."

Just when I was really getting somewhere, having cracked his cool-guy veneer, Maya and Emily came over and told me they wanted to bail. Great!

"Sam, this is Emily, and you remember Maya. They want me to leave." Not so subtly glaring at my friends.

"Nice to meet you." Extending his hand to them. "Why are you guys jetting?"

"It's just time." Maya said, shaking his hand. "Why don't you come with us?"

I knew I loved that girl!!!!

"Yeah. Why not come, Sam?"

"Hummm, I don't really know." Staring at me, trying to decide what I was implying.

"It could be fun."

"Yeah, I know. But, Lilly, I don't think that would be such a good idea." Answering cautiously.

"I want you to." Not really pleading, just being honest.

"I know, but I just can't."

"Okay. Whatever. Begging's not my thing, especially on birthdays." Chiding him somewhat sarcastically.

"Sam, it was a pleasure." Maya, saying her good-byes.

"Lilly, Emily and I are going to get our coats. We will meet you by the door." Disappearing back into the party.

"Okay. Grab mine too please. It was nice meeting you, Sam." Extending my hand toward him.

"Nice meeting you too. Happy Birthday, Lilly." Taking my hand in his.

"Thanks. Bye, Sam."

"Bye."

There Sam and I were, having already said good-bye but unable to stop staring at each other. Also, we both didn't realize that we were still holding each other's hand. What seemed like an eternity passed, and we remained silent. Everything else in the room fell away, the music, the frat boys, the occasional yells from another room, until all I could hear was the beating of my heart and the quiet pattern of my breath. Then, Sam leaned in and kissed me. Our first kiss, and I felt like I was rolling down a big hill inside a tire. It wasn't a friendly on the cheek, you're a swell gal kind of kiss. It was full, profound, and lip to lip. I almost fainted.

"You just kissed me." Breathless.

"I know. I wasn't planning to." Shaking his head. "Shit, we'll talk later. I can't deal with this now." Answering, and simply walking away into the crowd leaving me standing alone.

"What just happened?" Saying out loud to myself.

That was that. This happened in the middle of February. A week or so later, I began running into him everywhere: the PO, the street, the Underground bar. Everywhere I turned, he was there getting cuter and cuter with each simple exchange. Meanwhile, I proceeded to

104 extricate myself from my current relationship, rather messily I might add. It was a good thing that there weren't a lot of intimate strings to cut, because it turned out to be a bit of a disaster. I ended up calling it quits with my boyfriend late one nonsober night in a mean-spirited fashion and stayed awake until eight o'clock the next morning, freaking out for being such a bitch. I sat in Maya's bed, wrapped in her cloud covers, going over and over the horrible things I didn't mean to say. While trying to calm me down and get to sleep, she helped me see that it was okay to end a relationship I wasn't into and cool to pursue Sam, just not for a few weeks at least. It wasn't a great idea to bounce from one guy to another. That whole rebound thing. That was a Saturday and by Thursday of the next week, Sam was sitting on the steps by my room, holding my hand, and talking with me about kissing styles. I clearly don't always listen to my friends.

We were then a couple. It was that simple. The second time I slept at his house, I knew he was the one, because for the first time ever I had zero penis phobia. There was nothing gross or uncomfortable about touching him—I wanted to. I knew he would always make me feel safe no matter how naked we were. It's so strange how someone's vibe can just make you feel okay instantaneously. I can see why people get totally amped about believing in karmic connection. All that touchy, feely, line up the crystals, fate stuff really has some validity. Sometimes you just know. You can feel it deep inside you, and a light just turns on.

Since Sam had somehow figured out how to quell the phobic beast within, I figured he was the perfect man for the job. To tame and soothe my sexual trepidation, he had to have been doing something right. I decided that the big event would take place after spring break, which was in a few weeks. As you can imagine, from the minute we parted ways and went frolicking with our respective friends, all I thought about was him. All day, every day, it was Sam this, Sam that, until Maya almost gagged me with a woolly sock in the middle of the Cheesecake Factory after I ordered a chocolate peanut butter dessert named Sam's Special. The night I got back from spring break and first saw him, it was like I was a fourteen-year-old Leonardo fan who'd seen *Titanic* thirty times and now Leo was dropped on one knee before me declaring his undying love. There were stars in my eyes, and I was gone. It was just a matter of time. Somehow it was decided that April 9 was the night, and everyone, and I mean everyone who knew him or me, knew.

Sam's best friend, Alex, wrote for the *Brown Daily Herald*. His sports column was all about nonsports, like hacky-sack competitions or broom ball tournaments. It came out every Thursday, and this week's paper was all about a goatee-growing contest he had with Sam and the rest of their housemates. Sam had won and Alex wrote all about it. I think the copy read, "Sam Grossman, winner of the 212 Stuart Street goatee contest, will be awarded his much deserved and treasured prize tomorrow night, April 9." All my friends who read it instantly knew I was that much deserved prize, and I got so much shit. They made fun of me all day. Things got even more embarrassing when Maya and I went to the drugstore to buy some condoms.

"What kind should I get? There are so many." Scanning the rack. "How am I supposed to choose?"

"Just get the Sheik ones with spermicide." Grabbing a package from the shelf. "That's what they give out at health services."

"What about spermicidal jelly or foam? Isn't that what they say is the best combination?" Pulling a box down to examine. "It has been so long since I had those sex classes in high school."

"I'm not sure. Just buy it and we can read the thingy inside later. Might as well stock up." Maya, also grabbing a Today sponge. (This was before it was yanked from the market, and we all became familiar with the Seinfeld phrase "sponge worthy.")

"Puleeze! I'm definitely not using one of those." Looking at the flowery image printed on the box that hid its real purpose. "I can't imagine shoving that inside me. It looks a little large."

"I know, but this is fun. There is only one first time and it's your duty to go nuts and buy one of everything. If anything it will be a keepsake."

"I don't think when they created the definition for keepsake it included birth control devices."

"Probably not, but it is the nineties."

"True, but enough already. My comfort level is starting to drop."

"Don't worry about it." Knowing I wasn't just talking about the condoms. "It's going to be great."

"Easy for you to say. This is a major deal."

"I know, but I think you are making the right decision."

"Yeah . . . It's just scary to finally be here."

"It has been a long time coming." Winking at me. "My little Lilly is almost a woman."

"Cute, Maya. Let's go. I want to buy some other things and hide this shit or I'll die of embarrassment at the counter." Eager to get out of there.

"Okay. I need some toothpaste and tampons anyway."

As we wandered around the store, we picked up various items to cloak our real purpose. As if the store clerk wouldn't know! I bet every kid does this at some point or another . . . don't they? I sure as hell hope so, or I am totally giving away how ridiculously lame I am. Finally, we got to the counter, and the clerk began zapping our merchandise.

"What are we doing tonight?" Maya, asking as she pulled a magazine off the shelf to read. "I want to go out."

"You always want to go out."

"What's your point?" Thumbing through the pages.

"Nothing. I thought we were going to Ciao with Jack and the rest of the boys. Sam and I aren't on until tomorrow, so I am all yours."

"Thanks for squeezing me into your calendar." Poking me in the side and setting the magazine back down. "Do I get two hours or three?"

"Have I ever dissed you guys to hang with him?" Getting a little riled up. "I have *so* not been that girl!"

"Calm down, Lilly. I was just kidding." Playfully tugging my hair. "You have been very good about time spent."

"Your total is $25.06. Paper or plastic?"

"Plastic please." Handing him the money.

Before he had a chance to slide my purchases in the plastic bag, I heard a deep voice behind me call my name.

"Hey, Lilly. What's up?" Sam's friend Alex asks as I turn around abruptly.

"Hey, Maya." Another of Sam's roommates, Elliot, says.

"Oh! Hi." Maya, trying to swallow the beginnings of a giggle.

"Hey, guys. How's it going?" Me, trying to appear calm as my face contorts into that deer-in-headlights expression that is always oh so flattering.

"Good. Got anything special planned this weekend?" Elliot, asking while looking over my shoulder at my purchases still hanging out on the countertop. "Seems to me there's a party going on somewhere."

"Looks like someone's going to be real busy." Alex, saying with this devilish grin. "Something tells me you're spending the weekend at our house, Lilly."

"Nothing much. Just the usual." Maya sputtering the words out, trying to cover the obvious and save me.

"Well . . . yeah. . . . We gotta go. . . . Later." Grabbing Maya's hand, the finally full bag, and fleeing from the store.

We burst into hysterical laughter the minute we got outside on the street, and I began to hyperventilate. I was overcome with embarrassment. I bet even my toenail polish turned from pink to red.

"Holy shit!" Me, gasping, leaning over as I tried to catch my breath and stop laughing. "Oh my God!"

"Lilly, I can't believe that just happened!" Continuing to laugh hysterically. "Unreal."

"I can't believe you think this is so funny!" Giving Maya a good-natured shove. "I'm so fucking embarrassed. Why did that just have to happen? Not like having to buy the damn things was bad enough."

"Oh, please. That was so classic!"

"I wonder what they'll say to Sam?" Biting my lip. "This could be a land mine of humiliation."

"Probably nothing. Don't worry."

"Nothing?! Are you kidding me? They are going to have a field day!" Wincing at the potential jokes I was going to have to dodge. "This is prime material for them."

"At least it wasn't like in that movie where the guy without knowing it buys the condoms from his date's dad. Come on, let's go home." Grabbing my hand and pulling me down the street. "Emily's going to die when she hears about this."

Everyone thought it was so funny, and, well, it was pretty funny. Nothing like having your boyfriend's best friends see your birth control stash when they know you are a virgin and these are the first prophylactics you have ever bought with the intention of actually using. Someone must have been watching over me since there were no other major catastrophes to befall me before Friday. His friends were nice enough to keep their mouths shut. I owed them for that big time. I guess they felt a little sorry for me and were kind enough to forget what they saw.

When April 9 finally rolled around, Sam and I had an unforgettable evening, and despite the obvious physical discomfort that most women can relate to, it was perfect. A truly perfect memory. I consider myself so fortunate to have this first handled in such a delicate way. How many girls get to say that? He treated me with such respect, such tenderness, like I was a beautiful, breakable piece of art. He was able to make me feel at ease even in this horrifying yet wonderfully intimate experience. We listened to music, drank champagne, laughed and talked until the sun came up. Because my first time played itself out in an almost clichéd teeny-bopper romantic movie manner, I know it will continue to color all my future experiences. Knowing that a sexual experience can actually be like the dreamy stills of a film or the pages of a romance novel has me somewhat unwilling to accept anything less. I always want the hearts and flowers of my first time.

By the way, just for the record: (a) we never did use the condoms I bought because he got some also, and (b) the friendly presex group support did not cease after "it" had happened. I received a lovely card from my teammates extending their warmest congratulations. Hanging from the card was a brand-new pair of orange scissors. I think I still have those somewhere ensconced in a memory box from freshman year. I probably even have that Today sponge. Yes, I know, goofy, but if a girl doesn't keep mementos things just get forgotten.

HOWEVER, ALL THE feelings I associate with intimacy I don't need to place inside a box in order to remember. When I let myself misuse sex as a means to gain momentary satisfaction or a shadow of closeness like I did last night with Shane, I just want to curl into a ball and hide. By the time I got to Danielle and deposited the still warm latte in her hand, I was a bit of a mess.

"Looks like it's my turn to be the support beam." Throwing her arm over my shoulder. "Chin up, my dear Lilly."

"I can't. I have a zit on my chin." Tearing up. "It's really big."

"I thought you just did a piece on pimple prevention?"

"Thanks for reminding me." Scowling at her with my best tiger face.

"Easy. I don't think that is a zit." Holding my chin in her hand and inspecting closely. "I think you're allergic to something you used."

"Typical." Whimpering.

"Can I ask you something?" Eyeing me.

"Yeah."

"Be honest."

"What!"

"Did you use all the products at once?"

"Enough!" Slapping her hand away.

"Lilly." Shaking her head. "You . . ."

"I did! I'm stupid!" Interrupting her. "I'm upset and you are not helping!"

"Well, you can hardly see it." Examining my face again. "You need to cry on my shoulder?"

"Yep. Can you dig it?"

"Is it a double shot?" Holding up the coffee for inspection.

"Yep."

"I can dig it." Hugging me. "Let's go eat, I'm starving."

"Me too."

"You don't think that's contagious or anything?"

"You are such a bitch." Beginning to laugh.

We drove off in her little black Jetta with me trying to maul Danielle with a chin-rubbed finger.

"ladies" of the eighties

I have managed to jump off the spiral.
You can beat yourself up for making a
mediocre decision for only so long. Parisian trainer guy was years ago, and Shane
was fun and ultimately forgettable.
Danielle goofed around with me until I
felt, well, goofy. We ate copious amounts
of fried food, gossiped, and watched
another double feature of John Hughes
movies from under the covers of her
wrought-iron bed. Pretty soon, the throb
in my legs disappeared. As we read magazines, and talked about this and that and
not much of anything at all, I realized
that sometimes all you need is your girl to
hold your hand, make you smile, and tell
you how much better you would look than
Giselle, the model, in that outfit, even
though you know your girl is lying. I also
figured out that men couldn't hold a candle to the bonds between women. There's

114   a language that vaginas speak with a distinct accent that penises just can't nail down. (That is a weird sentence.) Anyway, that whole men are from Mars, women are from Venus thing is really true. Neither sex really gets anything but the gist of what the other is talking about. Maybe that's the point. Everything is a series of grunts and hand signals, a modern version of *Quest for Fire*. You just hope to find someone who at least speaks a third common lingo, comprehends your guttural groaning, and maybe somewhere in that the both of you understand something about each other.

A few days went by as they always do: work, eat, shower, and on Wednesday I needed my weekly movie fix. I searched for a partner, which usually is pretty easy since movies are my group's entertainment of choice, but for some reason I had slim pickings. Max was being beyond stubborn and would only see some stupid kung fu movie that I, on any other day, could have been swayed to watch, but we had no weed. Movies like that are entertaining only after smoking enough marijuana so that the action scenes spectacularly speed up because you have slowed down. Danielle had some dinner thing with a client, so I turned to Josh. He is an easy turn-to guy; he likes those schmaltzy teen romance flicks as much as I. Max was bitchy that I ditched him, but I was in the mood for something cute and corny, Josh was game, so I met him at the Beverly Center at seven.

"Hey." Kissing him on the cheek.

"What up? I got your ticket." Handing me the stub. "What happened to your bro?"

"You know how he feels about chick flicks." Walking

into the theater. "Last one I dragged him to was more annoying for me."

"Why?"

"All he did was groan through the whole thing. I had to keep elbowing him to shut up." Heading for concessions. "During every scene I had this running commentary from him. Want anything?"

"Water, please. Can I have some of your Goobers?"

"Sure."

I selected and paid for our treats and we proceeded in.

"Now I remember why I hate coming here." Looking at the maybe thirty-person room. "This theater sucks!"

"I know. I meant to comment but you got off the phone so fast." Picking seats in the third of five rows. "I don't think they have redone this in, like, ten years."

"At least we are alone." Looking around the room.

"How romantic. Wanna make out?" Josh jesting.

"Yeah, right!" Laughing. "You are the first gay guy who is going to shock everyone by sprinting back into the closet and going straight."

"I don't think so." Laughing. "You know how I feel about dick."

"Crude!" Laughing some more. "By the way, I got some."

"Really? Why didn't you tell me?"

"I am telling you now." Getting settled in my seat. "It was kind of lame and gross, so let's just leave it at that."

"Okay, but you needed it regardless." Reassuring me. (All my friends know my issues.)

"I guess."

The room darkened and the movie previews began.

116   Saved by the screen. As the silly teen romp played, I got to thinking about Josh. Josh as a general concept as the gay guy friend. Where do gay men fit in? They've got their pants full, but they also sometimes wear the proverbial skirt. They speak with a similar tongue, yet those tongues never want to touch your tonsils. They are a little of both. Everyone seems to be jumping on this straight women/gay men bandwagon. TV shows, movies, and magazine articles are always pontificating on the joys of this bond. They go on and on about how much easier it is for women to hang with boys who like boys. Gay men are more sensitive, more comforting, more fashion savvy. I'm in agreement on most of those things. Never have I had a straight guy besides my dad select the next hot T-shirt style or jean for me to purchase and tell me truthfully how I look in hot pants. Not that my dad, nor anyone else, has ever seen me in hot pants, but you get the idea. Josh is especially good at that. He has killer taste and a flare for finding Fred Segal accessories in more affordable stores like these Chinese feng shui bracelets made out of jade that he got in Chinatown for half the normal retail price. He's also the only person other than my mom whom I trust to go bathing suit shopping with, because he always comes up with the nicest way of telling me my ass looks like a overripe melon. It's great having a friend like him.

     Having a tight gay friend has opened me up to many more unusual experiences. They are neither good nor bad, just different. For example, a few days after our movie date, I needed a weekend break from the hetero world. Saturday nights are usually spent going to dinner, then a crowded bar with some friends, having two mediocre drinks over mundane conversation, trying to meet men, failing, and then going home alone to play Solitaire on my computer. I also needed to avoid any scenarios that could end up like my little cowboy fling, even if those escapades were few and far between. By staying away from boys who like girls, maybe I could disentangle myself one hundred percent from my double helix of bad sexual decisions. But I should have remembered that I never seem to get through an evening scot-free. Whether it's getting felt up by the wrong guy or running into the right guy when wearing the wrong outfit, you can rest assured it will happen to me. Let me explain.

Have you ever been fondled at a gay club? Well, it's a bit disconcerting. Do those hands reach out to touch you because they think, Ha! ha! I can get away with grabbing a girl's ass since I'm attached to a gay guy, or do the hands cop a feel because in that wig I'm wearing they think I'm in drag? Tonight, Josh talked me into going with him and some buddies of his to Stripper, this once-a-month hipster SilverLake gay club. I was game because Josh really begged, and I force him to so many boring straight events day in and day out that I owed it to him to join him in his scene. Also, I hadn't danced in a long time, ever since Danielle and I grooved late one night last fall at Bond's with a couple of twenty-year-olds. I especially dig dancing with gay men because they (a) are better dancers, (b) usually don't try to freak me and put their hands up my skirt, and (c) somehow always think I am Martha Graham, Twyla Tharp, and Janet Jackson all rolled into one smooth hoofer.

Each month there is a different theme at the club and this particular Saturday was "Ladies of the Eighties": Madonna, Pat, Annie, Belinda. My idols when I was seven years old. What self-respecting little girl didn't walk around with an armful of plastic rubber bracelets and a lace tie in her hair after watching the "Borderline" video on MTV? Stripper had a $20 cover charge and since there was no possibility of my meeting anyone, that was just a wee bit steep. If you got all glammed up, you got in cheaper. Dressed in costume it was five bucks, so you can bet your sweet tushie I was pulling out my fuchsia wig and the white plastic hooker dress I bought senior year in college for a Christmas cocktail party the girls and I threw.

THAT DRESS HAD hung like a cobweb in my closet for the last few years. There are just not that many places where white vinyl is appropriate. I do remember what a classic moment buying that dress was. Maya and I decided to sexpot it up for our holiday party. We went to the pleather and bad club-kid gear store on Thayer Street to find something tastefully inappropriate. Tap pants and chains were automatically out. We weren't going for the Hollywood Boulevard I-want-to-fuck-you big-hair look, just something racier than a prissy little black college cocktail dress every good coed had in her shoe box closet.

"Maya, I want to find something to go with those black-and-white platforms I have." Saying as we walked into the store.

"Which ones?"

"You know the ones my dad hates. I think I got them in Boston, freshman year, at the John Fluevog store on

Newbury Street. They are black with white stitching and look like Minnie Mouse shoes."

"I know them. By the way, your dad is so funny. Is he still giving you shit for constantly wearing shoes that dwarf all of us? I love it when he rips into you for that."

"Thanks a lot. You enjoy my dad's relentless teasing because he sticks up for you. He always protects the little guy. How many times do I have to defend myself? You can wear heels as well."

"I have heard that line before, every time your dad brings up this subject."

"Great, I'm a broken record."

"Not broken, just predictable."

"Fuck you."

On that kind note, we returned to our shopping, sifting through racks of scary dresses, or shirts, or whatever you call them. Since I had hangers of black clothing, I decided it had to be something white, winter white. I also instantaneously ruled out anything with Lycra, spandex, or any other body-sucking, butt-accentuating materials of torture. Luckily, there was this vinyl dress that didn't fall into any of those categories.

"What do you think of this one?" Holding up the white shift.

"It has potential, go try it on. I found a few too." Gesturing to the black scuba dresses hanging on her arm.

"Hey, since we're getting naked anyway, let's pick out something hideous for each other to try on."

"Okay, but what if we look terrible? Do we have to come out of the dressing room?"

"Of course, Maya. What fun is private humiliation?" Scanning the racks for Maya's getup.

Maya grabbed this red-and-black bustier leatherette dress with fringe for me, while I found this perfect leopard print Lycra pair of pants that had panels cut from the sides with a matching top for her to try on. Then we followed each other to the changing rooms. After a few minutes, we both started giggling.

"There is no fucking way I am coming out in this dress. I look worse than those fashion don'ts they print in the back of *Glamour.*" Calling over the dressing room wall.

"Whatever, miss what fun is private humiliation. You think I like pants that have no booty? On the count of three, Lilly, open the door and come out. One, two, three!"

With that, we both sprang from our chambers and stood facing each other, resplendent in bad dominatrix gear.

"Holy shit! Do we look bad!" Maya, giggling as she stared at our outfits in the three-way mirror.

"I don't think you guys look so terrible. Actually, I'm a little turned on." A male voice echoed from beyond. "Evan, what do you think?"

"Not bad. Could you turn a little so we get the full effect?" Another male voice asks.

Maya and I turned to see Jack and Evan, our buddies, standing by the register smiling. We paled like Casper.

"This is a joke, right?" Me, turning bright red.

"We're in a bad movie." Maya sputtering.

"I'd turn and run, but my butt! I can't turn around, it's hanging out."

"Mine too. I'm going to kill you!" Maya, turning her head toward me and throwing me the evil eye.

"Ladies, why so embarrassed? It's not like we have a camera or anything." Jack says and with that, Evan whipped out his instamatic, clicked the shutter, and fled the store laughing with Jack in tow.

"That didn't just happen. Please, tell me that didn't just happen." Stammering as I stood frozen to the black-and-white tile floor under me.

"It did, it definitely did. . . . Well, what now?"

"How should I know? This kind of shit only happens in movies. You couldn't write this."

"Whatever, you can write anything." Giving me an even nastier look than the evil eye. "You do know this is all your fault."

With that Maya turned, shook her little ass at me, and headed back into the dressing room. I followed, quietly got my clothes on, snatched up the white dress from the floor, and paid the bill. Maya followed suit and we walked out of the store praying there would be no major repercussions to this little incident. We were major hits that night at our party, although I don't think it was because of the new dresses we were wearing. Jack and Evan made sure it was the outfits we had on earlier that were the stars of the party. They printed up a hundred little flyers emblazoned with our tarty images and passed them out as coasters.

I HADN'T WORN that dress since the party. Bad karma. When I dragged it from the depths of my wardrobe grave-yard, I was reminded how ridiculous that evening was. At least the white dress still fit when I put it on, and for a bunch of gay boys and drag queens, it would be a definite knockout. All day Saturday, Josh and I prepped. Boredom makes you do such lame things. I was so bitchy, I made Josh drive all over town looking for these rhinestone thingies I wanted to glue all around my eyes. A little Madonna at the Oscars.

"Let's try Hollywood Boulevard. I bet one of those stores will have them."

"Why are you so obsessed? You drive me crazy."

"Whatever. Last week I drove your ass around apartment hunting, I think you can handle it."

"You are so sassy."

"Whatever, Joshua."

"Fine, sassafras. Let's go."

We went to all these skeevy shops dotting Hollywood Boulevard: wig stores, costume stores, lingerie stores, S&M stores. When the fifth place smelled like God knows what had peed, Josh stopped humoring me.

"That's it. No rhinestones for you. I feel like I need to shower just from standing in here. I hope the car is still there."

"Don't be such a paranoid priss. No one is going to steal the car. It's broad daylight. You think everywhere we don't live is a bad neighborhood. Anyway, just a few more places, please?" Whining a little to get him to go to this particular art store, which was where I should have gone in the first place, but Josh put his foot down.

"No way, we are done, especially after you essentially called me a snob. It is time to go." Losing all patience with me.

"I'm sorry, I didn't mean it . . . I'm desperate. . . . Please?" Begging.

I knew I had pissed him off when pouting failed to illicit any response except silence. I was just going to have to go without my little gems. Damn! To compensate for making him drive me around all day, I offered to doll Josh up. I even let him borrow my favorite black tank top and use my makeup. *Yuck,* I hate letting other people use my makeup ever since I read this article in *Vogue* about all the germs and bacteria that can grow in lipstick and eyeliner, but I felt a little guilty for being a brat, so I gave in. (You know I am going to go out to buy new mascara tomorrow.) I should have been more worried about the top, knowing Josh's spilling problem, but he was pretty good at taking care of my stuff.

Actually, he is really good at taking care of me in general. A one hundred percent totally reliable and trustworthy friend. I am lucky to have him around to bullshit with, chow down with at every lunch, and go shopping with. I just like to sometimes give him shit and make fun of him because he's this wacky, eccentric, goofy guy. My very own Shakespearean jester. Sassing him is too fun not to do it, and I can't resist throwing a barb whenever I can. Giving each other grief is our form of entertainment. And tonight, what girl could get a better date to match her prostitute style than a draggy Annie Lennox. Josh looked pretty funny with spiked orange hair and layered— and I mean layered—Viva Glam lipstick all over his mouth. We were quite the couple, and we were ready.

Of course Stripper didn't get hopping until eleven. It was only eight, and I was ravenous. Deciding to eat out, Josh and I, decked out in our club gear, went to one of our favorite Mexican joints for margaritas and fajitas. It didn't take me very long to remember what I had on. It was like

124   the eighth-grade prom, when your braces matched the pink poofy dress you thought looked good at Macy's, and every single one of your classmates turned to see the doof your mom had to bribe to take you as the music skidded to a stop and they all started pointing and laughing.

"Maybe I should have cooked us some chicken or something at my house?" Me, swallowing slowly.

"Whatever. I don't think we look that strange."

"Easy for you to say. At least your clothes are made from breathable fabrics. I look like a Japanese cartoon character."

"Actually, I think you look like that cartoon, shit, what was it called. . . . They were a rock group and went on adventures. Maybe they were called *The Misfits*?"

Josh tends to mix up pop culture references.

"I know what you're talking about, but I don't think it was *The Misfits*. . . . *Jem,* that's it. You really think I look like *Jem*? Truly, truly, outrageous." Singing their little tag line and shaking my hips.

"You just gave away that you watched that lame show. Didn't that come on when we were, like, thirteen?"

"Maybe, I don't know, but so what? I like the Backstreet Boys and the Spice Girls too. If I had gotten the call from Baby to replace Ginger, I'd have done it in a minute."

"Oy vey, my wanna-be pop singer friend."

"They have the best job in the world. They get to sing, dance, wear ridiculous clothing, and make millions of little girls happy. They know they're cheesy, but they dig it and relish the attention they get."

"Maybe, but I will never be convinced of their artistic merit."

"Me neither, but they are pure fun, a total guilty pleasure. One thing, though . . . don't tell anyone that I really listen to them. . . . Promise?"

"Fine, but if you start listening to Hanson I *will* be forced to tell all."

"Deal."

Finally, we were seated, and the hostess put us in a nice cozy table by the kitchen doors. The placement wasn't really that bad, because the people at the table next to us fell in love with my pink hair. Mind you, they were all small children under the age of five and probably thought I was a Power Ranger, but still it was nice to feel wanted. Josh and I made faces at them all through dinner, and we had them laughing, so it took some of the pressure off me being white vinyl and Josh wearing lipstick.

"I love that kids can embrace the strange and unusual," Josh says, giving the little girl a goofy face. "I want a baby so badly."

"Me too. I can't wait to be a mom. The older I get the more I think about it. Ever since I can remember, I knew that being a mom was my ultimate mission in life." Gazing at the kids in adoration. "There can't be anything as rewarding as seeing a little face look at you with pure, unadulterated love."

"At least all you have to do is find the right guy. I have to find the right guy, which is hard enough. Then I have to meet the right girl to carry the baby for me. My problem is twofold. It's going to involve such planning. Maybe you'll just have to have my baby for me."

"Maybe not. Even though I love you dearly, my friend, that would be just too weird."

"We wouldn't even have to have sex."

"I don't think so. Something about turkey basters being used for gynecological purposes gives me the creeps. You'll have to find a nice lesbian to help you."

"You never know, you might end up switching teams."

"If I did, it would be for an at-bat, not an entire season. Besides, there are plenty of girls who would help a cute gay guy out. It just isn't going to be me."

"That's too bad. I have always wanted to be a member of the family."

"You just want a wardrobe like mine."

"True. God, when you have a kid, your parents are going to go nuts. I can just see your mom buying out the store."

"My mom? No way. My dad will be in there buying twelve of everything in every color. My kid will own Patagonias in every possible weight and style."

"Your kids are going to be so spoiled."

"And chic. By the way, we are pathetic for talking about babies so much. I can't even fathom the responsibility of a puppy. And, as my mom says, 'don't get ahead of yourself.' I don't even have a boyfriend."

"Well, none of us do. Maybe I'll meet him tonight."

"Maybe I won't! Just don't ditch me or I'll kick your ass."

Josh and I finished dinner and just as we were about to walk out the door, I heard someone call Josh's name. I froze.

"Hey, Jonah, what's up?" Josh asking.

"Not much. Just grabbing a quick bite."

"Yeah, us too." Gesturing to me. (Asshole!)

"Hi, Jonah." Me, blushing.

"Oh, my God, Lilly. I didn't recognize you." Laughing. "What the hell are you wearing?"

"It's my new look." Trying to hide my humility. "What do you think?"

"You look like a Hollywood Boulevard he/she hooker." Touching my wig. "I have never seen you look so skanky."

"Thanks. That was the vibe I was going for."

"Well, you succeeded." Checking out the rest of my outfit.

"I made her dress up. We're going to this drag club." Josh interjecting. "I think she looks hot."

"I agree. It's just a little more Lilly than I remember." Cataloging and itemizing all of me.

"Well, it's been awhile."

"Yep." Still staring at me. "It has."

"Yeah."

"So . . ." Jonah, not knowing what to say.

"So . . ." Me, not knowing what to say.

"So . . ." Josh, trying to think of something to say. "Lilly, we've got to go. Jonah, take it easy."

"Bye, Josh. Lilly, I'll call you."

"Yeah, okay, bye."

With that I hurried out the door into the cool night. *Ugh!* Why does a girl have to run into a guy looking like this?

"That was in-ter-est-ing." Josh enunciating as he got into the car.

"Thrilling. I haven't seen him in months, and I run into him wearing cheap vinyl."

"It wasn't that bad." Trying to cheer me up. "He thought you looked hot."

"Yeah, hot like a hooker! To me that was like getting caught in an accident with dirty underwear."

"It was so not like that. Relax."

"Okay, Annie. Whatever you say." Looking out the window and sulking.

"Can you please just let this go? I do not want to deal with this version of you tonight."

"Fine."

"Promise?"

"I said fine. Just let me be a minute. God!"

Josh shut up and drove. So, despite the huge damper that interlude put on my evening, we headed off to Stripper to meet our friends (or really Josh's gay friends who think I am a really cute straight girl they'd marry in a second if I had a penis). We parked and got high, really high. I had to dampen and dull my Jonah headache. Do you think I would be able to deal with this scene sober? Not! We got to the door and tried to finagle the cheaper rate.

"Come on, we're in costume." Josh, batting his mascaraed lashes.

"All you have on is makeup. Sorry, in this post—RuPaul world that just doesn't cut it anymore." The doorman replied.

"She's Cyndi Lauper, I'm Annie Lennox. She *is* wearing a wig." Josh, continuing with the persuasion.

"Okay, since I'm a sucker for beggars, she gets in for five dollars, but, honey, you are full price. Next time, sweetie, let yourself go."

Josh looked a little dejected as we paid, but as soon as we walked in, his mood brightened. Then we realized what "in costume" really meant, and we both were pathetic excuses. There were drag queens there who were so fucking unbelievable! Huge wigs, platform shoes that put the Spice Girls' three-feet sneakers to shame, tight sequined dresses, and killer sparkly makeup. There was even someone dressed like Joan Cusack in *Sixteen Candles*. He had both the headgear and the neck brace that had prevented Joan's character from drinking water from the fountain. It was awesome. And, guess what? These Doublemint twin queens had on my rhinestones! I was so jealous—in the black light they looked so cool. Oh, well. Then the lights began to flash, the music began to blare, and the people started to spin. Love it when the maryjane kicks in. My grin widened, I forgot all about my encounter with you-know-who, and Josh and I took to the dance floor. After about seven songs and the development of a serious case of underboob sweat, Josh and I sojourned to the bar area.

"Josh, so, I am curious, is anyone here straight besides me?"

"No, but now you know how I feel most of the nights we go out."

"What about that guy over there dancing. He's cute and he keeps smiling this way."

"Not to be a dick, but I already talked to him. He's from San Francisco here visiting a friend, and he is smiling at me."

"Lucky you. I bet he is digging my stellar makeup job. You look sexy." Smiling at Josh as I moved closer to the bar to order a drink.

It was right here that I felt the fondle. A soft little caress and careful squeeze on my rump. Shocked, I turned to see two little gay guys smiling at me like nothing was wrong. I turned back to Josh and felt the frisk again. This time I was the Charmin.

"Umm, excuse me." Turning to face the smaller of the pair. "Was that just your hand on my ass, or am I imagining things?"

"I just had to reach out and touch someone." Grinning at me. "It was just out there. Bam!"

I swiveled my head left and right, trying to get a good glimpse of my goodies.

"Out there, huh?" Still looking at my ass.

"Yep. Nice and perky."

"Well, thanks. No one has told me I have a perky tush before." Spinning back to face him. "But, no more rubdowns, okay? My ass is now officially a hands-free zone."

"Deal."

"So, wanna buy this perky ass a drink?"

"My pleasure."

"Lilly." Extending my hand.

"Dominick." Shaking my hand. "This is Chad."

"Nice to meet you both."

My twin Twinkies and I ordered beverages, and then chatted for the rest of the night. What lovely gentlemen! Usually strange hands up my skirt don't turn me on in any way, shape, or form unless I want them there, but any guy, and I mean any guy, who says I have a nice ass gets a little leeway.

two for the road

Sunday morning I awoke, tossed a hazy gaze
at the dress and shoes laying like a chalk
outline on my floor, and searched around
my bed for the remote control. Beneath
three twisted blankets and a beaten pillow,
it lay, along with the portable phone, a
pen, and my wig. How all this got in my
bed is beyond me. I flipped on MTV,
tossed the wig onto the floor, and threw the
pen across the room, perfectly landing it
on my corner table. I am Michael Jordan
reincarnate. Reaching by the side of the
bed, I grabbed the Advil and water I always
have ready, downed two, and dialed.

"Hey, Maya."

"Lilly. What's up?" Answering the
phone on the third ring.

"Besides being exhausted from having
been felt up by a gay guy and running
into Jonah wearing my white vinyl dress,
I'm fine."

"Not the one we bought together? You still have it?"

"Oh, yes. That would be the one. I felt like an asshole."

"Well you were in like company."

"What does that mean?"

"Jonah. Why you care about how you look in front of that jerk is a mystery to me. He sucks."

"You are so overprotective."

"Maybe. Yeah, I know. At least I am not as bad as your father."

"No shit! After the Jonah melodrama, I don't even broach the subject of men with him. The dude and I will have to be well into a relationship, talking about china patterns, before I dare bring him up."

"Dude? What are we, chilling on the beach, ripping curls, and hanging ten, Betty?" Teasing me.

"Like totally, Betty."

"That is not even surfer speak. That's Valley circa 1983."

"Like, whatever, bitch. It's Sunday. I can't be up on all my jargon on this day of rest."

"But we are Jews."

"Details, details."

"So, felt up by a gay guy, huh?" Breaking off the conversation. "What happened?"

"Just a usual evening spent with Josh."

"Well, was it at least a good cop?" Asking with complete seriousness.

"You're nasty." Laughing out loud.

"Thanks, darling. I try. Look, I'm sorry I lashed out a bit about Jonah. He doesn't totally suck. The *dude* was hot. It's just my duty to try and keep you, Miss head-in-the-clouds, on this planet. I love you."

"I know. Just forget about it. Anyway, the real purpose behind my call was I have this random plan." Changing the subject.

"Do tell."

"I know your mom is coming in a few weeks and you are busy, but want to play hooky?"

"What do you mean?"

"Well, you know my mom and I are leaving on Tuesday for our little road trip to the Grand Canyon."

"Yeah, the annual mother-daughter love fest."

"So, we are going to meet up with my dad and Max in Vegas for this restaurant opening, and I think it would be perfect if you came to meet us," saying enthusiastically.

"Hummm . . ."

"We can shop and gamble and spa it."

"Keep going." Letting herself get convinced.

"Max is bringing some good weed and we can pretend that weddings and exes don't exist."

"Twist my arm, give me the details."

Fun, fun, fun. I love that I can still win her over with pot. Some things never change, and Maya's collegiate predilection for smoking was constant. The next few weeks are going to be so great. Maya and I get to tear up Vegas, and my mom and I always have unusual and terrific times on our little jaunts. I was hoping that this one would be no exception.

Tuesday rolled around, I picked Mom up in my car, switched to the passenger side, loaded up the CDs, placed all my maps carefully about the dash, and we were off. Luckily we had a six CD changer because Mom was not digging my grooves.

"Lilly, if I have to listen to one more whiny girl I am taking the first plane home and you can finish the trip alone."

"Whoa, Nelly. You're being a little harsh."

"Just switch it."

"I am not listening to Zydeco again!"

"What else do we have?"

"Joni Mitchell, some Dylan, Cat Stevens."

"Cat Stevens."

"Fine."

A tentative peace was reached again and we kept driving. Thank God my mom was a bit of a hippie back in the day, so I know we will always come together over early rock and roll. With my dad it was Meatloaf, Bob Seger, and sometimes Top 40, and with my brother, a little trip-hop or Green Day always united the car.

It felt good to get away and go on vacation. I got to put everything on the back burner. Shane, weddings, and Jonah all could float out the window and languish on the highway. I'm sure I would pick them up hitchhiking on the way home, but for now it was just Mom and me, a lot of road-stop food, and the largest cow patty tourist attractions. Sometimes you need to leave your life, take a break, in order to really see how silly and stupid all the things you stress over are. It sounds kind of simplistic and obvious, but getting away and gaining some perspective is a beautiful thing. Maybe it was just the desert air and "Peace Train" on the speakers, but whatever works.

On day three, Mom and I had one of our typical experiences. This time it involved an open road, a highway officer, a real hitchhiker, and a glass of Caber-net. Mom and I were spending the night in Santa Fe, and we had just had a great meal at the Coyote Café: four courses worthy of two cigarette breaks. Mom was driving, we were blabbing, and then there were flashing red lights. Soon, Mom was on the side of the road, praying she wouldn't get a ticket.

"Ma'am. Did you know the speed limit was twenty-five?"

"Yes, Officer, of course." Stammering and smiling. "Wasn't that what I was driving?"

"You were going thirty-eight."

"Really? I didn't realize. I'm sorry."

"Well, you were. Can I see your license and registration?"

"Of course." Fumbling in her purse. "I think what happened was that just out of town I saw this hitchhiker and I probably sped up a little to get away from him."

"Where was he?" Taking her information.

"Just a little way back at the bus stop."

"I'll be back in a minute." Walking back to his patrol car.

"Mom, I can't believe you. Terrific excuse." Chiding her. "Good try at getting out of a ticket. That will so not work. Traffic school here you come."

"Well, there really was a hitchhiker there. He looked potentially dangerous."

"Yeah, right. In that prepubescent way. He was, like, seventeen, probably just got off work, and you just completely busted him. I can't believe you."

"It just fell out." Starting to giggle. "Words sometimes tumble out before I can self-edit."

"So that's where I get it from. Shush, stop laughing. Here he comes." Shoving her.

"Okay, Ma'am, I'm just going to give you a warning since you are out of state."

"Thank you."

"Have you been drinking, Ma'am?"

"Just a glass of wine, Officer."

"I can smell it."

"I swear it was just a glass. I do have my daughter in the car." Gesturing to me. "I wouldn't do anything to endanger her."

"You'd be surprised how many drunks drive around with their kids. Be more careful next time." Leaving us in our luck. "I don't want to see you two again." Walking away.

"Nice, Mom. Way to go! I didn't think it was going to happen." Punching her arm. "But next time leave me out of it. I will have no part of your criminal activities."

"Promise." Winking at me. "That was good though, huh?"

"Here." Handing her a mint. "You obviously need this."

Mom flicked it into her mouth and promptly spit it out.

"Ugh!" Wiping her mouth with her hand. "What the hell is that? My mouth is on fire."

"They are supposed to be the latest in breath fresheners." Looking at the tin. "I hadn't tried that one yet."

"Well, don't. Is there any water by your feet? Or at least a napkin I can wipe my tongue on?"

"Yeah." Handing her an Evian. "I guess I will have to give that one a thumbs-down. I will even give you a little credit."

" 'Does not melt in your mouth, it actually melts your mouth,' according to Linda, Lilly's mother."

"Nice copy, Mom. I am writing that down."

"Thanks." Gulping the last of the water.

Believe it or not, we have not always had this grace nor aplomb in dealing with our road-trip follies. We seem to have improved in our old age. Thank goodness we aren't too perfect, because I do love catching a glimpse of my mom when she's just a little bit messy. Those are the best times, when you can see that your parents are a little smudged, a little bit disheveled. It makes them so much more appealing, because suddenly a vision of how they once were and how they used to and still do fuck up once in awhile pops into your mind. It's like a stage actor's face before he layers on all the thick pancake makeup, false eyelashes, and rouge. A clean, vulnerable, and incredibly human visage. I think parents shouldn't be afraid of being mortal, making mistakes, even cursing every once in awhile. If they have to put nickels in the swear jar too, it makes it easier on kids, makes everyone paddle the same creaky boat. I remember a poem I read by Dorian Locke, I think it was called "Small Gods." It was all about seeing your parents as bigger-than-life mythological creatures. My parents were never larger-than-life, they were just parents. Fragile, fearless, and fallible.

MOM AND I have become this sort of *Thelma and Louise* vaudeville routine. It all started two years ago, the summer after I lived in Paris. We ditched the men in our family, and we set out alone to conquer the Italian coun-tryside . . . or at least eat it to death. It was our first girl-girl trip. After gorging ourselves in Venice at this cooking school, we embarked in our little Fiat. Destination Paris. The initial plan was that we would alternate the driving responsibilities and spend a week eating, shopping, eating, shopping, and ultimately return to my apartment in Paris to puke. As it turned out, there was no way in hell I was going to get behind the wheel with all those aggressive European drivers. I'm a very mellow driver, easygoing, never cutting people off. I would be eaten alive, or grow gray waiting for an opportunity to merge. On the other hand, my lead-footed mother, as I affectionately called her, was just crazy enough to keep us safely on the road. Seeing how I wasn't driving, I became the navigator, which was a good thing because Mom was terrible with directions. It was a very good arrangement—in the beginning.

On day four of our little adventure, we decided to take a day trip away from our charming inn to visit Torino. After a nice lunch, some gelato, mine straciatella, hers coconut, a church or two, and a shopping stop, we headed back. Not wanting to repeat ourselves, we thought it would be a great idea to take little roads in order to see more of the surroundings. Things started off just fine. We were in the wine country and happily watched the grapes grow. Then, in a blink of an eye, we were very, very, very lost.

"Where are we going?" Mom, asking irritably. "I thought you said this was the way back to the hotel."

"I did, but all the roads seem to lead nowhere." Exam-ining the map more closely.

"I thought you knew which direction to go. Are you even looking at the map?"

"No, I'm not . . ." Sarcastically throwing her a sour look. "Of course I am! Do you think I am trying to direct us to Spain?!" Getting huffy.

"Calm down. Just look at the next sign and find it on the map."

"What do you think I have been doing this whole time?"

"Okay, relax. Here read that one." Pointing ahead of her while slowing down the car.

"I see it. Here it is, turn left . . . no . . . wait, turn right." Flipping the map over.

"How are you going to read it upside down?"

"Fuck! The problem is this map from the hotel has its logo right over where we are. We are probably only ten minutes away." Whining.

"Let's just take this road and hope it gets us there."

Just as Mom made her turn, we saw a brown blur come out of nowhere and smash into the front window. There was this loud, uncomfortable, jarring thump. We looked at each other, then at the window.

"What the . . . ? Mom, pull over."

"God, what was that?" Slowing the car down.

"I don't know." Getting out of the car and walking around. "It's a bird. It's all fucked up. I think you killed it." Peering at the ground.

A little brown bird lay on a cold grave, his wing twisted and small beak somewhere hidden beneath.

"I killed it?! It flew at the window! It's not my fault!" Coming over to look. "Oh, no."

140   "At least it was probably killed instantly, no suffering. Poor bird. I can't believe you did that." Getting back in the car quickly. (Dead animals give me the heebie-jeebies.)

"I didn't do anything. Actually, if someone hadn't gotten us lost, I wouldn't have been on this road in the first place and I wouldn't have been here to collide with that poor bird." Eyeing me as she got back into the car.

"Don't blame me, bird killer! You wanted to take the scenic route!"

"An hour ago you thought it was a great idea too!" Starting to smile.

"Well, are you going to move it?"

"What?" Mom asking.

"The bird you killed?"

"I'm not touching it."

"You can't leave it in the middle of the road. Cruel and unusual punishment."

"If it matters so much," looking at me, "you move it."

"Fine!" Jumping out of the car.

I walked to the trunk and fumbled around our things looking for something that could pass as a low-tech, fleshless version of my hand. An umbrella, perfect. I went over to Tweety and gently rolled him to the side. It was more like a shove, a push, then a roll, but a roll sounds so much more graceful and kind. I managed to get the bird on a bald patch of grass, threw the umbrella back in the trunk, and got into the car.

"I am now officially your accomplice."

"Thank you."

"Way to initiate me into your life of murder and crime." Eyeing my mom.

"Again, I will reiterate that the bird flew into the window."

"Whatever, bird killer." Starting to smile at the absurdity of the moment. I mean, here were two ladies in a small car stopped in front of a dead bird in the middle of nowhere. Definitely not normal.

"Lilly, you do realize we are still lost. . . ."

We did get back safely, just as night was falling. Lucky for us, or we would have been sleeping in the car and that would have been mighty uncomfortable in the two-door. I don't think we got lost again on that trip, even when we went to return the rental car in Paris, which was a major feat. Nor did we kill any more unsuspecting forest creatures, unless you count the giant spider I found in the bathroom of our hotel, which I sent to a watery rest. You kill once, and well . . . it gets easier and easier, especially when eight hairy legs are involved.

OUR SECOND ROAD trip the following year was through France's Loire Valley. One day, Mom had her mind set on seeing troglodytes who lived in this little hole-in-the-wall town I obviously couldn't find on any normal-size Fodor's map. When I finally found it on a random pull-out page in one of our other guidebooks, the town literally turned out to be set inside a hole! Despite an incoming rainstorm, we finally reached this pinprick. It was one little farm which was the entire fucking town. Houses, toilets, wine presses, ovens, plants, and animals were all set inside the limestone beneath the ground. After wandering through cave after cave filled with actual people's personal belongings, Mom leaned over and whispered to me.

"This is not what I thought this was supposed to be."

"What do you mean? This is what that dumb book said."

"I know, but I thought troglodytes were something else."

"What did you think they were?"

"I'll tell you in the car."

She sure sparked my interest, but I had to pee. I went in some sketchy potty, and then busted a move to the car. In my hurry to get back to Mom's story, I stepped in a big pile of wet chicken shit, which was a major nasty bummer. Luckily, I spied a hose and washed it off before getting back into the car.

"Okay, I'm waiting." Tapping my fingers on the dashboard.

"I thought they were supposed to be cave dwellers."

"They were."

"No, like cavemen, like a new culture."

"Are you kidding me?" Laughing, then laughing harder, realizing the implications of her statement.

"No, I thought they would be . . ."

"Like creatures from the *Wild Thing* book?" Finishing her sentence.

"Exactly."

"Mom, you're a freak! I can't believe you would think there were little trolls, running around France living in tourist attractions. Besides, the only wild things around are snoring mothers by the name of Linda." Giving her a jab.

"Cute, Lilly. Anyway, it's just when I read about it last

night, those little dolls with the fluorescent tufts of hair popped into my head."

"I knew you were drunk after dinner. Please, go easy on the wine tonight. I'd hate to see what other creatures you conjure up."

SO CARS AND wine and weird ones became tradition. Now there would be the blame-the-poor-hitchhiker story to add to the mix. We managed to get to Vegas without further difficulty and relatively crime-free if you ignore the insect death trap our front window had become. Maya was already there when we arrived. It was the first time I had seen her since the news, and she looked the same. Same black pants, cute lightweight embroidered button-down, worn-in jean jacket, and black Kate Spade purse. Same girl. Same friend. Thank goodness.

"Hi, honey. Congratulations!" My mom, hugging her. "Mike and I are so happy for you."

"Thanks, Linda. The orchid you sent was so beautiful."

"Hey, babe." Hugging her too. "So, let me see the ring."

"It actually is getting fixed. One of the stones was loose." Squeezing me back. "You will just have to wait and see it."

"Bitch. You know that was the only reason I wanted to see you." Pinching her side. "It's all about the diamonds."

"You are such a jerk!" Laughing. "Lilly, let's get this party started. The slot machines are starting to call my name. Maya, Maya, Maya!"

"Well, they will have to wait a bit. I had Mike's office book us massages at the spa," Mom says. "Lets go change and we'll head over."

"Linda, remember when you, Lilly, and I went to that sketchy spa in Calistoga?"

"Oh, yes! It was interesting smearing mud all over my daughter's ass." Winking at me. "I hadn't paid that much attention to those cheeks since you were a baby."

"And they told us people came there with their coworkers!" Me, exclaiming. "If you thought it was weird rubbing my butt, imagine that it is the person you share a cubicle with!"

"That place was so bizarre." Maya, laughing. "I did have a good massage though."

"I think this one might be better." Mom, smiling. "I heard the spa was just redone, and I think we are getting that new hot-stone treatment."

"Perfect." Maya and I reply in unison.

After Maya, Mom, and I got rubbed, and loved, we walked around the casino a bit. I hit the blackjack tables while Maya tried her luck at the slots. Mom went off to meet my dad, and soon it was time to get ready for the evening. Maya and I started the night innocently enough at a cocktail party with my parents and their friends. The guest list read like a who's who of Hollywood, and the people-watching was fantastic. Young stars with younger models, older stars whose charisma only got better as they aged, and other business types enjoyed the spectacle. Maya and I, having already gambled a bit, loved the scene, and the lovely break it offered to our slimming wallets. But after a few hours we were ready to bail.

"Maya, can we stop at the room before we do anything? These heels kill." Taking off a shoe and rubbing my stockinged foot.

"Sure, but what do you want to do anyway?" Downing the last of her white wine. "The world is our oyster."

"Whatever. You pick where we are going to go diving for pearls."

"Do you want to smoke first and then decide?"

"Did someone here mention marijuana?" A male voice says from behind us before I can answer her.

We turned to see this actor guy grinning at us with this very cute cinematic smile. I of course perked up a bit, seeing how I was a sucker for those actor boys. Bright teeth and thick brows make my knees melt.

"My name's Andy," he said, extending his hand. (Like we didn't know who he was. His face used to grace many a rag sheet. We'd have had to be living on those French underground holes to mistake him for someone else.)

"Maya, and this is Lilly." Gesturing to me. "She's having a little shoe problem."

"I noticed. They're great though." Pointing to my heel.

"Thanks." Me, responding midrub.

"It's really nice to meet you two. I can't tell you how happy I am to see some younger people around. You here for the opening?"

"Yeah." (He digs my shoes! I haven't worn them since you-know-when. I think they might be troublemakers.)

"So what are you guys doing now? I did hear you mention getting high, didn't I?" Lifting one sexy eyebrow to punctuate his question.

"You're correct, but we hadn't really made any plans yet."

"Well, I just got this stuff sent to me from Amsterdam and brought it. Why don't I get it and meet you in your room?"

"Quite the plan maker." Maya, eyeing him.

"It's easy when it comes to pretty girls and bud." (Cheese ball!!)

"Room 1512. See you soon." Maya, walking in the direction of the rooms.

You could tell by the way we walked and the slight glow emanating from our faces that we felt a little "hey there" sexy since some actor whom we dug as preteens wanted to hang with us. Granted, he was super lame, aging, and his lines smelled like ripe brie, but he was still hot in that used-to-be-famous way. Who doesn't deep down want to kick it with a teen idol? I always have and will love cute boys. Actors usually happen to be cute, and although lately I have moved on to musicians like Jonah, I still have a soft spot in my heart for film stars. John Cusack, are you listening?

Maya and I headed upstairs, I changed my shoes, and we primped. Instead of waiting for Andyman, we decided to get a head start. For some insane reason, bud from Amsterdam didn't seem potent enough. We had to enhance our trip with some extra LA kind. I rolled a perfect joint and handed it to Maya.

"This trip was exactly what I needed." Maya, taking a hit. "I have been losing my mind a bit lately."

"No kidding." Grabbing the joint. "My mom and I had a great time driving. No distractions or worries. Nice open highway."

"It's cool that you guys get along so well. I think we have special relationships with our parents."

"I know. Imagine being one of those kids who fights all the time? That would seriously suck." Handing her the joint.

"It doesn't make sense to me. I think that is why I picked my guy. Ted gets along great with his family."

"My mom always told me to watch how boys talk and interact with their parents because that's a sign about what kind of man they will be."

"It is so true." Walking to the mirror and fluffing her hair. "How do you think I should do my hair for the wedding?"

"Well, you don't want it all down." Walking over to her and taking the joint. "Then it gets in the way and you have to futz with it. I think half up and wavy would look pretty."

"I guess it all depends on the veil." Holding her hair in different styles. "Is there more?"

"Yeah, finish it, I can't deal with the roach."

"Nice joint, by the way."

"Merci."

JOINT ROLLING JUST happens to be a Lilly specialty. A unique talent I have cultivated over the years. One night in college, my friend Jack and I were sitting around Emily and Maya's room, smoking and talking about music. I was again on the defensive about my taste for girl rock, and was trying to justify its merits while rolling us a joint. At first Jack wanted to roll it himself, but the conversation got so heated that he bailed from the task to prattle on about how great Phish and the Dead were. I took over, finished, and then let him light the joint, hoping it would shut him up. Sure enough the conversation lightened.

"I really hate the music you listen to."

"How original."

"But now that I think about it, that doesn't really matter. I have to give you credit for standing by it like you do." Jack, exhaling. "I'm sorry for giving you shit all the time."

"Wow! Coming from you that's a big compliment. Thanks so much!" Sarcastically exclaiming. "What caused this big change of heart?"

"Well, any girl who can roll a good joint deserves a break."

"How generous of you." Laughing as smoke poured from my mouth.

After that moment, Jack never rode me about my chick rockers, and he always let me handle the joints.

THE ONE I ROLLED for Maya and me had been pretty good. Before we really knew what hit us, we were high as the proverbial kite. Then the doorbell rang and Andy was standing there, grinning, and holding this big FedEx package in his hands.

Trying to play off being stoned is perhaps one of the dumbest things a person can do. Once you fixate on getting yourself straight, you immediately start freaking out and making yourself paranoid. In attempting to curb the THC in the bloodstream, you make it circulate that much quicker, due to racing hearts and intense focus on sobering up. It was very evident the minute Andy walked into the room that we were a mess, and no amount of acting could pull this off. Luckily, instead of needing Maya and me to participate in the conversation right away, our actor boy was content to dominate the flow of communication.

"My friend had to go through such lengths to get this into the country. It was so James Bond. He had to send it to some other guy, who sent it to a false name at this random PO Box in Hollywood. Then he had someone FedEx me a key. When I finally got the goods, they were wrapped all high-tech *Mission Impossible* style. Lots of plastic and tape and boxes within boxes. I mean, you know how bad it would be if I got caught smuggling bud in from Amsterdam? The *Enquirer* would have a fucking party. By the time I actually got around to smoking it, I was kind of upset with myself for risking it, but then I tried it and knew it was all worth it, big time. I bet it will be the best you have ever had. You guys are very fortunate to get to sample some."

By the time he was done with his monologue, he had rolled a fatty and lit it. I don't even think he noticed that Maya and I had yet to speak. We sat there, smiling, letting this guy blab on and on. He was rather pompous and ignorant, but we were too incapacitated to jump in and interrupt his soliloquy. For the next five minutes, we passed around the joint, and little by little Maya and I lost our shit. First, I got this vicious body tick. I could feel every muscle twitch, and the moment I tried to concentrate and stop it, it would pop out in another body part. I bet no one else could see the Mexican hat dance jumping through my veins, but I certainly felt it. Maya got all fidgety and started pacing around the room. Not really pacing, just getting up, getting water, sitting down, tying her shoe, getting up, getting a sweater, sitting down, adjusting her hair. Then, stupidly, Maya and I caught each other in the eye and we just broke up.

The giggle started quietly enough, like the laugh you try to swallow at a movie when only you and the friend you are with find something funny while the rest of the audience is crying. The only problem was this laugh was too big to choke down. All our trying to be cool party girls for the hottie only made the entire situation funnier. Pretty soon I was on the floor laughing my ass off, and Maya had tears running down her face. I don't think we even realized that by this point Andy was sitting there with his face whitening like a carton of chalk.

"Are you guys okay?"Andy, fidgeting.

More laughter was our only response. I think I might have even started hyperventilating.

"I guess you guys aren't used to such strong shit."

Laughter.

"I think I'm going to take off."

Laughter.

"See you guys tomorrow."

Laughter.

"Bye."

He left in such a hurry, with the door slamming behind him, that it only made the whole situation more ridiculous seeing how we totally blew our chance to play it cool. The guy couldn't wait to ditch the freaky girls who

weren't able to handle their bud. Maya and I were in hysterics, rolling on the floor, when Max came into the
room; it was a two-bedroom suite and we were sharing. I
can't begin to imagine what we must have looked like.
Disheveled with our skirts bunched up around our
waists, choking back tears and guffaws, and unable to
look each other in the eye. So not ladylike.

"What the fuck is wrong with you guys? Man, does it
reek in here." Going to the bathroom and putting on
the fan.

"Oh, my God." Maya, trying to catch her breath.
"Oh, my God."

"I have snot running everywhere." Me, running to the
bathroom for a mop.

"You guys are so stoned. Maya, your eyes are blood-
shot. What happened?" Max asked. "Did you smoke all of
the pot I brought?"

"No, I shoved it in Lilly's bag over there. Sorry we
started without you. I think we just did way too much. That
guy came up with this Amsterdam stuff and we had already
smoked, and we smoked more and then we just lost it."

"Lilly, you smoked with Andy?" Calling to me.
"Right on."

"Yeah, this will be a funny story one day." Calling back.

"One day? It is now." Maya added.

"I bet this will make it even more funny." Max, nodding as he fashioned his own joint.

"What?" Maya, asking, then calling over her shoulder,
"Lilly, are you okay in there?"

"I think so," coming out of the bathroom. "I just
started tripping out on my face in the mirror. I started

making all these fish faces and testing out smiles. I'm totally fucked up."

"Max says he has something to add to this ridiculousness."

"I heard." Going to the bed and lying down with my legs dangling off the side. I closed my eyes and could swear I was flying.

"Guess who's married and here with his wife and toddler?"

"No?!" Maya, mouth agape, eyes bugging out. "No way!"

"Yes! She's been in the room chilling tonight but will be at the restaurant tomorrow." Max, laughing. "Your new little friend is a total sleaze."

"What a freak. Lilly, can you believe that after he started out mac daddying us? Lilly!" Maya, yelling.

"I heard you. Imagine being this high around a toddler."

They continued chatting, and I faded out of the conversation. In my mind, I was Supergirl cruising the Strip dressed in a hot pink spandex suit, darting in and out of the neon lights, and soaring high with a matching hot pink cape flapping in the cool night air. I was so wrapped up in my flight around Vegas I didn't even hear the phone ring. Luckily, Maya did, and it was Randy, the son of one of my parent's friends.

"Hello . . . hey, Randy . . . What? . . . Where? . . . Maybe . . . Lilly . . . *Lilly!*" Yelling to me.

"What, what?" Asking while lifting my head up a notch but still not opening my eyes.

"It's Randy."

"Hi, Randy."

"She says hi. Hi back." Calling to me.

"Hi." Repeating, lying back down, and continuing my flight.

"He's calling."

"So?"

"So he's going somewhere."

"Okay, where?"

"Oh . . . Randy, where again, I spaced out . . . They are going to Drink."

"I don't want to drink."

"No, that's the place."

"Is there drinking at Drink?"

"Yes, probably."

"I don't want to drink."

"Okay, okay. You said that already. We don't have to drink."

"Good."

"Do you want to go?"

"I don't know."

"What do I tell him?"

"I don't know."

"Shit . . . Hello, Randy . . . Hello? . . . Still there? . . . Fuck." Maya stared at the phone. "He hung up on me."

"Okay."

"Will you please say something else!"Coming to the bed and standing over me. "It's making me crazy."

"Okay."

"*Ahhhhhh!* Enough!!!!!! Get up!!!!!! I have to get out of this room!!" Yelling, grabbing my hand, and dragging me off the comforter.

It took me a minute to remember where my feet were,

154 and I almost pitched over when she pulled me up. I opened my eyes and the room swayed a bit, like I was on a seesaw.

"I feel like a floating marshmallow. Where's Max?"

"He left before Randy called. Didn't you hear him say good-bye?"

"Nope, too busy flying."

"Flying? I think there might have been something in that pot. I feel thick, like I'm walking through cotton, and you look like you're on acid."

"I'm scared to go outside."

"Me too, but we just have to." Letting go of my hand and grabbing our purses. "On the count of three we make a break. One. Two. Three."

With that we burst from the room and ran giggling to the elevators. It took one trip down to realize I had no shoes on.

"Uhhh, Maya."

"Yeah."

"We have to go back up."

"No way! I can't deal with that room."

"I have to." Glancing down at my bare feet.

"What?" Tossing me an annoyed look.

"Guess who forgot to put on shoes?"

"Lilly!" Pressing the button. "You're on my last nerve."

"Sorry." Grinning. "I was flying."

"You're a freak." Starting to laugh despite herself.

Take two. Action. By the time we got into the casino, we knew it was going to be one of those nights. Everywhere we turned there was something absurd to trip out

on. The bad makeup girls, the chimney smokers with
their butt-filled ashtrays, old men talking to extremely
young pay-for-your-pleasures, little old ladies doling
change into dime slots, and young hipsters carefully
unfolding their crisp hundreds for all to see. I don't even
know how long we walked around, or how many words we
spoke. We had both sunk into this very stoned, very personal, mind adventure. We knew each other was there the
whole time, but there was no interaction until the
munchies struck. At the all-night café, milk shakes and
French fries loosened our tongues.

"Whoa, what a night." Maya, stuffing a fry into her
mouth. "That fiancé of mine is going to laugh his ass off
when I tell him."

"I feel like I was walking around hell." Taking a sip of
my shake.

"Me too." Popping another fry. "Everywhere I turned
there was something weirder to focus on."

"Sorry I lost speech. It was all a little too much."

"Not a problem. You didn't see me doing any Chatty
Cathy impersonations."

"I think I'm finally coming down." Taking a deep
breath. "That was, by far, the strongest shit I have ever
smoked."

"I know. Thank goodness it's almost over. I couldn't
take much more."

As we chatted about our observations, my parents
walked by.

"Hey, girls."

"Hi." Planting kisses. "Did you win?"

"Some," my dad answered. "What did you guys do?"

156   "Not much." Maya, giving me this secret undercover look.

"Yeah, not much, not much at all." Throwing Maya a perfectly appropriate, perfectly Vegas, devilish, sinful wink.

rocks, rings, and things

Maya and I got to continue our bonding, since as soon as I returned from the trip to Vegas it was time to head up north. When I got off the plane, I finally got a glimpse of the goods.

"Damn, girl, nice rock!" Exclaiming as I jumped into the car. "You could blind someone with that thing."

"Is it too much?" Kissing my cheek. "I haven't gotten used to it yet."

"No, it's amazing. I want one."

"In time, my dear girl, in time." Pulling the car out onto the road. "You have that killer ring anyway."

"What killer ring?" Eyeing her. "I definitely would remember diamonds, especially boy-given diamonds."

"Dummy, the ring on your finger." Pointing at my hand. "Don't tell me you don't remember it."

"Oh, yeah. But it isn't as important as yours."

"That, I totally disagree with. To me, that ring symbolizes major growth for you. It is an artifact from a very specific point in time."

"I guess you're right. I never thought about it that way."

"Years and years from now, like my engagement ring, it will be this object that reminds you of something really intense in your life. Maybe it's not about marriage and forever, but still."

"You are so wise, chief."

Maya was referring to my little blue sapphire flower ring I bought myself a couple of years ago as the reward for winning a bet and spending an entire summer toiling away at a construction job that left me with calluses big enough to be mistaken for fingers. It hasn't come off my finger since, and I don't really notice it anymore. Actually, I only think about it when someone else points it out, or if I snag it on my sweater. It is, though, like Maya said, very important to me. It is a tangible memento of what was not to be and what will and shall never be again. If the ring could talk it would tell the long saga of my first love. Remember Sam? The guy with the great hair, my first? He's the guy responsible for me having this pretty ring. No, he did not buy it, I don't think he ever really gave me anything bigger or smaller than a bread box, but it was a bet I had with my dad about him that led to the inevitable purchase.

I like to compare myself in this sorry little tale to Bart Simpson. I know it's a stretch, seeing how he is yellow and animated, but stick with me a little. There was only one *Simpsons* episode I really remember. In college, I always tried to avoid the Sunday night *Simpsons* rush. I just wasn't sucked in by Bart's antics or Lisa's sad sax, and besides, Maya, Jack, and I liked doing the Sunday night movie thing. In my opinion, driving out to Seekonk, Massachusetts, and seeing a flick was the best way to wind down a hangover Sunday. After a too long, drunken weekend, it was a perfect respite. Darkness, Coca-Cola, and candy. Even now it's still a tradition, it just doesn't have the wild drunken preamble, since getting trashed is pretty much a thing of the past—or at least trying to be a thing of the past. One Sunday, though, when no new films opened, I caught a *Simpsons* episode that ended up burned into my brain. It's amazing how enduring and perfectly human animation can be.

Sarah Gilbert of *Roseanne* fame voiced this older hip wild child who becomes the Simpsons' baby-sitter. She was this rebel teen with whom Bart instantly falls in love. As they pal around, admire the anarchist streak in each other, and talk about crazy stunts, Bart falls deeper and deeper. Every tiny nice thing she does, Bart, like the rest of us tend to do, takes it to mean that she too is stirring in the loins. As the show progresses, Bart and the rebel girl chill in his treehouse, and Bart lets her in on all his secret gear and gizmos. Then, one day, she comes over and climbs into the treehouse window all dressed up, having finally ditched her combat fatigues for a dress and lip-stick. She goes on and on about being in love with this older bully guy, and as she continues to talk, we see her morph into Bart's inner dialogue. Here, she reaches her hand into Bart's chest à la Spielberg's *Indiana Jones and the Temple of Doom,* and violently rips out his heart while cack-ling, "You won't be needing this anymore!" and smiling savagely as the dripping heart beats on.

This classic TV memory is a perfect metaphor for a common disaster: when the one you love, loves you not. Sam ripped out my heart. It figures he was the first to tear me to pieces since he was the first to tear . . . that was kind of crude. I should have known better, but when does that ever happen? Like the rule I mentioned before, I'm already well over the cliff before I know there's no safety net beneath and no reason for me to have jumped in the first place.

Our relationship was doomed from the beginning. Sam was a second-semester senior when we met. If that doesn't spell disaster for a second-semester freshman virgin, I don't know what does. On top of that, Sam was the heart and soul of his group of friends. Always being the guy's guy, he was the glue that held all his buddies together. They looked to him to be their rock and salvation. He had never really had a girlfriend before me and was expected to hang out whenever his friends with girlfriends needed to take a break. Twenty-four-seven he was available and ready to hang. A pattern like that is hard to alter. When we started dating, Sam faced tremendous pressure to be there for his friends while still being accessible to me. I commended his loyalty, but it was totally destructive to our relationship. How can an eighteen-year-old girl compete with four years of ritualistic fraternal male bonding? I didn't have a shot in hell.

There were warning signs all around, flashing, beeping, and screaming, but I chose to play dumb and dumber. I didn't want to admit or notice how bad it was going to become. It's that masochistic streak all humans seem to share. We met at a party, I had a boyfriend, he sort of kissed me, and we were together a few weeks later sharing my first postcoital secrets. For a month or so, it was pure bliss. Then it was May, and graduation loomed. I knew things were going to go from bad to worse when I first told him I loved him, and let's just say he didn't respond in kind.

"I can't believe you even had the balls to use the ominous 'L' word. That's super intense. I wouldn't have."

"Why? Love, so sweet, so simple."

"Yeah, but you are never supposed to say it first." Stating matter-of-factly. *"Plus, love is a word always in italics."*

"Kind of like you?" Joking.

"Maybe." Winking. *"Seriously, love exists completely separate from reality, from the day-to-day. It's an enigma. If said to and heard from the right lips, it can make you feel lovely, like you are inside a chocolate cake. But, if said to and not heard from those same lips, it can make you want to ram into a brake-test wall at full speed without a seat belt. Love is power and you become helpless to its whims."*

"I agree. That's why if you feel it, you feel it, and you can't help but say it. The beauty is in its power. We are the only culture that balks at its utterance. For something so essential, we avoid mentioning it whenever possible."

"Because it's scary shit! What? Do you want to scream love from rooftops? Become a caterwauler of romantic bliss?"

"Why not? Better that we choke on the word and let it fester within? The fear and potential disappointment oxidizing and oozing, until we are too afraid of vomiting even to open our mouths? That is not for me no matter how much it sucks to say it to a blank face."

I love love. I love to be in love, to be in like, to have crushes. I jump into every possibility because it makes me feel shiny. Even if brief, I like that sparkle. It's better than the best drug pharmaceutical companies can offer. I'm addicted to it. It's like peaches, and summer, and candy. I just wish that I could bottle it up and give it away. Then I wouldn't be alone. I wouldn't be afraid to share it and use it and feel it. Sam's reaction to my first use of the word was a slap in the face and a perfect illustration of how few love to love like me.

I had been rolling it around my tongue for a few days before I decided to unleash it. I told him after a very sweet and intense evening spent at his fraternity's semi-formal. The day began simply enough: woke up hung-over, wandered to class, had lunch, bought some black nylons on Thayer Street to wear with my dress, stopped at Sam's house for a kiss, ended up getting stoned, went to my Evolutionary Bio section, felt like an idiot because I was too high and understood nothing, walked home, and began primping. I looked like a million bucks that night. A wraparound black chiffon Nicole Miller dress, waved hair, and red lipstick applied carefully with a tiny lip brush. My mom still keeps the picture in her Filofax, despite her ill will toward Sam. That's how much Mom liked the photo. Anyway, we went to the dance, got trashed, hooked up like mad on the bus ride back, and then wound up at his house for a long night of lovemaking. Afterward, as we were lying there totally beat and content, I decided I was going to make my move.

"What a great night, Sam." Snuggling into the warm crook of his arm. "I'm so happy."

"Yeah. I think I'm in my own little nirvana right now." Kissing my head and squeezing me tighter.

"Really?"

"I have my girl, I just had amazing sex, I have some pot, a bong, and the Doors are playing. It doesn't get better than this."

Thinking this was my perfect opportunity to whisper those three words, I opened my mouth and let her rip.

"I think I love you." Whispering into his chest.

"What?"

"I love you."

Silence.

Silence.

Silence.

"You're so sweet." Kissing my head again.

Fuck.

"See? Total destruction."

"But at least I said it, and he knew it."

"Lucky for him." Scowling.

"Never mind." Sighing, rolling over so as to keep my back toward him and not allow him to witness the small tear forming in my eye. "Forget I said anything."

"Forget? It's not like you can take that back." Trying to roll me back over to get me to look at him.

"Whatever."

"Please, look at me, Lilly."

"Fine." Wiping my eyes and turning back toward him.

"God, you're so cute."

He began to kiss me, not noticing how much his less than special response hurt my feelings, and pretty soon we were having sex all over again. So much for my resolve.

I got a "you're so sweet" and "you're so cute" when I told him I loved him. I stupidly thought that would be enough. Lo and behold, it wasn't. As the weeks went by and the end of May drew closer, Sam and I were hit-and-miss. If there was something better to do with his friends, I was told to meet him after, and every time I tried to make plans with him, he flaked. Like the Wednesday night he promised that the two of us would hang, just us. I went over there in the early evening, and we were supposed to go see *Like Water for Chocolate,* this really romantic flick I had heard was awesome. "Supposed to" are the key words in that sentence, in case you weren't sure. Right after I got there, his posse began straggling in, one by one. Soon it was me and six of Sam's buddies sitting around and movie time came and went.

"Sorry about the movie, Lil." Apologizing, when he finally noticed the time. "We'll go another night."

"Whatever." Nonchalantly, trying to downplay my resentment. "It's no big deal."

"Lilly, just hang with us." Alex, suggesting. "We're way more fun than a movie."

"Sure." Smiling, despite being completely unsatisfied and unhappy.

Hanging out with them entailed the six of them trying to see if the marijuana they had grown in their basement could be made into dip—you know, the stuff you shove inside your lip and then spit up like an infant? I know that sounds really stimulating, but I quickly and quietly slipped into the living room to watch TV. As I stared at the screen, I could see them from the corner of my eye as they sat crouched around a coffee table in Sam's room, crushing up the pot leaves, mixing them with Skoal, and stuffing the unsightly wads into their mouths. The amount of spit and drool in that room was more than a litter of puppies and a dozen newborns could create in a day. I sat there getting more and more peeved, and sadder and sadder, not the easiest thing in the world to pretend you're not feeling. Especially when you are me and my face reads like an open book. On top of that, there wasn't even anything to watch except bad exercise-machine infomercials.

"Lilly, what are you doing?" Sam, calling out to me when he finally realized I was no longer in the room.

"Not a whole hell of a lot," I said under my breath. "Just watching TV," calling back so he could hear me.

"Come in here with me."

"I don't think so. I'm just fine out here."

I guess I wasn't so convincing because Sam got up and came to sit next to me.

"What are you watching?"

"Nothing special." Keeping my eyes glued to the TV screen as I continued to channel surf.

"Come here." Pulling me into a kiss.

Let's just say that it was the nastiest kiss I have ever received. Dip and pot are just not what you want scenting the saliva. It tasted like garbage—at least I think it did because since I'm not a dog, I have never really tasted garbage before.

"That's so gross!" Yelling at him a little too loudly. "You're such a jerk!"

"What did I do?" Smiling this cute, pretend-innocent grin.

"I can't believe you sometimes." Getting angrier, as everything that had been pissing me off quickly rose to the surface. "Is that supposed to be endearing? Do you ever think before you do things?"

His nasty-ass kiss was the straw that broke the camel's back, and there were already a lot of fucking straws weighing me down.

"All I did was kiss you."

"With a mouth full of crap!" My face getting redder and redder. "I can't believe you!"

"Why are you so mad?"

"You just don't get it." Extricating myself from the tangle of his arms. "I'm going home."

I got up and grabbed my coat. As I buttoned up, I started walking to the door. I was already outside before Sam did anything. I think all that pot and dip must have turned him into a fucking imbecile!

"Are you mad at me or something?" Lumbering to the door after me. "What's going on?"

"No. Nothing." Not even turning around as I continued walking away. "See you later."

"You can't get mad at me for this."

"Whatever."

With that I hurried down the porch steps. As I walked home, I felt huge hot tears on my cheeks and wished I had had the guts to tell him how I was really feeling.

"What a wuss!" **Cursing myself.** *"When did you become such a wimp?"*

"I don't know. It's like I was afraid to use my own voice."

"I know the 'rents never taught you to kowtow to any-one, but you were doing it anyway."

"It seemed to be happening without my permission."
"Life never happens without your permission."

It was my first love, and all I could think about was if I made one false move, asserted myself in any small way, it would all just vanish. He wouldn't want to be with me if I called him on his shit.

Everything we did revolved around his schedule, his plans, his friends, and I remained the ever supportive smiling girlfriend despite being taken for granted. I was deathly afraid if I said anything to him or demanded anything of him, he would be gone. I couldn't imagine being without him. He was everything to me; everything centered around him. If we were good, I lived on cloud nine; if we were bad, I lived on a rock in a leper colony. I became a shell, so fragile, so insecure. Why did I let him have such power over my emotions? Why did I give myself up so quickly? It's not like I wasn't aware that I wasn't getting what I wanted or needed, but I just didn't know how to change things. Furthermore, I was scared that if things did change, I would be left with less than what I had already, which in retrospect wasn't really that much at all. I was such a mess when I finally got home to my dorm. I headed right for Maya's room and she didn't know what to do with me.

"What happened?" Maya asking, pulling her blond hair up into a ponytail as she shut the door. "Lilly, you look like shit."

"It's just so fucked up. I'm fucked." Choking on my tears. "Everything's a mess."

"Why? I thought you guys were going to the movies? Spend a little time together tonight?"

"I thought so too until all his boys showed up."

"Did he tell you to leave or something?"

"No, but it was just so obvious that he didn't want me there, and the more I stayed the more pathetic it made me look."

"You are not pathetic."

"Please, I sat watching bad TV alone in the living room while they played with some pot project. That's, like, the definition of pathetic."

"So what happened? Did you tell him you were upset?" Maya, trying to get the story out of me. "Was there any face-to-face?"

"Face-to-face?" Me, getting confused. "He did kiss me with dip stuffed in his mouth."

"No, not sucking face, dork, but confrontation. And, by the way, dip? He's vile."

"No, of course not. I'm too scared to. It's getting out of control."

"Sam is being such an asshole." Maya lamenting, pulling me into bed with her. "What are you going to do?"

"I don't know. The closer graduation gets, the more things just suck. I don't want to be all demanding, but don't make plans with me if you want to do other things." Getting riled up.

I could get my anger groove on in the company of my friend.

"You should say that to him." Maya, thinking out loud. "He can't read your mind, and he should know he's fucking up."

"But I can't. I don't want to make it a big deal."

"Big deal? It already is a big deal. This is ripping you apart. If you think it's bad now, it's only going to get worse if you don't deal with it. Call him and tell him, or he is going to keep acting this way," Maya advised. "Don't be afraid to tell him how you feel."

"All that sounds really easy, but . . ." Getting quiet. "I don't know."

"You have to do something. I hate seeing you like this. I can't stand watching my friends get tread on." Maya, commiserating. "Guys can be such dicks."

"I know but that's why we like them." Trying to make a feeble joke.

"No, we like them because they have dicks." Maya, finishing my joke.

"True." Attempting a giggle.

"That's a little better. Lilly, you can't cry because Sam's totally clueless all the time. Most men are. If they flake it's like, 'Oops, sorry, forgive me. It's not my fault I spaced.' Then, if you get all emotional on them, they think you're the one who's being ridiculous. Why we like them I will never know."

"A girl just can't win."

"No shit."

"I just don't know how to act."

"Just act like yourself."

"You're right, but that's easier said than done. Fuck . . . I don't know. . . . I guess I'll talk to him later when I'm not so upset and slobbery. If he's already freaked out about anything, my calling and crying is just going to make it worse. No one can stand a hysterical mess."

"You need to stop worrying about him being freaked out and think about yourself a little more." Maya, giving me a bear hug. "Besides, I really don't want to see 'worse'!"

After rented movies and girl talk, I managed to mellow a bit. I took some of my girl's advice and I got some balls. I tried to convince myself that it would all be okay, and if I said what was on my mind, he would understand how I was feeling and try to change. When I did eventually get the courage to call Sam, he already knew I was upset and was prepared for the convo.

"I just can't promise you that it won't happen again. With graduation coming, I want to spend time with my friends as much as I can." Telling me all matter-of-factly. "They're a big priority."

"I understand that, I really do, but where does that leave me?" Gnawing at the black rubber phone cord. "Do you want to spend time with me too? It sounds like I'm not a part of your life."

"You are, and of course I want to spend time with you. That isn't what I'm saying." Backpeddling. "It's all getting so intense. Everything is so extreme."

"Well, what do you want me to do? All I know is that I want to be with you. That is the only thing that makes sense."

"I don't know. I feel all this pressure from everyone. Nothing I do is enough for anyone. I'm being pulled in a million directions. I can't deal."

"I'm sorry."

"You don't have to apologize. You didn't do anything wrong." Softening. "None of this is about you."

"It feels like it is. It feels like it is all about me."

"Well, it's not. I swear. I love being with you. You make me relax and able to breathe a little easier."

"So?"

"So." Taking a deep breath. "Tomorrow night, just us. Okay? I promise."

"Okay." Believing him enough to release the phone cord from my vise grip and let myself inhale again.

Of course, I then let everything that pissed me off melt into thin air, and I was fine again. Scary how men can have complete control of your emotions. Like they have this *Wizard of Oz* control panel with big buttons, color coded and labeled for each of your feelings that they then press at their own whim. Hey, let's make her happy today. Oh no, wait, she was happy yesterday, let's make her cry.

The next night Sam did come through. We snuck out of his house with a big blanket and climbed up onto the roof of one of the school buildings to chill. There, we had a view of the sky and the stars, and it was very romantic. Except for the fact that I had on a bodysuit without snaps that impaired our physical contact, we had a great time together. We sat and talked and held each other under the moon, and I fell in love with him all over again. The next few nights were fine too, but then he went and totally dissed me for his friends yet again, telling me we would meet at this party but then never bothering to show up. I was trapped in this cycle for the next few weeks. Then it was graduation week, and things completely exploded.

For a long time, I thought it was all my fault that things got even worse. I felt I blew it by giving him the wrong present. I had pulled out all the stops and made him an album filled with letters, notes, songs, and pictures. Anything that was a reminder of our relationship. Essentially, I cut out my own heart and served it up to him on a beautiful Tiffany tray. Every single thing he had made me think about or discover in myself was in that book. I think there were even a few tears caught between the pages. I should have known that for a guy who was already feeling tremendous pressure and stress, this type of emotional display would push him right over the edge. After I gave him the book, everything disintegrated, and I cursed myself for the new can of vulnerability I had opened up. It was too much for him, and soon we were over. I blamed myself for his inability to deal.

"Why do you always go and blame yourself for others' faults?"

"I think we all do. It's not just me. When someone you love fucks you over, instead of getting mad and realizing it was his fault, you tend to start apologizing for your own behavior."

"But it is their behavior that should be apologized for."

"I know, but maybe we think we can fix it and solve the problem if we think we did it. Maybe if you hadn't called that last time, or kissed him that hundredth time, or cried in front of him when you were scared, or visited him bearing ice cream and a smile when he was studying for that last big test."

"Those are all incredibly sweet and wonderfully nice things to do."

"When you are in the throws of being broken up with, though, all those nice things are signs that you pushed too much." Stating clearly. "You made him go to places he didn't want to go, so if we make things right, we could get him back. Force him to reevaluate and change his mind."

"Why want him back in the first place?"

"Maybe it's because I'm just a spineless sucker."

Sam and I had no sweet good-bye dinner, no romantic good-bye sex. The last time we made love was on a threadbare, orange, Salvation Army couch in the basement of his house while his roommates milled about upstairs. Sad how you never know it's the last time when it's happening. You only know later, when you're left with a shitty memory and couch burn on your butt. There was no conversation about what was going to happen or what had happened. He didn't even introduce me to his parents, nor include me in any of his graduation plans. I began to feel cheap and depressed. All I got from him was a hideous breakup in the middle of a loud raging party. It was Saturday night, and his house had a huge blowout. I went there with a group of friends and tried to have a good time. I don't even think Sam said more than two words to me. He would have paid more attention to a one-night stand. Some friends left and just Jack, Maya, and I stayed.

Well, time passed, and my friends and I got bored. It became so clear that Sam was ignoring me on purpose, trying to pretend I didn't exist. We said a ghostly good-bye. As my friends and I headed down the stairs to leave, I decided I couldn't take it anymore. I had to go talk to him. I went back upstairs to the third floor and pulled Sam from a roomful of his pals. Everything that came next took place in the fucking hallway.

"This is so stupid. Why are you ignoring me?" Chewing on my lip, a thing I do when I am nervous.

"I'm not ignoring you." Staring at me with a blank face. "What are you talking about?"

"Yes, you are! You have said three words to me all night. It's like I don't exist!"

"Don't be so sensitive."

"Sensitive! 'Don't be so sensitive' he says. . . . Sam, are you planning on making any effort to see me or even talk to me?" Swallowing hard.

"Not really." Saying with that same dead stare. "I just want to spend time with my friends right now."

"That's great, but what about me?" Feeling my face begin to burn. "What about us?"

"I don't know." Looking down. "I want to hang with them as much as I can. I can't handle any 'us.' I really don't want there to be any 'us.' "

"So this is good-bye?" Choking back tears. "This is it?"

"Yeah. I guess so." Avoiding my gaze. "I just don't get attached. This has all been much more intense for you."

"You're saying all this meant nothing to you? I mean nothing to you?" Now fully crying. "Who are you?"

"Lilly, that isn't what I meant. You do mean something to me. We just aren't on the same page. I don't know how else to deal with this." Still not looking at me. "I don't really know what else to say."

"When were you planning on sharing this with me, or was I supposed to guess that my boyfriend was bailing?"

"I don't know." Shuffling his feet. "It's like this whole situation is a rotting tooth. At first, we were wonderful and romantic and everything was fine. Over time, an infection started to grow, and we or really me started to ache. Then everything started to really hurt, so I just have to remove it altogether to ensure the health of the rest of my mouth."

"So now I am a rotting tooth? You just called me a rotting tooth! I'm a fucking infection to you! No one has ever said something so horrible to me in my life."

"Lilly, no, it's not like that. You aren't an infection." Running his hands through his beautiful hair. "Fuck. I can't say anything right. I just cannot deal with this anymore." Getting really somber. "I just can't."

"Are you even going to kiss me good-bye?"

With that he pulled me to him and kissed me. It was a salty and sad kiss that put the nail in my coffin. I began sobbing uncontrollably. I couldn't let go of him. I grabbed onto his sleeve with all my might, thinking if I kept myself physically attached he wouldn't leave me. If I had had handcuffs I would have locked us together and swallowed the key. If only I had been into S&M. I wonder what all the people walking by must have thought! I was totally losing my shit. The walls were swirling, nothing felt real.

"Shush. Lilly, please don't cry." Stroking my cheek with his thumb. "Please. You are so special."

"I can't help it." Sobbing loudly.

"You have three years left here."

"What the fuck does that mean?" Still hanging on to his arms, crying. "What the hell are you talking about?"

"You have so much to look forward to."

"Sorry, just not thinking about that now."

"I don't know what to say." His voice cracking.

"You said that already! Are you even going to miss me?!"

"Of course I will. This isn't easy for me either, I just have to move on or I'm not going to make it through graduation. I can't do this anymore. I have to let go. You should too."

Here is where I wish I had been the older version of myself and could have told him he was a selfish bastard who was full of shit. How everything was about him. How he was insensitive and disrespectful. How he was ugly and bloated. How he smelled and had a full mouth of rotting teeth that I hoped one day would all fall out simultaneously. How pathetic he was for bailing. How real men don't play games with innocent virgin's hearts. How much he had hurt me and didn't deserve me. How miserably he handled the whole situation. How I would rule one day, and he would regret every sorry word he ever spoke to me. But these moments, unfortunately, are never do-overs. Instead, I kissed him again and ran out of the house in hysterics while my friends tried to catch up and prevent me from getting hit by a car. I wandered through the streets blindly, unable to breathe and wanting to die.

I don't think I stopped crying for days. My face was a faucet, continuously dripping. After the initial shock, I did calm down a bit. I went on to spend the rest of the summer crying myself to sleep listening to Shawn Colvin's "Stranded" on repeat. It was such a bad breakup that a year after it happened, I realized that he had tainted almost twelve months of my life. Danielle and I tripped one weekend at Brown our sophomore year, and we had an intense conversation in a fraternity bathroom about how I could X-Acto knife the last year from my life and label it "Sam." I knew I was fucked. My relationship with him colored over most other things, I was so consumed by it. It took me a long time to get over it and move on, even though I knew it wasn't worth all my emotional turmoil.

I once heard you were supposed to linger over someone after the breakup for double the duration of your time together. If you dated a year, you could wallow in it for up to two years. Whoever made that one up is full of crap, if you ask me. Depression does not follow a timetable, nor does it make logical sense. It takes a long time to reconnect the heart to its proper muscles and veins when it gets ripped from your chest. Just ask Bart.

WHEN I HEADED into my second school year of I-still-miss-him-and-taste-his-kisses-even-when-I-have-tasted-other-lips depression, my dad decided to take matters into his own hands. My dad is super protective and super caring. He once even broke a car mirror and cut his finger in an angry reaction to some ugly doof I thought I liked who had broken my heart again. I think that the Sam thing is the singular event he'd like to pretend never happened to his little girl. He would do anything in his power to make it okay. I think for a minute he even considered having a hit put out on Sam, but thought, nah, not intense enough.

Before I went back to school junior year, we had a family powwow. Dinner and drinks to bid me adieu. For some reason, Sam came up.

"Why are you still talking about that guy?" Max asked, annoyed. "He's old news. What was it? Two years ago?"

"It's just that I know his little sister is starting Brown this year." Defending myself.

"So?"

"So, I wonder if he is going to come up and if I should be nice and call her or something."

"Why bother?" Max, dismissing the conversation. "Why should you be nice to her or anyone related to him? Guys who mess with my sister do not deserve 'be kind to others' behavior."

"I don't know, Max." Mom, piping in. "It isn't like you and Holly had a happy ending, and she still calls Grandma to talk. Grandma loves those calls."

"That's not the same thing. Holly fucked up, not me, so she should kiss ass. Sam broke up with Lilly. She shouldn't go out of her way. She bent enough for him. It's called self-protection."

"Maybe being a bigger person is better?" Me, musing out loud.

"Yeah, but only if the desire is pure." Max, stating assertively.

"What do you mean? Pure?"

Playing innocent was always a great disguise. Batting big brown eyes, playing dumb, and then turning with fascination to the steak sitting before you like a bone.

"Are you planning on being nice to be nice, or because you hope it grapevines back to him so he can feel guilty for dumping a girl as cool as you?"

Was I so transparent? Of course I wanted to just be nice because I am a really nice person. I didn't want him back at all, nor did I care what he thought anymore. I was over it. Really, I was. . . . I have always been a terrible liar.

"Probably both." Answering meekly. "Actually more of the latter."

"He already regrets it," Dad saying matter-of-factly.

"Men always do when they get a good one and screw up. I 179 bet he comes back to you."

"You are joking, right, Dad?" Asking in disbelief. "You think he's going to want me back after all this time?"

Why was my dad putting me, Sam, and together in the same thought?

"Dad, why are you planting that seed in her head?" Max responded. "It's obvious she isn't over him. Encouraging this is a really terrible idea."

"I don't think I am planting anything that isn't already there. Look at her face."

Big eyes again, and a big ol' blush. I hate talking boys with my dad and brother. They just wind up knowing too much, and you know they are picturing you naked and doing the nasty.

"I remember that I disappeared on your mom for about six months before I came around to my senses," Dad continued.

"That's true." Mom nodded. "But, I agree with Max. This needs to end, not continue. It is so unlike you to support this infatuation. It was just a little while ago that you wanted to kill the guy."

"I know, and that hasn't changed. Trust me. But I have my reasons." Dad went on assuredly. "Shall we make a bet, Lilly?"

"Sure, but what are we wagering exactly?" I asked, confused.

My dad speaks in mysterious ways. Was this a Jedi mind trick or something? What was he trying to accomplish?

"I bet you three hundred dollars that Sam comes around and wants you back within the year."

"What do I have to give you if he does?"

"Nothing."

"Nothing?"

"Exactly. It is a gentleman's bet on your part."

"I don't get this bet at all. Basically, if he doesn't come back, I win three hundred bucks . . ."

"And if he does come back, she pays no money, and she sort of wins too because she gets the guy." Max, finishing. "Dad, bad bet."

"I'm not so sure."

"Whatever you say, but, Lilly, I would shake and count your winnings already."

We shook, finished dinner, and packed me off to another year at school. Time ticked on, the leaves changed, the first snow fell, finals set in, Chanukah came and went, parties and kegs entertained, leaves reappeared, pot and parties entertained, finals set in, and time ticked on. I never heard a word from Sam or any other Grossman. He sort of vanished from my life, from my thoughts. I had new crushes and new crush mes, and he just wasn't relevant anymore. I didn't need him as a crutch, and I didn't really miss him anymore. It was a memory. When my dad gave me the bucks after I returned home from school, I had forgotten all about the bet. I think this was the message my dad was trying to send me.

The bet didn't make a hell of a lot of sense back when we made it, but my dad has weird logic sometimes. I think that by making a horrible situation into something I could profit from, even if it meant profiting off him, my dad took control of my grieving process. He created a situation in which no matter how it ended, I won. It was his

way of softening the blows he couldn't deflect, easing the
pain he couldn't prevent. Somehow he knew that by the
time the bet wound down, none of it would matter anymore. If Sam had returned, I would maybe not even want
him, or if I did we would have a newfangled relationship.
If Sam never called me again, I would get over it and forget. If I didn't get the guy I wanted, I'd still get something
nice, and I could still walk away with more than I had
before. Dad created a little play where I was the star, I was
the winner, and I was the one with the better hand. Dad
rocks.

So I combined some of my own money with my winnings and I bought myself a ring. A very tangible memento
of my entire first relationship. What Sam took from me
when he broke my heart could become what he gave to me
when he broke my heart. I could smash an entire history
into a piece of jewelry, like Maya said. She was right
because just looking at the ring in the car with her made
me remember this entire tale. A simple ring doing all that.
Maya's ring did and would come to represent her life story
too. She would look at it and remember all the little things
we forget when we get tired and bored, all the words we
don't always say, all the nuances we sometimes ignore but
are the very things that make us fall in love the hardest.

APPARENTLY THOSE BASIC things like time and place can
be easily forgotten. When I fall deep into my memories as
I just did I tend to lose sight of the immediate things
around me. Luckily, I am not sprawled in a ditch somewhere, passed out, with a bleeding cut on my head from
the sign I didn't see myself run into. The last place I

remember was the inside of Maya's car at the San Francisco airport, and now I'm sitting in a bridal store surrounded by meringues. I'm pretty sure that none are made of egg whites and sugar beaten into a frenzy, but they look quite tasty and edible. Swirls of marshmallow white and dips and twists of marzipan cream float around me like the dance of the sugar plum fairies. I am on a plush-velvet settee holding a satin slip so soft it feels like cocoa butter. I feel I am in one of my meditations just before they go askew. Oh wait, silly me, here comes that part. My black cargo pants and leopard-print tank look harsh next to all the pretty confections. I look like a club kid trying to interview at a corporate office. I do not fit in; I feel out of place. Ugh.

Maya, on the other hand, looked really happy, if not a little ridiculous swathed in taffeta and ribbons. Her face glowed and shone like the flush of great sex, or when you get a facial and your face looks like a polished car. Maybe this marriage thing was good, or maybe it was just good for the skin. Wedding dresses looped and swooped about her, their trains rustling against the beige carpet and their bustles hugging her gentle curves. They had a music all their own, playing hearts and flowers along the bones of their corsets. All of a sudden, she looked like a grown-up. I was the gangly, awkward, kid sister. My friend was such a woman tied and laced into the fantasy gowns of our childhood, and I was sitting there wondering if I would ever get to grow up at all.

"Maya, I feel we are in that scene from *When Harry Met Sally.*" Resituating myself on the couch. "This is such a Nora Ephron moment."

"Which one?" Looking at me through the three-way mirror.

"The one when Meg Ryan goes with Carrie Fisher to pick out the wedding dress, and Meg starts crying when she sees her friend all decked."

"You're going to cry?" Turning around to face me. "Are you okay?"

"No, I'm fine. No tears." Smiling. "But I could use some M&Ms."

"Then why does this remind you of that scene? The whole point of that scene was Meg's breakdown about her friend getting married and her losing to someone else the guy she thought she was going to marry."

"Details, details. Give me a break. It's just that looking at you in that dress is such a trip. You're a big girl now."

"I am. Scary thought sometimes." Turning back to the mirror. "What do you think of this one?"

"You're beautiful." Walking to her.

"I think you might be right."

"Nice ego." Tickling her. "You make a great bride."

"I love you." Kissing my cheek.

"Me too." Hugging her.

"Smile girls." Maya's mom says as she comes from the front of the store holding her camera.

"Could we have tried to have a more Velveeta picture taken of us?" Maya says as she looks at her mom.

"Nope, but you know what they say?"

"What?"

"Velveeta . . . it's the cheesiest." Smiling for the camera.

thirty days and counting

After finding the perfect dress, Maya's mom took all of us out to the perfect dinner. The usual suspects were there: Maya, her fiancé Ted, Emily, Evan, and Jack. It was so nice to hang out with the crew again. They of course always get to spend time with one another since they all share the same zip code, but I never get to see them all at once. Soon we slipped back into the old-school groove, and I had them rolling with my tales of cowboys and shoes. After three bottles of Napa Valley wine (red), and a four-course meal (organic, farm-raised, and homegrown), we were all flushed, full, and hyper like a team of teenage cheerleaders drunk for the first time on screwdrivers and wine coolers. Our chemistry clicked and sparks were flying. Maya's mom excused herself after dessert and left us to our own devices. I guess we were acting juvenile, but that's what happens when old friends reconnect and imbibe.

We headed over to this karaoke bar somewhere in the Mission and ordered another round right away: shots of tequila to go with the sing-along to come. The place was dimly lit with green walls and tons of mirrors. Wrapped around painted pipes and scattered along the moldings were small white Christmas lights. The mirrors made you feel as if you were inside a prism. The bar was on the left and toward the back was a small stage set with microphone, video monitor, and a wooden stool. We found seats easily since the bar was virtually empty except for two couples and a handful of single guys drowning in their beers. A tall Asian man was singing Cher so effusively the veins on his neck were bulging and I, for sure, thought a band of sailors à la her "Turn Back Time" video were going to jump out from behind a door and start gyrating. We settled into our seats and poured over the songbooks lying on the tables.

"Lilly, what is it going to be this time?" Maya asked as she flipped through the book. "What will the karaoke queen select?"

"Maybe some Go-Go's." Looking for titles. "I think I have done Madonna to death."

"I am not singing." Closing the book.

"Yeah, right. Maya, wait until that shot kicks in and then we're going to have to pry the mike from your hand."

"Nope. Don't think so." Holding fast.

"Ted, you should have seen your fiancée when she came down for my birthday last year. At first she protested, then guess who was singing her heart out with anyone who would let her join."

"Lilly, that is so not true. Ted, don't believe a word she says."

"I have pictures! You practically decked Danielle in your overeagerness to control the mike."

"I think I am going to have to go with Lilly this time, honey." Ted, grinning. "I have seen your inner diva many times before."

"So have we." Emily, Jack, and Evan agreeing in unison.

"Fine, fine. If you all are dying to cover your ears and suffer, I am game. Pick anything." Pushing the book toward me.

I toiled and toiled, searching for the perfect bad song. Then I remembered one Danielle and I did a few weeks back that went over like a lead balloon. No one but Axl Rose should sing "Paradise City." You need to be on a major speed high to be able to spit out the words fast enough. Watching Maya boldly struggle through it on this night made me love my friend even more. What a trouper!

Shots and beers flowed, and soon it wasn't just Maya up there. Just about every one of us banged out a few numbers, and then some. We completely monopolized the machine, and when we did look up from our own little recording session, we had cleared the bar. Oops! I think we sang just about every song on the hit list. The night ended with us still singing "Living on a Prayer" as we entered Maya and Ted's apartment. Emily had already been dropped off at home and Evan retired to his temporary room, so it was just the four of us. Maya and I shared a bong hit while the boys looked for something to watch on TV. Some things never change. Ted and Jack settled on a movie, and soon it was just Jack and I on the couch watching. I guess for Maya and Ted, karaoke was a major turn-on. Then we weren't watching anymore, and we were starting to do stuff we hadn't ever done before. Things were getting strange and heading for undiscovered territory.

"Are you holding my hand, Jack?"

"I think that would be an affirmative." Squeezing.

"I thought so." Squeezing back.

"What are we doing, Lilly?" Caressing my fingers.

"I'm not sure." Doing the same to his. "Should we stop?"

"I don't know." Not letting go.

"Me neither." Still holding on.

Sam wasn't the only boy important to me freshman year of college, Jack was there too. Boys in college weren't always boyfriends. That was one of the best things about school, you got to form these really intimate and intense friendships with members of the opposite sex. Platonic love flourished within coed halls and bathrooms. I have to admit, for a girl who didn't have a lot of guy friends before college, this whole platonic vibe got a little confusing. Sometimes I naively mixed up my emotions and put a few relationships into jeopardy thinking they were something they weren't.

A couple of years ago I thought I found the perfect road test to avoid this potential problem. I had read that you should wait thirty days before pursuing a romantic relationship with a friend. According to the article, you had to let your entire hormone cycle run its course, or you were at high risk of humiliating yourself due to bad judgment on account of increased levels of estrogen, or maybe progesterone, racing around your bloodstream.

Thirty days was supposed to ensure that what you thought you were feeling was the real deal and not some psychotic episode brought on by insidious PMS. I thought this made perfect sense, so I took this bit of *Cosmo* advice to heart and began applying it whenever my stomach began to flutter and make my logic back flip for someone who up until then I looked at like a brother.

I kept employing this rule in my relationship with Jack. Sometimes I couldn't stand him, and he thought I was the bomb. Then there were other times I wanted to jump his bones, and he ignored me. There were even a few times when we stopped speaking to each other altogether. In the moments when I did want to pursue something more and I started my countdown, something inevitably would interrupt it. A new hottie on the horizon for me, a new girlfriend for him. After awhile, I kind of forgot about him. It just wasn't meant to be.

The article probably should have appended the rule and said that once you forget about the friend, that's when things really get exciting. When six years of sexual tension finally combust, people better run for cover. All that pent-up energy and unused aggression makes for a pretty expansive explosion. I mean, when two cycles cycle up, who knows what can happen? It's one of those moments when both of you could be the world's most atrocious kissers with tongues like limp pickles flapping about or fumble around bra straps and buckles with hands full of thumbs, but because this is an experience you both have always thought about, it doesn't matter. Tonight you are Debbie Does Dallas meets Ron Jeremy. Even if it's something you have kept far away on the back burner of your brain as I did, it's still electric and quite volatile. I was finally getting to satisfy my curiosity. Jack and I had decided sometime in the evening to ditch the chains of friendship and look at each other as potential sex slaves and porno partners.

"Hey, where are you?"

"I'm here."

"Aren't you going to comment?"

"Why?"

"Because you always do right before the kiss."

"Not always."

"Liar. Always." Affirming. "So?"

"Party on, Garth." Encouraging, giving the thumbs-up.

"Really?" Not fully believing.

"I'm just as curious as you. It's been a long time coming."

"I am a little uncomfortable with us agreeing with each other about a boy situation."

"I think it is a sign of growth. It's like a new beginning for us."

"How romantic. What happens when we start saying the same things?"

"I'm not sure, really. I'll think about it." Musing. *"Better start paying attention!"*

"No problem."

I squeezed Jack's hand again and we started to readjust our positions on the couch, inching closer and closer together. I'm glad I waited six years and never tainted this possibility with lame college fondling. If we had done any sort of consummation earlier, the whole scenario wouldn't have been so sexy and appealing. How rare is it to find virgin friend flesh after college? College friends know you in this incredibly intimate way that can never be duplicated, and to kiss someone who knew you then and thinks he knows you now but doesn't really is the safest and most fun random night a person could have. Sort of a one-night stand minus the creepiness of a total stranger touching you but still smooching with someone you've never explored. With Jack, I had none of the potential for the shame spiral, because we knew each other, we were close, we were friends, and no matter what happened, I would see him again. Jack wasn't going to become another Shane or Alain because this was some-thing we were just supposed to do and that gave me a sense of comfort. If I couldn't fearlessly and without complications hook up with a guy I offered my virginity to way back when, I was more screwed up than I initially imagined, and I just wasn't going to allow that to be true. For once, I could feel strong in this decision to follow my desires. Maybe that's why my inner voice and I were start-ing to speak the same language. Maybe this was the begin-ning of something new for me.

JACK AND I MET the second day of college, in line to get ID cards. The wait was excruciatingly slow, and my new friend, Emily, knew the guy Jack was with, so we all began chatting the way only freshmen can. I think that fresh-men friendliness is a true talent. Somehow you find this super strong iron nerve inside yourself, and you can say hello and shoot the shit with anyone. For a short time, you can be ballsy and walk around waving and smiling a Vaseline smile like a pageant girl without feeling like a member of the Partridge Family. After that first conver-sation, Jack, Emily, and I realized we were on the same floor, same hall even, and became immediate friends.

192 Later that day, we bonded at some freshmen unit meeting about racism or drinking, or maybe it was sexual assault. I don't really remember, but does it matter? After the meeting, Jack and I hung out, and he talked to me about his girlfriend from home until three in the morning. Not to get ahead of anything, or myself, but I was in love! Never in my life had a cool, cute guy wanted to talk to me. Never being one of the hip kids in high school, my guy friends were all awkward, shy, and nerdy like me. Here, I finally had one of the guys I always wanted to know, and to know me, sitting in his J. Crew checked boxers telling me his life story and asking me for advice. God, I loved college! At last, it was my time to shine.

Time passed, and Jack and I did many ridiculous things together, yet always friend things (to my chagrin). Getting drunk, going to dinner, sitting on the green getting high, watching *The Untouchables* one thousand times, and smoking my cigarettes on the steps in the wee hours before dawn. In the back of my head, as we got closer and closer, I thought this was how real love began. The scratchy first minute of a record before it gets going, carefully collecting, measuring, and chopping the ingredients for a mouth-watering feast. But, I was *très* naive. My puppy dog crush was not the least bit attractive to him, and he kept close enough to remain inside the friendship but far enough away to keep me outside his bed. When I met Sam and fell in love for real, Jack and I finally hit a groove that was satisfying to both of us. He liked my boyfriend's ability to get him pot, and well, I just really liked my boyfriend. The only problem Jack had with the situation was that Sam was a senior and graduation loomed in the not too distant future.

"I've been thinking. What are we going to do when Sam graduates?" Jack asked me one day. "I think that might be a problem."

"Really. What do you mean 'we'? I think you mean 'me.'" Staring at him. "Since when did you become so invested in my love life?"

"Since your boyfriend became my best source for bud. Who are we going to get pot from when he leaves?"

"You are joking, right? This is about bud?"

"No, not at all." Responding with a straight face. "You are just going to have to start sleeping with someone else as soon as he leaves."

"Excuse me, is the idea to pimp me off?"

"No, but now that you mention it. . . . I'm just trying to find a new angle on a connection."

"And I get to be the new angle. Lucky me." Sarcastically. "So, I prostitute myself for weed?"

"That seems fair to me." Starting to laugh. "Everyone wins."

"And what part do you play in all this? Do you already have a list of possible drug dealers for me to fuck around with?"

"Lilly, I don't need a list. You seem to attract all those sketchy stoners anyway."

"Really?"

"Yeah. Henry, Scott, Sam. You like that grungy thing." Laughing harder. "Don't look so upset, so far it has been beneficial to both of us."

"You are a real asshole." Starting to grin.

"Thank you." Kissing me on the cheek.

Thank goodness, sophomore year, Jack found his own connection. I got to keep my pants on. He was sort of right, though, about the sketchy guy thing. For some reason, I liked that alterna-boy look: disheveled, funky, and a little out of it. I think it was my way of rebelling against what was expected from a nice Jewish girl from a nice Jewish family from a nice little city by the beach. Mismatched men kind of roughed up my good-girl image. Sometimes I think I walked around with a big blinking sign on my head that said, "Sketchy guys and tokers hit on me and find me attractive. Suck me into an unfulfilling pseudorelationship." For a time, wherever I went, this type seemed to gravitate toward me and position himself next to me by the punch bowl.

Anyway, junior year, Jack left school for a while, needing a break, and to some degree we lost touch. In our case, absence did not make the heart grow fonder, it just sort of made the heart forget. We stopped being the kind of friends that were a part of the important stuff that goes on in life. When we'd chat on the phone, the conversation stayed on a shallow, bullshitty level, as if the trust we had in each other had been swallowed by the distance between us. We never talked about things that made us think, or things that kept us up at night lying in bed. A little piece of the magic we had together broke off and filtered out to other people.

When Jack returned to school and we began our senior year, things were fine. We hung out and spent time together, just never intimate one-on-one time. Other people had fallen into the slots we used to reserve for each other. At times, I got so jealous of Maya and Emily.

They had managed to never have any sort of sexual vibe with him, so they never got into any alienating space like me. They were his ear for everything that didn't revolve around college basics, like who was sleeping with whom, or when the next Phish show was. Then things began to change again. For some reason, this particular friendship was an active amoeba, a gremlin that changed shapes when exposed to light, water, and food. By becoming less than best friends, this mutual attraction began to surface. I was no longer a lost little girl needing advice, nor the ear of a chill guy, and I had developed more of a womanly vibe that he finally began to notice.

After a few weeks of halfhearted flirting (we'd hang at parties, go grab lunch alone, all the things we used to do when we were freshmen), a sexual energy began to twirl around and dance in the Providence air. At first I didn't really notice that anything was different. I had just gotten out of a relationship that was, to be kind, very mediocre, and I had a huge crush on a grad student in my Sentimentalism class. The boy I was trying to forget and the one I was trying to get to remember me were maxing out all my boy concentration. I had my hands full with friends, school, and other men, so there wasn't really any room for that friend crush thing to spread out, slip in, and inhabit me all over again. Then one night . . . It's always one night where things change, never one morning or one day or one afternoon. Why does all the juicy stuff happen during the wee hours? Watch, I'll meet my husband at nine in the morning, just because that will be when I least expect it. So one night, things really changed with Jack and me, and I began counting to thirty.

Our friend Evan was having a cocktail party at his

196 apartment. We all trudged over there en mass, about
twenty of us dressed in our finest cocktail garb smashed
carefully into two cars. I happened to be wearing a very
tight, slinky fuck-me dress I had bought a few years back
to wear to a semiformal. It did me no good at that dance
since it failed to woo my intended suitor. When an outfit
falls short of its supposed goal, it must be tossed to the
back of the closet to collect dust. It must spend time in
wardrobe purgatory, and think long and hard about its
inappropriate behavior. The ensemble doesn't even
merit the plastic cleaners bag treatment. It is just not
worthy.

It had been a long while, so I thought that maybe it was
time to break it out of bad-dress prison. It had served its
penance. Maybe it had developed some of the magic I
thought it had in the first place. It was a Betsey Johnson
long, red crushed-velvet number, and hugged just about
every single one of my curves, and a few I would have
liked not to show, but you can't win them all. I had done
my hair up in this haphazard arrangement of twists,
braids, buns, and bobby pins, and I layered on the red
lipstick. It was one of those nights that I wanted to be
kind of trampy. I was among friends, so what harm was
there in flaunting what I had? Sometimes a girl just
needs to do the hoochie mama thing and remember she
can be sexy if she wants.

We all got to Evan's and drank up a storm. Shots and
wine, beer and vodka. The party buzzed with that high,
loose excitement of best friends all getting trashed at the
same time. In this scenario, everyone's inhibitions fall
away because everyone in the room is on a common level,

a common wavelength. Jack and I began to flirt around Evan's round kitchen table. We were going head to head, downing tequila shots in this sick let's-get-as-fucked-up-as-possible game. It's not surprising that our hormones began raging the minute we poured good old José Cuervo down our throats!

"Cheers!" Jack, raising his full shot glass toward mine.

"Cheers!" Responding by clinking and throwing back my third shot, which tasted like fire. "Ugh. That sucked. It's definitely going to be my last for a while." Sucking the rind off the last of the lime slices in front of me.

"Wimp. You were the one who started this shot thing in the first place." Trying to haze me like a frat boy. "You can't bail from your own game."

"Why not? If I started it, I can end it. If I don't stop drinking right now, I'll get sick, throw up, and embarrass myself in front of my dear friend Jack." Sucking harder, searching for just a little more citrus to dull the taste of the tequila.

"You're being such a woman." Pushing harder. "Take off the skirt."

"Thank you. I'll take that as a compliment." Not caving in. "Besides, why would I want to waste tonight in the bathroom after I went to all this trouble to get babed?"

"You are looking very dressed up tonight." Pointing to the dress. "Is it new?"

"No, but I haven't worn it in forever. Usually it makes me feel a little self-conscious." Adjusting my strap.

"Don't worry, you look great."

"Thanks."

I began to blush. (It took a lot to get him to compliment anything, much less me.) My face mottled into the color of my outfit.

"Is it hot in here?" Feeling my own cheek. "I'm burning up."

"Must be the tequila. Want to go outside for a smoke?" Finally giving up making me drink more.

"Sure."

When we went outside, the steps were already crowded with friends, and our first little interlude of the evening was interrupted. When Evan's party ended, we all decided to get back into the cars and head downtown to a bar. Before we went, Maya, Emily, and I made the boys stop back at our place so we could change. The tight dress and heels thing worked for a nonthreatening friend fete, but it was time to get a wee bit more comfortable. I don't like looking like a total slut in front of strangers. They might get the wrong idea. I did, however, try to keep a small part of my sex vibe going since it was obviously working. I just wanted to be wearing more clothing. By putting on my tight shiny black Olivia Newton John in *Grease* pants and a tight black cotton T-shirt with a red Chinese character emblazoned on the front, I was dressed enough to feel at ease, but had enough oomph to hopefully still get the guy.

Once dressed, we raced outside to the waiting cars and headed down the hill. After we parked and began roaming the streets of Providence looking for the perfect spot to continue our happy vibe, we met up with some very amusing Providence inhabitants. In the first bar, there was the bachelor toga party we accidentally walked into and then promptly walked out of when they thought we were the entertainment, and another bar with flannel-clad go-go dancers shimmying atop the pool table to "Love in an Elevator." We finally settled on Skipper's because it was relatively empty when we walked in and for a group of twenty that was really what we needed. It took us only about fifteen minutes to realize that Skipper's was a gay bar, and that was when this woman decided I was her dream girl.

"Hey, my name is Jo. Can I buy you a drink?" Asks a tall, broad deep-voiced woman.

"Thanks, but I already have one." Gesturing to my gin-and-tonic sitting on the bar.

"What's your name?"

"Lilly."

"You have great freckles."

"Thank you."

"Are you here with anyone?"

"Yes. She's here with me." Maya, answering, and coming up behind me. "Hi, love."

Maya and I had this deal to pretend to be lovers whenever someone we didn't want hitting on us made their move. The only problem with this little arrangement was that usually the image of the two of us together was only encouragement to keep tossing out lines.

"So, are you guys together, together?" Jo asks, really interested.

"Yeah." Maya, putting her arm around me. "Honey, I leave you alone for one minute and look what happens." Leaning toward me.

At this point, Maya and I began whispering into each other's ear and giggling at the gibberish we were coming up with to enhance our couple act. I stroked her arm, she rubbed my neck, I played with the cherry in her drink, and she held her cigarette out for me to smoke. Jo got the message and took her drink to the other side of the bar. I felt a little guilty, but I was drunk, and it was too funny pretending to be Maya's lesbian lover.

"What would I do without you, baby?" Batting my eyelashes and cooing to Maya.

"I don't know, I don't know." Laughing, giving me a hug.

The evening progressed, and we closed down the bar. When we all unleashed ourselves outside, the gang of us became a tidal wave of energy rolling and crashing down the street. We were singing, laughing, skipping, and throwing snowballs at each other. By the time we reached the cars we were wet, happy, and soggy messes, but the evening refused to end. At two in the morning we were just getting started. We headed off to Barnes Street and attacked one of our friends' house. Jack and I reconnected and found ourselves on the couch sitting very close together, sharing a bong.

"So I saw you with your new girlfriend at the bar."

"Oh, yeah. I was tempted to go home with her, but Maya put her foot down."

"Watching you and Maya flirt was very interesting."

"So you saw that?"

"Yep. Evan and I commented on how nice it looked."

"Really? Have a fantasy of the two of us going at it?"

"Who doesn't?"

"Probably me . . . and Maya."

"Too bad."

"Sorry, you can't win them all."

"I'd settle for one."

"Which one?"

Before he could answer, Maya sat down on the coffee table in front of us and began chatting away. As I feigned rapt attention, I kept looking at Jack to see if he meant what he had almost said or if he had just almost said it in the spirit of jest. He kept averting his eyes whenever I'd catch them, and in that instant I knew. I was going to kiss him.

I'm never right about these things. I mean, I was right about the fact that he did want to kiss me, but I was dead wrong about it actually happening. That's how it always is for me: I have this huge problem with closing the deal. Something always gets in the way or I fuck the situation up entirely. I go left when I should go right, I run when I should walk, and I wink when I should just be blinking. Never have I truly gotten it all right. When we all went over to Jack's house, and even after I sat on his lap in the crowded car and we did the hand squeeze thing we were doing now, I totally blew it. BIG SHOCKER. Maya and I and about five others were still hanging out, smoking, talking. After about twenty minutes, Maya stood up to leave.

"Lilly, let's go." Getting her keys out.

"What?"

"I'm going home. Come on." Taking my hand and pulling me off the couch in one fell swoop.

"You go ahead." Sitting back down. "I'm going to stay a little longer."

"I'm hungry and I want some company making mac

202 and cheese. Everyone else is asleep at home." Giving me this pleady kind of "If you don't come, I will make you feel guilty for days" look.

Then she just stood there in the middle of the living room waiting. There was just no ignoring her. Fuck!

"I really have to go?"

Nodding, grabbing my coat for me.

"Okay, okay."

"Good night, boys." Maya, helping me on with my jacket.

I let her talk me into leaving. As I walked to the door, Jack and I caught eyes. Written all over his face was "Why are you leaving now? I want you to stay." There was nothing I could do. I had been suckered into bailing, and there was no turning back. Sitting down again would have been an impossibility. I tried to write that on my face, but that was a hard one to translate into a facial expression. Then I was out the door, walking home, and walking away from my one moment. I knew there would never be another night like this one, but I still let the flame of hope burn just a little bit. He was the same guy I had a crush on years back. Now that I had a taste of what might be, I couldn't let it go right away. Deep down, I knew I had no chance, but nonetheless, I still started the count.

A few weeks passed, and before I could even get to the end of my hormone cycle, Jack started dating Tracy. When I found this out, I guess my hormones went into double time, because I decided to murder Maya. I had the plan all thought out and everything. It was one of the few instances I wished she had paid attention. All I wanted was a kiss or two, and she gave me the "Heisman," the cock block named after the player immortalized in metal on the Heisman Trophy. The design, a player who's positioned with both hands up ready to receive the pass, could also be read more subtly as, "stay away from me." Chicks just aren't supposed to do it to their own quarterbacks! I had my hands up ready to grab the ball and run, Maya's were up as well telling me to back off because she was never passing. I was even angrier when she eventually told me that she knew what was going on that night with Jack and me and had intercepted on purpose. Bitch! Apparently, when we left Skipper's, he had said to her that we were going to definitely hook up, but it could be a potential nightmare. I guess Maya made it her own personal mission to avoid the nightmare and ensure my inactivity. She benched me in the last five minutes.

That's what happens in college when everyone knows everyone else's business. People tend to stick their noses into places they don't belong. They pull the strings and leave you dangling like a limp puppet. I got over it eventually, because once I had a little hindsight I thanked God she was so intrusive. Maya was right to intercept. Jack would have flipped out and stopped talking to me, which was his habit after kissing his friends. I knew this since I had watched it happen before. He wasn't mature enough to handle it. I would have therefore been left with nothing but the memory of one alcohol-induced hookup. Moreover, if Jack and my friendship had fallen apart back then, I wouldn't have had the pleasure of experiencing this San Fran fling thing.

In San Francisco, years after graduation and with no

204   clocks nor calendars counting out days or hormone cycles, Jack and I just went for it. Without college grapevines or consequences, we could explore our curiosities. No strings, no expectations, no seven hundred and twenty hours in a month to twiddle our thumbs through. It was just him, me, a green couch, and *Threesome* glaring on the TV. Sometimes magazine advice should remain trapped inside slick pages and glossy covers and be left to sit by the toilet in case of emergency.

let the girl sing

I'm exhausted. San Francisco was not what I expected. I seem to be on a roll now with men. Maybe I will find a real date to the wedding after all. Optimism is good, right? My lips are chapped and I have the remnants of all those aforementioned mints my mother hated on our road trip to categorize and review. It's a good thing I bought that espresso maker a couple of weeks ago, because now that it is four shots later, I am jacked up and ready for the last taste test. Coffee is probably not the best thing for me, seeing how I haven't really conquered the ability to fall asleep normally yet, but a girl has got to do her job.

Three hours, a myriad of mouth rinsings, and two more espressos later, it is two in the morning and sleep is an impossibility. I'm convinced the meditation has to

206   start working some time soon, so I'm willing to give it another try. I have to get some rest or I'm going to have to bump up the concealer article I was planning on suggesting. At least then I would have enough makeup to cover my drooping-to-my-nose undereye bags.

Okay, I'm in bed, covers tucked in all around me, and my favorite Calvin Klein nightgown hangs to my knees. Sarah McLachlan is in the CD player, and I am trying to bliss out. Breathe. Mellow out. Breath. Inhale. Exhale. Relax. I am on the edge of a lake. It is early morning and dew hangs on the trees like perfect bubbles. I am walking along the edge and staring out onto the glassy water. Everything sparkles and twinkles in the sun. I smell the pine trees, and I close my eyes taking in the invigorating aroma of nature. I open my eyes. I'm staring at a moose. It's huge. I hear a bleat. I turn around and see another smaller moose. I'm between a mother moose and her kid. I'm dead. I'm going to be killed by a moose, how humiliating. It charges. I'm awake. I'm sweating. I will never sleep again.

Despite making peace with *mi amiga* and knowing I can enjoy the engaged version of her, I can't find REM anywhere. I thought resolving things with Maya and having a sweet hookup would have calmed me down, but my brain just can't turn off. Even though I feel really good about things, something is still off. I just don't know what it is. I'm stuck right now in this place of stasis, anxious and antsy, floating in a drop of glue, and dying to jump out and experience a major change. I am no longer a girl, all innocent and cute, but I certainly ain't a woman, all worldly and knowing. I know something is coming to rock my world, make me into a righteous chick (the best word I could think of for the in-between phase because "giman," "girman," and "womirl" get caught on the tongue), but fuck, get here already!

Making up with Maya and feeling better about myself must be steps toward it, but where's the adventure? The training is getting tedious. Now I know how the Karate Kid must have felt. "Wax, on. Wax, off." I guess I just have to find the benefits of being a night owl. I can watch a slew of the B movies on cable that I love and get turned on by the gratuitous yet sleazy sex scenes. I can do the crossword puzzle with a dictionary by my side and get all the clues right. I can rearrange my closet and color coordinate my fifteen pairs of black pants. I can take a hot bath with aromatherapy oils and smell like Martha Stewart's garden. I can ramble on and demonstrate how neurotic I am. I can get cranky and tired and bratty.

Going to work when you're burnt and crispy is too complicated. Every sound is jarring and every movement makes your eyes scatter like a drop of oil in a hot pan. The battle-ax forgot the coffee, and I hate her. I seethe at my desk, blindly editing the previous night's prose, and then I run when the clock strikes five. Get me out of there. Tonight, I'm going to a party with Danielle. No matter how tired I am, even the rules girls say you should never turn down an invitation, so I will trek there yawning if I have to.

GOT THE WEIRDEST message on my machine. It was a "call" of sorts, but one I didn't consider before. Jonah

208 called me out of the blue. I guess he liked the pink hair thing after all. I replayed the message five times.

"Hey Lilly, what's up? It's Jonah. Thinking about you. Call me anytime."

Brief, but enough to roll me backward into my crush-dom ever so slightly. The fact that even though it took him awhile to call me, he did, after saying he would, made me pause. Those obsession boys can always take away your breath and make your head spin. They connect to this very primal, very passionate zone in your body that has a will of its own and never grows up. Even if you know how things ended and how nothing was right, you always have a soft spot in your heart for their druglike hallucinations. They are always easily remembered.

As previously mentioned, Jonah and I didn't ever consummate our relationship, nor did it last very long, but it inhabited every bone of my body for a while, feasting on me like a parasite. I lived, breathed, smelled, and tasted this man. His few kisses tattooed themselves onto my lips like permanent makeup. Why is it that the ones you know are going to smash you to bits are the completely irresistible ones? Nothing about him screamed boyfriend potential. Much to my chagrin, I couldn't deny that I was and am a boyfriend girl. As it is already known, I don't feel comfortable in sexpot shoes, even if they make quite a nice outfit sometimes. A guy like Jonah was a whirlwind ready to pick me up and toss me to the wolves when the monsoon season ended. I let myself get taken away.

He continued to hold some sort of spell over me despite the fact that I thought I had given him up. I can even pinpoint the exact moment I thought I fully broke the chains. It was about a year ago, and what follows may sound corny. Having a life-altering experience at a folk-rock concert sounds a little too Woodstocky even for me, but you can never plan when or why a phenomenon like that will occur. It might take you by surprise in the shower or in the car or at the supermarket, and you can't ignore it and simply walk away. Events like this force you to listen and beg you to take notice and learn. Mine happened to find me at the Lilith Fair, and there was nothing I could do about it. I couldn't very well say, "Hey, I just can't be enlightened here because people will think I'm a cheese ball." I had to let it happen.

It makes sense that a lot of things came to a head the night I saw my idols grace the stage for the first time: Sarah McLachlan, Paula Cole, and Tracy Chapman. I had been looking forward to the Lilith Fair since before it even existed. All my favorite artists together singing to me. Ah, dreams do come true. Maybe I'm too typical—the all-American girl who cries at night, staring at the ceiling of her room, while listening to Sarah or Tori or Alanis spill their guts out. I can't help being constantly suckered into their vibe. I like being a girl's girl: I am damn proud my favorite color is hot pink and that I sometimes like wearing rhinestones, ribbons, and bows. I constantly hear people moan and groan over the latest Natalie Imbruglia or Liz Phair type to get their boppy, poppy little infectious tune on every radio station across the country, yet it's obvious someone other than I must be listening. Lilith Fair haters can say what they wish, but girl music speaks to millions and surely talks to me every time I'm in the kitchen, at the gym, on a hike, at a club, in a bar, in bed. . . . You get the picture.

It was over the duration of the post-Sam summer when I discovered the magic and power they could wedge inside the lyrics of their three-minute songs. They found a way to soothe me as I was nursing a broken heart, and these songs became my lifeline. Somehow these singers could express in a perfect little sentence my intense misery, anger, jealousy, love—everything. Their words floated over and around me until I was singing instead of them, and I had the means to get over it and get on with my life. If I traced the different songs that meant something to me, it would read like a chronology of my emotional growth. It could tell me when I was sad, when I was hopeful, when I wished on stars, and when I felt good enough to just be. The music marked my journey. That's why I am such a fan, a true fan.

But I would have to say that I was not among a typical Lilith fan group that day. It was four guys—my brother, his friend Robert, Josh, Jonah—and little ol' me. Three of the four had zero clue who was playing, and Josh, well, Josh was a whole other story. He was perhaps more into it than I. We had spent months conquering the transatlantic time difference with e-mails and letters about the concert. We conversed back and forth while I was in Paris about who would get the tickets, if we should travel to other cities to see more than one show, and whether we could somehow get backstage passes. Then there was the matter of picking out the group who could join us, because bad vibes would just ruin the whole thing. I, of course, wanted to bring Jonah. It was soon after he had decided we weren't kissing anymore, and I got to thinking that a night of heartfelt lyrics and unrequited love songs might be just the ticket to get myself back where I wanted to be: resting in his sexy embrace. I was also determined to experience Lilith with a man I liked since it would, once and for all, signify that I had conquered the music.

To go to a concert and hear those same words with someone who had the power to crush me might appear sadistic, but I felt that sitting there with him would prove I would always be okay. A guy who affected me on such a visceral level could hear where I was coming from. If he could open himself up to their words, maybe he could also open up to mine, and I could find my own voice through the process. If I could share this with him and expose myself so completely, it really wouldn't matter how things ended because I had been so totally honest and open. He was being given access to my most private and personal space. From his response I would be able to see how he felt, and there would no longer be any maybes.

We got to Lilith late, which pissed me and Josh off, even though Max was this mad map reader and got us down to Irvine by the most back roads way in record time. We were late because the rest of the boys got going a little too leisurely. And they say girls are slow motivators! Anyway, everyone but Josh decided to partake in some X as we walked into the arena.

"I don't want to take a whole one. I don't think I want to be that fucked up." Me, looking around and smiling at all the funky hippie chicks. "I love this place."

"Just take part of one." Jonah, handing me a piece of the pill he broke in half. "We can share."

"Max, you and Robert can have the rest." Giving them the other two pills I had with me.

"How strong is this stuff?" Max, rolling the dose between his thumb and forefinger.

"I'm not sure. I got it from Tony's brother, and he said it was pretty good, not like that shit we had Thanksgiving."

"Nothing will be as bad as that." Max said, swallowing it. "That was such a bad trip!"

"I actually had fun, except for the spontaneous projectile vomit."

"You were lucky you were in the bathroom already."

"No shit. If it had been witnessed, I wouldn't have gotten to kiss David." Remembering and grinning. "He gave me a great massage. Lotion and everything."

"How fair was that? You kiss some random guy, and I get to deal with the crumbling of my relationship." Shaking his head.

"I guess that was sort of the beginning of the end for you and Mandy."

"No, but it should have been a sign. Whatever. I don't want to think about that now."

"I hate to interrupt this trip down memory lane, but let's go in already! You guys are so busy chatting, we're going to miss the rest of Paula Cole." Josh, taking off in the direction of the stage.

We found our seats and began to get into the rhythm of the concert. I was sitting there talking to Jonah about who knows what, thinking in the back of my head, "When is this stuff going to kick in?" An hour later Jewel was on and I lost the ability to speak. I was convinced that if I opened my mouth, I would throw up everywhere. Imagine listening to "Who Will Save Your Soul" trying to contain nausea the size of a sumo wrestler, because next to you is the man with whom you are so infatuated that if you did anything repulsive like vomit, he would surely never want to kiss you again, ever. As the sun set, my eyes began flipping out. God, was I a mess. I couldn't focus, and everything was swimming, water ripples and all. So, not only was I ill, I couldn't open my eyes for fear of seeing Jonah become some small blue Smurf. The only thing that snapped me from this place of utter hell was Max rushing past me.

"Where are you going? Are you okay?"

"Gotta go."

"Okay, where are you going?"

"Don't know. Gotta go."

And with that Max disappeared into the crowd. Luckily for me this little reality check brought me back to earth, and as quickly as my bad trip started, it vanished. All of a sudden, Jewel was gone, the air was no longer viscous, and my lunch retreated back from the tip of my tongue. Everything was beautiful and bright and Jonah was smiling and I think I saw God.

"Lilly, you look pretty happy." Jonah, smiling. "What a great smile."

"Yeah, everything is great. I think I'm finally at that fluffy marshmallow buzz you get when you X." Rubbing my head, enjoying the scalp tingle.

"Me too. I think I've been here a bit longer than you though. It looked like things were a little touch and go back there."

"You could say that. Jewel just didn't sit well with me, if you know what I mean. I'm fine now. I'm happy you're here."

"I'm glad I came too. I think it will be good for my music to expose myself to other kinds of artists."

"It's nice to be able to share this with you."

"Yeah . . ." Blushing a little and fidgeting. "Who's on next?" Clearly changing the subject.

"Tracy Chapman."

The lights conveniently went out, and she walked onto the stage. It was probably a good thing because he did not seem to want to travel on that happy vibe with me. That's the one real problem with drugs. They make you say things you shouldn't. If I had not been saved by the darkness, I would have probably gone on to tell Jonah how I felt, why it meant so much for me to be here with him, why he meant so much to me, why I wanted to kiss him all the time. None of that would have been wise since we were friends, just friends. Anything I said to encourage our pursuing a more intimate relationship would have sent him running even faster in the other direction, and I was sure his sneakers were already laced and ready. You may ask why I stuck around if I knew he wasn't really interested in me on a girlfriend level. I have no idea how to answer you. What makes us stay? I bet if I came up with a solution for that one and began hawking it as an advice book on QVC, I'd become a millionaire. Until then, I just accept broken hearts as part of my daily bread and keep on trucking.

As soon as Tracy walked onto the stage and began singing a cappella, I forgot all about my troubles. She ripped through the entire audience like a freight train, delivering a sound so pure and true that everyone immediately shut up. We all were transfixed by her presence; she inhabited every single ounce of space. As she contin-

ued with her set, she brought the audience to their feet
with the most beautiful rendition of "Fast Car" ever, and
a jamming "Give Me One Good Reason." She was so
moving that Jonah and I started holding hands without a
second thought. For her to be able to hold all these fans
in the palm of her hand and inspire affection from this
guy next to me was truly amazing. I was in heaven until
she began to sing her final song, "Baby Can I Hold You."
All of a sudden my bubble of bliss began to burst, and
everything began to spin out of control. I was on a
turntable doing 360s. Her voice rang out and every word
she sang pierced directly into me like a nail from an
automatic nail gun. It had been so long since I had heard
that song.

Sam and I used to listen to Tracy Chapman when we
made love, and the track she was singing now was our
favorite. We would play it on repeat, over and over again
while we fell asleep in each other's arms. After he broke
my heart, I couldn't bear to listen to it, and every time I
was sadistic enough to try, it destroyed me. It was "our"
song, and now, years later, it was turning me right back
into that eighteen-year-old lovesick little girl after only a
few notes. This huge wave of nostalgia crashed on my
head, drowning me, and I began crying. As I turned to
look at Jonah sitting next to me, smiling this dopey grin,
I wanted to puke all over again. What was he doing here
with me? Why had I let him come? Why did another guy
have his claws digging into me? I had to get the fuck out
of there asap. Everything was instantly so wrong.

"I'll be right back." Me, choking back the tears and
wiping my eyes.

"Are you okay?" Jonah, asking politely.

"Sure." Standing up. "I just need some air."

"Do you want me to come with you?"

"No!" Answering a little too quickly and a little too loudly. "Stay here and enjoy the show."

With that, I took off and left the arena as fast as humanly possible. My head was on fire, sparkling and flashing with visions of Sam and Jonah and every other stupid boy I gave my affection to. A high-definition video montage played, recalling every sweet time they touched me and every time they fucked me over. I moved through the crowd in slow motion, weaving in and out of bodies as I remembered those two guys. It all seemed so alive, so fresh, as though it all just happened yesterday. I started to hallucinate and began to see visions of these men everywhere, especially Sam. In my drugged state, every dark-haired flannel-clad guy looked exactly like him even if the one in front of me was fat and balding. I got frantic and tears pelted me like tiny bombs.

I finally reached the bathroom and rushed into the nearest stall where I promptly threw up. Actually, I couldn't stop throwing up. Kneeling there on this nasty-ass-seen-too-many-muddy-shoes floor, I threw up for about five minutes. The ragged chokes and dry heaves followed one after the other, steamrolling me into submission. My face was a mess of saliva, snot, and tears. Then someone knocked quietly on the door.

"Are you okay in there?" A female voice, whispering.

"Yes . . ." Choking.

"Are you sure?"

"Yeah, thank you." Catching my breath.

"Do you need anything?"

"No, it's okay."

"Here, take this." Handing me a pack of gum under the door.

"Thank you." Grabbing it with my sweaty palm. "That's really nice of you."

"No problem. Can I do anything else?"

"No, no. I'm fine, really."

"Okay, take care." Leaving me alone again.

Here's to the kindness of strangers, because that little interruption broke the sick spell and I refocused. What the fuck was I doing on the floor of a concert-venue bathroom? Somehow, amid the toxic disaster all around and on me, I could see clearly for the first time in awhile. I had this pure epiphany. I was going to be fine. Not just fine in the sense that I wasn't nauseated anymore, but fine in general. Really profound, I know, but that was it. Sam or no Sam, Jonah or no Jonah, with or without, there was just me and that was fine. A pretty lame moment of self-realization probably brought on by drug intake, but who cared? Like I told the gum lady, I was fine, and it was that simple. No more tears or regrets, it was time for all that to be dead and buried. As quickly as I hurdled into the pit of despair and panic, I regained composure and calm. The situation flipped on a dime. I slowly stood up, wiped my mouth, and walked out to the mirror. I threw some water on my face, primped, popped a piece of gum, and smiled. I had just puked out the old Lilly, watched her flounder in the bowl, and then flushed her to China.

As I walked back to the seats, my grin grew. I felt hollow and clean and confident. I knew when I sat down next

218 to Jonah that he really didn't matter at all. I didn't need him to validate my music or me in any way. I could and would do it all myself. Who gave a fuck if he dug my chicks or me? My life was not about figuring out a way to reach him and make him understand me or want me. That would just be a big waste of time and energy.

"Lilly, where have you been?" Josh, asking in that concerned friend way.

"I just needed some air." Smiling at him. "Has Max gotten back yet?" Changing the subject.

Just as I said that, Max came walking down from the top of the stands.

"Perfect timing. We were just talking about you." Telling him as he sat down.

"What was with the sibling exodus?" Josh, asking. "You both bailed rather quickly."

"Yeah." Jonah, chiming in.

"Max, where did you go in such a hurry, and where did you get that ridiculous hat? You must be tripping hard because your eyes are like saucers." Me, ignoring any comment directed at me.

"I had to just go. I felt really ill, but when I got to the bathroom, stared down the toilet to puke, and leaned over, all of a sudden I was fine. It just clicked over. I wandered around, bought the hat, some CDs. Things are just great right now."

"You are a freak." Josh says to Max.

"You are also lucky. You got to win the face-off with the toilet."

"You didn't?" Josh, eyes widening as he looked at me.

"Yep, I did."

"Are you okay?" Jonah, asking all sweet. "I would have gone with you."

"I'm great actually. No problems whatsoever."

"You are taking it quite well. I'm impressed." Josh, responding. "I don't think I would be so chipper after throwing up."

"It was really enlightening."

"Throwing up was enlightening? Max, I take it back. Your sister's the freak. This is why I don't do drugs."

The lights again conveniently turned off and the next performer began. I didn't have to explain about my epiphany and the nice stranger who facilitated my discovery. Everyone would have thought I was a big flake anyway, and who needs that? Keeping all this to myself was the better solution. It was an important moment only for me and that doesn't always translate especially to brothers, friends, and a guy who didn't know he had just lost his spot on your idol mantel.

The rest of the concert was super, and we all left totally satisfied, the only thing bringing us down was the hour-and-a-half ride home. When we got back to Jonah's and the rest of us got into our own cars, Jonah lingered by mine before going into his house. When I hugged him good-bye, we had that awkward moment of do we or don't we like we always did even though we were "just friends." This time I didn't stare like a wounded puppy, hoping he would plant a big wet one on me. I just smiled and hopped into my car, leaving him standing on the curb with this puzzled look on his face. Loved it! Little did he know just how meaningful my trip to the bathroom had been. Inside my car, I had all I needed. My

220   girls were waiting to kiss my ears and sing me all the way home to my perennially empty but now content bed.

That night I released Jonah, or at least I thought I did. I gave up all the hopes I had for us to be together and become this blazing couple. Months past, and for the most part, my epiphany stuck, which is pretty cool because you can never be sure that will be the case if they occur when you are on drugs. I moved past him and the girl I was when I longed for him. I had matured and become more of who I was supposed to be. I . . . I . . . I . . . I may be a little bit full of shit. There's just so far a potty epiphany can take you.

house of cards

"You are definitely full of shit!" Trilling.

"Give me a fucking break." Rubbing my temples.

"If a new viewing of Pink Flamingos made you puke, and seeing him in a bad outfit made you freak, what do you think this phone call is going to do?"

"Make my head explode?"

"Well, not in a David Cronenberg kind of way, but maybe in that we were just getting the house neatly in order when a tornado just blew right through it kind of way."

"It sounds like I am Dorothy."

"Not likely. We know how well you do with nice high-heel shoes." Smirking.

I had no jazzy comeback since here was Jonah's voice on my machine saying he was thinking of me and checking in, and I could not bring myself to hit erase. What is that saying from The Godfather? "Just when I think I'm out, they pull me back in." My body was starting to buzz. How quickly I turn into a puddle of melted Jell-O. Damn it! Fortunately, just as I picked up the phone to ring Jonah way too soon for it to appear like he didn't matter anymore, which was the vibe I wanted to project, Danielle showed up to get me. The "call" would have to wait.

"Guess who called me today?" Getting into Danielle's car.

"Who?" Getting into the driver's seat beside me.

"Blast from the past." Pulling on my seat belt and flicking down the visor to check my lipstick.

"Sam?" Starting the car and blasting a Garbage CD.

"Nope."

"Nathan?"

"Nope."

"Just tell me already, this is a tiresome game." Tapping the steering wheel.

"Jonah." Bopping my head to the song.

"Reeeaaalllly?" Overemphasizing her syllables. "What did he say?"

"Not much. Just the basic hi/bye message."

"How many times did you play it?"

"None of your business."

"Wait a few days to call back, unless you already did, which is highly possible in your case."

"Fuck off. I'll call when I want to."

"So you did call! Always the eager beaver."

"No, but I almost did." Answering meekly. "Instinct."

"Stupidity."

"Whatever. Just drive."

"Don't get like that." Turning down the music. "Like I'm one to talk. There will never be the wrath of Danielle chastising anyone."

"I know, I just get defensive."

"No shit." Eyeing me. "Look, Lilly, I don't think you're stupid for caving or wanting to cave. I've always known that you and Jonah weren't through. I saw how he looked at you, and I could tell there was something real there."

"There was, wasn't there?" Musing out loud. "I don't think it was all one-sided. I felt a connection. I felt something different."

"Yeah, but don't take that the wrong way. He still really sucked and broke you for a little while. You can't forget that. Proceed with caution. If I have learned anything this year it is that."

"How are you doing?"

"Okay, I guess. Some days are better than others. I still do taste bile every time I see a photo of them, but I could swear she has gained ten pounds. You know how fond Tom is of the whole wine and dine dance."

"Yeah, I agree. In the last issue of *Interview* I definitely saw some cellulite on her upper arms." Grabbing Danielle's hand and giving it a big squeeze.

"You saw it too?" Squeezing back.

"Oh, yeah. The girl has some serious upper arm waddle." Holding on tight to her.

"So, all I can say is, be careful."

"You're right. I just can't help getting a little hopeful. I want something real to happen to me. I want to be loved."

"Ah, my girl. The perpetual optimist. Maybe this time

224 the glass will be full, and if not I'm here for you, I always got some good lovin' to give."

"Thanks, *ma petite chou.*" Kissing her cheek. "Oops." Rubbing off my lipstick mark.

We finally got there, and the party was your basic sit in the corner and pretend to be having fun event. Everyone stared at everyone else, sizing up the competition, and puffing up their chests like big blue peacocks dressed in feathered jeans. Drinks were guzzled, random tidbits of movie information and gossip were traded, cigarettes filled up ashtrays with matches and butts, girls adjusted their tube tops and their flat-ironed hair, and I got bored. The fake smile thing gets so old. Even though I was single, and flirting would be beneficial to the cause, I just couldn't muster the energy to bat my eyes and talk to anyone but Danielle.

"Why do we come to these parties?" Observing the scene. "It's not like we ever have any fun."

"I don't know. Maybe it's the free liquor." Holding up her full drink.

"But we don't even really drink anymore."

"Yeah, right."

"Well, we only drink on special occasions. But, seriously, why?"

"The cute boys?"

"And they would be where?" Pointing to the crowd. "All the ones here are plastic."

"Yeah, but plastic can still be hot."

"Hot plastic melts."

"Details, details. It's better than staying home."

"Is it?" Wondering. "I don't think so. At least at home

you have a plush seat, a place to set your drink when your arm gets tired, and easy access to the remote."

"True."

"How much longer do we have to stay?" Looking at my watch.

"I don't care, but we should stick around a little while. Maybe we will meet some interesting people."

"You always say that and yet we always sit in the corner talking to each other all night."

"No, we don't."

"Yes we so do. We have probably met two interesting people in two years of parties like these."

"I met Tom at a . . ." Danielle, starting to say.

"Yes. Exactly my point."

"Fine, fine." Taking a last slurp of her drink.

"I'm bored."

"Let's blow this pop-stand." Danielle, grabbing her purse. "Hungry?"

"Always."

Danielle and I hit Swingers for a late grilled cheese with tomatoes and fries. Then we headed home with ever dampening buzzes and wasted outfits that would now have to be dry-cleaned. What a pisser! Why is it that I always get dolled up for parties that treat me like yellow wallpaper? When I got home, I played the message again—couldn't resist. Then I decided I would wait three days to call him, and I marked it on my Filofax. That would be a huge feat since I am the girl who calls back before she even gets the call in the first place. Three days, I can do it. . . .

I crawled into bed and hoped to get some shut-eye.

226   Laid my head on the pillow ready to be taken to la-la land. Breathe in. Out. Listen to the murmur of the bugs outside. Breath. Relax. Smile. Dream. Ahhh, there is a room filled with white flowing curtains and red roses. Candles drip with wax and set the room aglow with a soft peach porn-star light. A lone violinist plays Bach in the corner. I feel calm and collected. A slight wind blows the curtains and tickles my face. I am a Harlequin woman. All corsets and ribbons and bows. A high canopied bed leans against the back wall. I tuck myself into the silky sheets, rubbing my hands down the sides of myself. I am relaxed. I am almost there. I close my eyes and feel the warmth as the soft focus of a Lifetime channel Jackie Collins miniseries covers my body with good angles. I feel something on my foot, a delicate caress. It pleases me. I'm almost there. I open my eyes. It is a spider. A big hairy tarantula playing footsy with me. I am freaked. I am frightened. I am awake. Again I will never sleep.

SEVEN HOURS AND no real sleep later, I am at work falling into my keyboard. What the hell is going to get me through the day? This seems to be a recurring theme. Hopefully my boss will never get wind of my less than alert performance. I think I am going to suggest a test of NoDoz or Uptime for our May end-of-school issue. Every self-respecting crammer needs to know the best way to perk up at four in the morning, as does every self-respecting need-to-get-through-the-day-somehow insomniac. How clever I am! I'll disguise my cloudiness with a stellar idea. I really should be researching sleep aids instead of sleep preventers, but if meditation, warm

milk, and guided imagery couldn't help, I might as well
fuck it and be more productive with all the extra time.

And how did I spend my time? Instead of trying to
work, all day I dialed Jonah's number then hung up
before I hit the last digit. These days with caller ID and
star 69 you can't be too careful. Those pesky little inno-
vations have become the bane of my existence. I think the
phone company majorly screwed over teenagers and
young adults. They have made crank calling, the I'm-
too-nervous-to-speak-so-I-hang-up-fast call, and the
I-have-to-see-if-he-is-home call impossible. When I
was a wee lass, you could call that unreachable guy with the
perfect after-braces smile and side-swept bangs just to
hear his voice, and then slam the phone down when you
lost your balls without any repercussion. Now everything
is so traceable you get called out on your nervousness and
ineptitude immediately. You get caught with your hand
in the cookie jar since every fucking call is coded into the
damn phone. The days of innocent phone calls are long
gone. I hate that. Now we all have to grow up.

It wasn't until a few days later in the privacy of my bedroom that I let the call go through. After about five rings I
was going to hang up, then I heard that familiar baritone.

"Hey."

"Hi Jonah. It's Lilly."

"Heeeyyy." Accentuating the "hey." "What's up?"

"Not much."

"Not much? We haven't really talked like forever and
you say 'not much'? There's got to be a ton of shit going on."

"Well." Stuttering a bit. "Just tossing out a standard
reply."

"Since when have you ever been standard?"

"Since when have you ever been so direct?" Getting my wits about me. "What's with the drill? I don't remember you being so interested."

"You're right." Laughing. "I'm a little pumped up right now. Just downed three cups of coffee."

"Writing?"

"Yep. How'd you guess?"

"You always drink way too much coffee when you write. How's the album?"

"Great. It's pretty much done. It comes out in a few months. I'll be going on tour then."

"So what are you writing?"

"Some new stuff. I can't just stop because my album is finished. Actually, I'm using that cool journal you gave me last Christmas."

"Glad you are using it."

"Of course. I think of you every time I open it up."

"How sweet." Melting ever so slightly. "You sound so focused. I'm impressed."

At that moment, I pictured him hunched over the little red book, pen caressing paper, pages being turned with ink-stained fingers, and I did a little more than melt. Now, I was swooning.

"Thanks, I am. It's all good. How'd that outfit do you? It was pretty wild."

"Great. I met some nice gay boys who loved my ass so much that they couldn't resist giving it a rubdown. That was interesting."

"Very. I personally could never get behind the whole butt-groping thing." Jonah, ruminating. "I just don't understand men who feel the need to frisk."

"That's a good thing. Shows you're evolved and not one of the Neanderthals lurking out there. Do they think they are going to get somewhere with that?"

"Yep, they must. At least they usually get a response."

"I had this girlfriend in college who used to do it to guys just to turn the tables. We'd go out and she'd become this mad butt pincher."

"No way." Beginning to laugh.

"She'd do it and flee of course, so I would be stuck standing there, unknowing, and looking very guilty."

"Are you sure there is a friend in this story?" Jonah, teasing me. "It sounds like one of those 'I have this friend' things."

"I swear. I was just an innocent bystander." Giggling. "I was no butt pincher."

"Sure you weren't. I'll be sure to wear butt pads the next time I see you."

"Who said I would want to pinch your butt?" Laughing fully. "Anyway, it's been awhile. . . . What can I do you for?"

"Can't a guy just call to say hi?"

"Sure, but that's too ordinary for you."

"I just wanted to reconnect. Seeing you reminded me how much I missed your voice."

"Really?" (He *missed* me?!) "You've become such a softy in your old age."

Swooning harder as I imagined him that night walking to his car, running his hands through his beautiful hair, and thinking about me in white vinyl. Now I was swaying.

"I've become a lot of things." Getting seriously quiet. "I know that you probably have minimal tolerance for me after all the shit I pulled, but maybe you'd get a drink

230   with me anyway. There's so much I want to talk to you about."

"Are you sure this is Jonah, the guy who used to run from me when I got the slightest bit serious?"

"It's me and I'm done running."

There was a long silence now that my tongue rolled out of my mouth and I became a baby before speech was learned. Forget swooning. Forget swaying. Now I was falling.

"What?"

"I'm done running away from things. I've changed."

"You've changed?" Repeating what he said.

"Yeah."

"What does that mean?" Trying to figure this all out. "Should I be taking these big bold statements to heart, or are you trying to fuck with me again?"

"Why would I want to do that?"

"Well . . ."

"You're right, you have every reason to feel totally weirded out right now. I must sound crazy."

"I'm a bit lost for words." Stammering into the phone.

"You? Never." Sarcastically.

"Fuck you. Just because I get chatty every once in a while doesn't give you free rein to tease me. You just laid all this shit out there, and we haven't even said hello in months. I don't get it. This just isn't the conversation I anticipated." Trying to breathe.

"I know, but I figure why beat around the bush. I wanted to get right to the point."

"Are you high or something?"

"Nope, that's part of what has changed." 231

"Really? God, I'm on repeat. Sorry."

"No problem, and yeah I'm done with that. Listen, can we get a drink and really talk?"

"Okay. When?"

"I'll pick you up in an hour?" Asking but really telling.

"You're quick."

"Just call me the Flash. See ya soon."

With that he hung up.

"What the fuck was that?"

"What the hell is going on here?"

"Who the hell was that?"

"Maybe alien abductions do happen."

"We are in trouble."

"We?"

"Yes, we. I face planted right along with you."

That definitely was not the guy I used to spend nights agonizing over, trying to get him to open up to me. I'm about to get sucked into Jonah's world again. What am I getting myself into? More important, what am I going to wear? The doorbell rang after half my clothing had been spit from my closet. I grabbed the closest things: jeans, black heels, pink studded belt, white tank, and a fifties tight red cardigan. Matching, doubtful, but I didn't want to keep him waiting. I flipped my hair into a half bun, half ponytail, grabbed my favorite Stila gloss on the go, and opened the door with a smile that hopefully was free of the aforementioned grapefruit gloss. With purse in hand I sailed out, and tried not to stare at him even though he had never looked quite so cute.

Our drink turned into an eight-hour, early-morning,

marathon conversation drenched date. It was something out of a perfect eighties nerdy-dork-gets-girl movie, except the scenario was tossed on its head. Here was the guy I pedestalized (It can be a verb, can't it?) twirling words and compliments around me like an ace baton thrower. We went to this little bar, the Game Room, and in a dark corner, in a blue booth, with a candle half lit between us, he made me start to like him all over again.

"So you are still using my journal? Well, it's not really my journal, it's your journal. I just gave the journal to you." Me, rambling.

"Yes." Looking me in the eye and smiling. "*The* journal is the only thing I write in. I'm almost out of pages."

"Good, I'm glad." Grabbing my drink and taking a big gulp. Help!

"Lilly, relax." Smiling more.

"I am relaxed, I'm fine." Saying a little too quickly.

In my aggressive reassurance, I proceeded to whack my glass and dump my entire Jack-and-Coke all over the table and down the front of his vintage yellow-and-white checked snap-down shirt.

"Oh, shit!" Reaching for the fallen beverage. "I am so sorry."

As my face flamed like Cherries Jubilee, he just grinned and undid his shirt. He took the entire mess off and wiped the table, pushing the ice to the floor.

"No harm done." Wiping the last of it. "I didn't really like this shirt anyway."

"I am so sorry." Eyeing him in his gray undershirt. "Good thing you are wearing layers. What is that by the way?" Trying to recoup. "Every guy I know can't just wear one shirt. There has to be this artful arrangement of thickness and texture before they can even walk out the door."

"Well, sometimes one is too thin. You never want the nipple effect." Placing the ruined shirt on the floor under the table. "Then sometimes a V-neck alone can give you the wolfman look, which is even worse."

"Wolfman?" Starting to giggle.

"Yeah, when your chest hair gets all condensed and smushed, so it puffs up over the collar."

"That's bad." Laughing.

"That is why we layer." Grinning at me. "This is my last one though, so, please, Lilly, be careful with the rest of your drinks this evening."

"Waitress!! Another!!" Laughing harder.

With the ice literally and figuratively cracked, I remembered how to be myself. We hit two other bars and then sat on my floor drinking beer and talking about life and love and everything we were and are afraid of. We always could talk, that was one thing we had been good at, but there was something else behind his words. They all came out tied to their own little life rafts, buoyed by the weightlessness of complete honesty. It sounds strange, but there was a force lurking beneath everything he said. Maybe you could call it purpose. He had figured himself out, quit smoking pot, and found out how to express himself without it. His music reached a new level of intimacy and wholeness. He was clear and focused and one hundred percent present. I was blown away.

I don't even remember if I spoke. I'm sure I did because I don't recall the conversation being one-sided, but it was all so intense I just don't feel as if I was there. Have you ever been in a scenario where everything is so electric and energized and perfect that it doesn't seem real? Have you ever ended up outside yourself watching as this buzz radiates from you like aurora borealis in a dark summer sky? Has everything seemed surreal and alien, existing in some other time and space, until, just when it gets so bizarre and you are about to trip out, it becomes so real that you realize you are experiencing a completely harmonious moment? Have you ever wanted to pinch yourself just to be sure you're still breathing? After spending that night with Jonah, I had bruises up and down my arms.

Just when you think that you are out of the game, the rules change and you become a star player. Maybe some other chick breaks a nail or gets a bad haircut. Maybe someone decides to grow up and ditch the diapers. Maybe there's overtime, and the all-stars are tired and sprained. Or maybe the thousand and one wishes you made on the night star actually get to come true. Whatever the reason, I was back in play with the guy with whom I so wanted to play, so long ago. Maybe this was the adventure I was waiting for. Jonah somehow morphed into that ideal image of him I created years ago in Paris before I even really knew him. Somehow, he became capable of giving me what I wanted. I got blessed. I was getting to be Julia Roberts, and I was loving every minute of it. If it's a dream, do not, I repeat, DO NOT, wake me up!

The next night, or really later that same day since he did not leave my place until five A.M., he showed up at my door with a bottle of wine in one hand and a cactus tied with a pink bow in the other.

"I come bearing gifts." Walking in and giving me a kiss on the cheek.

"For me?" Taking hold of the plant and spinning it around. "No one has ever given me something with spines before."

"Well, I figured it was very representative of our relationship."

"What? Full of tiny prickers that leave lingering pain if you don't remove them?" Eyeing him.

"No. I'm sorry about . . ." Stammering out a response. "I . . ."

"Oh!" Interrupting him. "I didn't mean it like that. No subtle dig. It really was just a cactus metaphor."

"Okay." Clearing his throat. "Well, what I was going to say was that it reminds me of us because a cactus can grow and thrive without a lot of water and attention. Even if it gets neglected on a shelf, it can blossom and still develop into something beautiful." Jonah, blushing slightly and running his hand through his hair.

"Oh my god!"

"Oh my god!"

"He just blushed!"

"I know! He *blushed*!"

"Who is this guy, Lilly?"

"No idea. But I am hearing really romantic, flowery words streaming from his mouth, aren't I?"

"Uh, yeah. Think so. We have been known to hallucinate every now and again."

"True. Maybe he will keep going so we can confirm."

"Ears on alert, Captain."

Realizing that I had not spoken in about a minute,

236 and had left him hanging, I quickly walked to the counter, deposited the plant, and swallowed.

"Thank you. It's perfect." Placing it by the window. "I love it."

"Good." Setting the wine down on the counter.

"You know, Jonah, I once pushed a guy into a cactus."

"What?"

"Yeah. Weird memory. I have this flash of being nine and on some school camping day trip. We had free time and were all playing *Buck Rogers.*"

"Man, I loved that show!"

"Me too. Anyway, he was the villain and I was supposed to push him away from me, so I did. Well, the fact that we were on a little bridge slipped my mind, and I pushed him right off. He fell about four feet into a huge cactus."

"You are kidding? By the way, do you have a bottle opener?"

"In the drawer to your left." Grabbing two glasses from above my head. "No. The poor kid had to have some nurse pull prickers out of his ass for hours!"

"You are an evil girl." Sassing me.

"He was the bad guy! He was after me!"

"I'll keep that in mind if I ever decide to chase you anywhere." Opening the wine and pouring it into the awaiting glasses.

"You seem more of the Buck Rogers type anyhow. The guy who gets the girl instead of trying to abduct and torture her." Picking up one of the glasses.

"I will toast to that." Jonah, clinking with me.

"To what?" Taking a sip.

"Getting the girl."

Now, I blushed. I took another swig of wine to give me

courage, and I leaned over and kissed him. I melted, he melted, we melted, and then and there, we fell.

We were inseparable from that night on. During the day I would float to work, kick ass there, and rush home to meet Jonah. We'd go for dinners and coffee and watch movies. We'd laugh and kiss and hold hands inside the hippest of bars. We were a "we." I never before had felt comfortable with the idea of being a "we" in public. There was something unnerving to me about hand-holding and PDA. Even though I have always wanted a boyfriend, I used to get freaked by the idea of being perceived as having one. I think I was wrapped up in other people's notions about quality and if the guy I was with was a good catch. It is part and parcel of the self-consciousness I constantly try to shake.

I remember going on this date a few months ago with a sweet guy. It was our third or fourth date. When we got out of the car to walk to the restaurant, he took my hand in his for the first time. My initial reaction was not one of "how nice and cool, I'm with him," it was "alert, alert, alarm sounding." All I could think was that I was not an "I" anymore, I was part of a "we," and I hated it. It made me feel invisible, like I wasn't my own person. I felt sublimated.

With Jonah, I felt I was "me" and "we" at the same time. I know I'm throwing around pronouns repeatedly right now, but that's the easiest way I can describe it. Being with Jonah wasn't subtracting from me and my focus, it was adding a rich layer of dependence and support. He was writing like mad and I was too. We were rocking, and we weren't even sleeping together yet. Sure, there was lots and lots of foreplay and canoodling (love that word), but

238   I wanted to wait. I had relayed to him all about my shame
spirals and the whole angel/devil thing, and how sex was
just such a complex issue for me. As much as he turned
on all my buttons, I wanted it to be right and perfect and
Sam-like. We decided to wait and see what would happen
if we focused on talking and not tonguing. I was living my
fantasy.

On our seventh date (yes, I know it was the seventh
because I was counting them with a little orange x in my
date book), I officially dedicated myself one hundred
percent to the relationship. It's not often that a girl really
gets to be seen by a guy for all her glory, for all her worth.
I usually spend time reining in different parts of myself
in order to mold into the situation. With Jonah, there
was no need to bend because he sent me all these signals
that he was watching and waiting and wanting everything.
The day began with him bringing me an iced latte just
how I liked it, with a sprinkle of Equal. Then we went
shopping on Melrose, and everything he picked out for
me or I picked out for him were exactly the things we each
would have picked for ourselves. He found me this vintage belt with a Farrah Fawcett buckle and I found him a
snap-down shirt to replace the one I destroyed on our
first date. We were in sync.

Next came dinner and him ordering a double order of
chili fries for us to share, remembering from way back
that I'm addicted to them. After that, we went out and
met his friends at this club, and despite the great day, I
was still a little nervous. It's always weird meeting and
greeting the guy's friends for the first time. I wondered if
they knew about me and what they knew. I wondered if

they would like me, accept me, think I was cool enough, cute enough. Basically, I was just worried. But then Jonah made everything perfect. We walked in, and two of his buddies, Mark and Tim, were already there sitting at a booth in the corner.

"Hey, what's up?" Jonah, as he slid into the seat and pulled me next to him.

"Nothing much." Mark answered. "So, I take it this is the famous Lilly." Reaching for my hand and kissing it. "We have heard much about you."

"Really?" Kind of surprised. "Nice to meet you."

"You've been keeping our boy occupied lately." Tim, chiming in. "We thought he was abducted."

"Nope, just been chilling with my girl." Kissing me.

"Did he just say his girl?"

"I think so."

"His girl! And he kissed me in front of them!"

"Calm down."

"I can't. I feel like bursting into song."

"Definitely don't do that."

"He just called me his girl in front of his best guy friends. Boys don't do that unless they are serious."

"True, but if I catch one note of melody falling from your lips, I'm taking over."

I nuzzled into Jonah and squeezed his leg under the table. I had never been anyone's girl before much less his girl in front of his guys. I floated through the rest of the evening, sitting on a cloud created by this one small statement. I am such a dork! When we got back to my house, after making out on the couch for what seemed like hours, I had to ask if he really meant what he had said or remembered that he said it in the first place. I can never seem to leave well enough alone.

"So," wiping a lock of hair out of my eye, "you're girl, huh?"

"Yup." Not even hesitating. "And, I can be your guy. With your permission of course."

"Of course." Rejoicing. "What caused this change of heart? You were so anti all this before. So not into being in a girl-guy thing."

"You."

"Me?"

"Yeah, after we had our brief dating thing, then our sort of friend thing, and then when everything sort of totally disappeared, I realized how much I missed you. Our conversations, your smile, your energy. When I was with you, there was no one else I wanted to be with, no other moment to be in. I knew I had to get it back."

"Why, then, did you blow it off in the first place?"

"At the time, all that was too much for me. I just wasn't ready to be what you needed or what I thought you needed, so I stayed away."

"I didn't need you to be anything but what you were."

"I know, but I didn't know what that was. Who I was. I wanted to be someone who earned the affections of such an amazing girl, and back then I was a flaky stoner who didn't know jack."

"And now?" Tracing his cheek with my finger.

"Now I want you to need me. I want to give you what you deserve."

"Wow." Staring at him, overwhelmed. "This is intense."

"Yeah, I guess it is." Kissing me. "Thank you for giving me another chance to make this work."

"Your welcome."

Hook, line, and sinker.

Everything from then on proceeded with such ease that I kept waiting for the other shoe to drop, and yet I never heard the crash of a heel. It was a magical, intimate time and because of that I didn't want to tell anyone at first, not even Danielle. Even though I knew she would be cool, it felt wrong sharing things right away. Also, everyone else had listened to countless tirades about him in the past, their ears clogged with his name and deeds. They would all give me a zillion and one reasons not to go back there, and make me feel small and lame for wanting to be by his side. It was hard to think of excuses for how I was spending my time, but I got creative. I used my family, writing, illness, anything to make up for my disappearance. So far, it was working, but it was getting exhausting. I decided Max would be the first one I told. He knew my modus operandi by heart, so maybe he could understand my rekindling this old connection.

We went for sushi as we always did. After a sake and a slew of Max-centered stories, I exploded with the news.

"So, I kind of have a boyfriend."

"What?" Setting down his glass abruptly. "How do you have a boyfriend?"

"I just do."

"That's not going to do it. We talked yesterday and the day before that and the day before that. Did you meet him last night?"

"No, it's been about a month." Saying quietly.

"Who is he?" Getting a bit riled. "Nice to keep secrets."

"I haven't told anyone. It just didn't feel right to talk about it."

"What is wrong with this guy then? When you don't want to talk about boys, something isn't right with the world."

"Nothing's wrong with him. He's actually pretty wonderful."

"Okay, if I have to ask once more who he is, I'm leaving."

"Jonah."

"Jonah?" Eyes widening a bit. "Musician guy is your boyfriend?"

"Yep."

"I'm confused. Didn't he bail, like, years ago and leave you bereft?"

"Big word there, bereft." Laughing at Max. "Yes he did bail, but that was my fault too. You were the one who made me see that anyhow. Don't you remember the lecture?"

"Which one?" Moving his water glass so the waitress could set the sushi down. "As the brother I lecture you a lot."

"No shit." Stirring the wasabi into the soy sauce. "You told me how I lose sight that two people are in the relationship, and I make it all about me. I never pay attention to what he is telling me and then push him even further away trying to get them to see it my way."

"Oh yeah. You hated me for a day because of that one."

"I did, but in the end I realized you were right." Stuff-

ing a spicy tuna roll into my mouth. "It took me a little
while to assimilate it."

"So, Jonah has changed and you have changed and
now you are in love?" Dropping his yellowtail into his
sauce boat. "So corny!"

"Something like that. It feels good to be corny."

"Well, good." Picking up his glass. "To you getting
laid."

"Eventually getting laid. We haven't gone there yet.
We are taking it slow."

"I recommend speeding it up." Clinking my glass. "I
think you need to enter the adult world of regular sex."

"Yeah, I know. I just really want it to be right." Taking
a sip of my drink.

"Well, the way this whole scenario is coming across
seems to scream keeper, so I think you may be in luck."
Grabbing another yellowtail sushi with his fingers. "If
some guy is waiting a month when he obviously is seeing
you, and probably most of you, most of the time, he is in
it for the duration."

"I think you may be right. Sometimes when and where
you least expect to find anything worthwhile becomes the
best place to start looking."

"Just be sure to keep your wits about you, and you
know the three of us are having dinner very, very soon.
Like tomorrow soon."

"Yeah, yeah. The big brother test. Jonah's practicing
so he gets everything right this time."

"Here's to him succeeding."

After dinner, flushed from my first foray into admit-
ting all, I went home to take a bath and chill. Jonah was

244 busy schmoozing some record folks, so we were having a night apart. I had time to relax and relish. Maybe the rest of my friends would be as supportive as Max. Maybe Jonah and I could have a happy ending. Maybe we all would get along and rejoice like a Greek chorus. Maybe I'm a little drunk on sake and I need to tone down my fantasies a wee bit . . . *Nah!* No way is fantasy girl going to tone down anything. As I was walking to my door in this distracted state, something moved behind me in the bushes, and I screamed.

"Shush . . . Lilly easy, it's me." Maya says, stepping out from behind a plant. "Sorry to scare you."

"Fuck me!" Catching my breath. "Thought I was a goner. You can't do that to girls who live alone and constantly worry about night stalkers and rampant rapists attacking them."

"Don't be so dramatic. It was only a little scare." Giving me a hug. "Sorry."

"Little, big, they all make me gray. Any new white hairs?" Smiling at her and squeezing tight. "What the hell are you doing on my doorstep at nine at night? You know, Dorothy, you aren't in San Francisco anymore."

"Oh, Lilly." Bursting into tears.

"Was my joke that bad? What is going on?" Fumbling for the keys.

I opened the door and grabbed Maya, pushing her through. I took her purse, pulled her jacket off, and threw them on my kitchen counter. I put my arm around her shaking shoulders and walked her to the living room.

"I . . . I . . ." choking on her tears, "I . . . I . . . think it's over."

"Over?" Realizing I still had my purse slung over my arm. I set it down on the floor. "Over what?"

"My relationship, this wedding, everything." Sniffling. "It's so fucked up."

When I got a good look at her face for the first time, I could see that she had been crying a lot. Her face was streaked and runny, stained with pink blotches from a long session. I have never seen Maya look so wrecked.

"What happened?" Settling her on the couch. "This just doesn't make any sense."

"It doesn't make sense to me either. I think he may be cheating on me." Spitting out her words. "The asshole might be cheating on me."

"Whoa. That I just don't believe. Ted loves you more than *Monday Night Football.*"

"I thought so too, but I'm convinced otherwise." Wiping her nose and then her hand on her black pants.

"Kleenex?"

"Yeah."

I got up and went to the bathroom. I hunted around for a tissue, but all I could find was a full roll of toilet paper.

"Here." Tossing the roll in her lap. "Why?"

"Well, for starters, we haven't made love in, like, a month." Taking a breath and blowing her nose.

"Maybe it's just the stress of the wedding. I've heard that happens to a lot of couples." (Not like I know that many soon to be married couples, but it seemed like a logical thing to say.) "You are both probably just too busy."

"Too busy for sex? No way. We have never been too

busy for sex. That is one place we always have gelled. Ted and I really like having sex with each other."

"A little too much information, but go on."

"I keep seeing all these random receipts from all these girl stores in his wallet."

"Maybe he's buying you things?"

"That was my first instinct too, but no gifts have come my way."

"Saving them for the wedding?" Trying anything at this point.

"He came home the other night smelling of perfume, perfume that was not my scent."

"Sister?"

"Lives out of town."

"Mother?"

"Ditto."

"Friend?"

"I know his girlfriends, and they don't smell like that. He's also been evasive and weird and . . ." Starting to cry again.

"I don't know what to tell you. Have you talked to him?" Unrolling some more toilet paper for her.

"No."

"That would be a first step. You can't just run to another city and ignore him."

"I know, but maybe this is a sign that we are all wrong and shouldn't be getting married. Maybe he's not the right guy for me." Looking at me.

"That's a lot of maybes. As much as I didn't want to accept you two together, I never could deny the look on your face in that wedding dress. You love this guy so much, and he literally makes you glow when you are around him. If he's cheating on you, yes, fuck him, good-bye, but my gut is telling me this all is a big fancy charade you have conjured in your head."

"I don't know."

"Getting married is scary as shit, not that I would know, but I can imagine."

"It is. I'm overwhelmed."

"Somehow, I kind of don't fully believe everything you just laid out." Swallowing. "I don't think you do either."

"Nice, my best friend doesn't believe me." Maya, getting mad and red. "You think I made all this up?"

"Kind of." Inching away from her, expecting a blow. "Everything you said about 'I think my man's cheating' sounds too textbook. It's like a bad Jerry Springer show. No guy would be so obvious. Maybe this whole running away to your single girlfriend's pad is your little freak out, not his major fuck up."

"I don't know."

"I think you may be looking for something wrong when it isn't there."

"Why would I want to do that? How long have I been planning this wedding? I don't want to ruin what we have."

"It could be a defense mechanism. Like it's easier to believe he's messing up and to blame him, because if you are the one who's skittish, then it calls into question everything you believe in."

"What does that mean?" Looking at me. "You think I have cold feet?"

"Yeah, I really do. You, like me, have always been so gung-ho about getting married, and everyone knows it. If you started to balk at the idea of committing and doing the whole 'I do' thing, you'd look hypocritical."

Maya was quiet after that for a little while, except for the occasional sniffle, and I wondered where in the hell I had gotten all those pearls of wisdom.

"I really hope you are right."

"No shit."

"Because if that schmuck is cheating then you just probably convinced Maya that he isn't."

"I really do think I am right though. Well, I tend to think I am always right, but that's an ego thing that I can't help. I just know that if she were me and I was feeling nervous about marriage when it was just around the corner, I'd feel stupid saying it because it is something I want so badly."

"That's true. Everyone would think you're nuts and blow off your concerns."

"Exactly." Nodding my head. **"I'm right, I know it."**

"I just want you to know that it's cool to be nervous. I understand the irony of a girl who once compared herself to Martha Stewart on speed flipping out about doing the deed, but don't blow this on account of that."

"So, you are saying this is all coming from that 'be careful what you wish for' thing?"

"Yeah, I do."

"I guess I never thought about it that way."

"I've gotten good haven't I?"

"You're sort of Dear Abby but younger." Looking at me, squinting.

"And cuter, thank you very much. Maya, what is really going on with you?"

"I'm just scared of all this change and growing up stuff I am dealing with. I feel like everyone expects me to be perfect at everything, and I don't know what the fuck I'm doing most of the time. In my head it is all so easy, get the ring, the dress, the temple, the flowers, the registry, but it's too much. I'm still just a kid."

"No one expects you to know it all except you."

"Looks like we switched positions."

"What do you mean?"

"Usually, I am the overprotective caretaker."

"Don't worry, it won't last." Giving her a hug.

"I think maybe it will." Squeezing tight. "Can I use the phone?"

"It's about time you called this fiancé of yours and tell him where you are."

Maya walked into the other room and I heard her dial, say hello, break down, and start talking. I went into the kitchen and poured two glasses of wine and smiled. I liked what I had done and who I had become. To go from evil bitch, jealous and unsupportive of my best friend's new life course, to masterful Yoda helping her stay on that very course was a pretty cool feat. Things were changing, and my little house of cards was slowly being erected and cemented with imaginary paste.

"I think this may be my cue."

"Cue?" **Asking. "As in, exit stage left?"**

"Yep, I think you can handle things from here on out."

"But . . ."

"No buts. As the 'Wish I' in our relationship, there is less

and less I wish you wouldn't do. I mean, I wouldn't do. We wouldn't do. Whatever. Regardless, you are doing just fine."

"Excuse me? I don't know what to say." Stuttering. "Imagine, me being at a loss for words. Things are getting very strange around here. First, I have this special, sweet verbally committed and communicative boyfriend. Second, I give stellar advice to my best friend who usually is the one with the astronomical words of wisdom. And, finally, you pat me on the back and relate that you are preparing for an imminent departure. I am at a loss."

"No, you aren't, and that is the beauty of it all."

I let out a sigh, scratched my head, and smiled. The adventure was here, and it was time to savor and loll about in my total and complete chickdom.

i'm in the pink

I don't think I really have ever had quite a
day like today. It was weird and embarrassing and wonderful and sexy and without a doubt the best day of my life. After
spending the day shopping and giggling
with Maya, she was ready to head back up
north. After depositing her on a plane
back to her one and only, who wasn't,
thank God, cheating on her, just putting
together a surprise wedding trousseau of
all her favorite things from all her favorite
shops, I decided to go get her bache-
lorette party gift. I figure since they made
up in spades, there still would be that
raucous time we were planning to have
again in Vegas. So I hopped into my car
and made my way over to Hustler, the
megamall of sex toys situated smack-dab
in the middle of Sunset Strip. Something
seemed safe and less embarrassing about
hitting this kind of store at two o'clock on

252   a Sunday afternoon. Some may say it wasn't a very pious thing to do, but I'm Jewish. Saturday is our day of rest.

As soon as I walked in, I realized how out of my element I was. Whether it was the buzzing vibrator I could swear I heard as I walked in or the two old grandpas in cowboy hats holding up Kama Sutra honey dust for inspection, I felt a chaste tide of embarrassment swell. As much as I talk about sex, it still is something that rattles my nerves to some degree. That's why Jonah and I are waiting. I have had to cut through a lot of past bullshit to feel comfortable. This store presented sex in such a here-is-your-dildo-to-go-with-your-cappuccino way, it made me feel like miss hang-up girl. If people could buy plastic massaging pussies and inflatable butt plugs, why couldn't I just relax and let myself enjoy being a sexual being? There were people out there doing crazier things than I could imagine even in all my horniest fantasies. And, for the record, I have never fantasized about a butt plug.

I walked around carefully, taking in the array of plastic pleasure devices. Who knew girls would be into sticking something squishy and purple up their you-know-whats? I'll leave the French ticklers to the less shy. Knowing I had come this far, I couldn't wimp out and sought to find the most elegant and tame vibrator for part of my gift basket. Maya would have probably balked at the squishy ones too. Well, maybe not after her "Ted and I really like having sex with each other" comment, but there I go thinking about what they are doing in bed and that just does not work . . . at all . . . ugh . . . at least it isn't as bad as imagining your parents going at it like rabbits. I wonder if they have any toys? *Ahhh* . . . Why am I wondering about that! Lilly, stop, mind must go blank and carry on. Get on with it. Shit, there's my cell. If my phone ringing when I am in a sex store picking out vibrators ain't an *L.A. Story* moment, I don't know what is.

"Hi, Lilly." My mom chirping.

"Mom!" Starting to laugh. "I was just thinking of you!"

"What about?"

"Oh, nothing." Chuckling to myself as I stared at my basket of goods. "What's up?"

"So, I got some interesting news from your brother this morning."

"Okay. And?"

"And, Jonah?" Tsking ever so slightly. "Lilly, what are getting yourself into?"

"Bed, I hope." Snickering at my wittiness.

"Lilly." Not getting my joke. "Come on."

"Seriously, Mom. We are dating, what more can I say. It's been about a month and so far I am happy. Really happy."

"A month?!" Shocked. "You kept a secret for a month! Even though I am a little peeved at being the last to know, that is rather impressive of you."

"Thanks, but don't be annoyed. Max was the first person and that was last night! I just knew I would get all these questions and advice, so I wanted to wait and make sure. I wanted everything to be a little more settled before I told anyone."

"Are you sure this time that it is real and not some fantasy you conjured up in your head?"

"Yes, no. I don't know." Pacing around the aisle. "We are figuring it out. I really am fine."

"Okay, I just don't . . ."

"I know, Mom, thanks." Interrupting. "Look I have to
go, but I will call you later."

"I love you."

"Me too." Hanging up.

I feel a small weight lifted from my shoulders now that
most of my nearest and dearest know about Jonah. Well,
at least those tied to me by blood and DNA. Once again,
I'm on the up-and-up with my family, and keeping anything from them is a major strain. Everything else
should be downhill from here. Back to the task at hand.
Where was I? Oh, something tamer than a purple passion penetrator. It wasn't hard to find since this store
seemed to pride itself on the something for everyone
vibe. I picked up some crotchless panties, a feather
duster, one of those spiky dog collars, and some minty
massage oil. It was when I came to the lubricant aisle that
I had some trouble. The suburban middle-age mom
beside me threw me off, and I started on the whole
parental vibe again. When she started asking me which
was better, the pina colada slip-and-slide or the extra-
slippery magnum lube, I had to bolt. She had morphed
into my mother, asking me what would turn my dad on.
Yuck! I hurried to pay and of course found out I had no
cash and had to charge. Love the big Hustler charge I am
going to have on my AmEx next month. Maya had better
dig the gift.

Not wanting to be a total prude, which maybe I am, I
did buy for myself as well. Maybe somewhere deep down
that was the impetus for the present. I'm-getting-all-
this-for-my-best-friend-who-is-getting-married-next-

month is the best excuse to investigate and test out your own curiosities. I got home and immediately opened my package. It was slim, pearlized pink, and about six inches long. I secretly hoped there would be operating instructions inside, but no dice. All it had was a how-to on battery installation. That blew, because I had no idea about how to use this wiggling piece of plastic. Did it actually go inside you? On top or under your underwear? Was it supposed to simulate sex or masturbation? Is there a difference? I mean, since it was sort of shaped like a weenie, did that mean it was supposed to act like one? Was I the only girl who wondered? These are not questions you can just ring up a friend and ask. It makes you admit too much and wait too long to try it out. I obviously wasn't going to wait. Hey, I get that kid complex when I get a shiny new toy—must play at once!

This wiggling piece of plastic is my new best friend. Sorry, Maya and Danielle. You have been replaced. Jonah, you better get a move on because you might get ditched as well. Let's just say no girl should be without. Something tells me this new saucy mood I'm in is going to be just the ticket for a repeat Vegas adventure. If I can go to a sex store, purchase, and pleasure myself with my first vibrator, maybe I can lose some of my inhibitions. My little pink friend was the first step.

As I was going for round two, the phone rang.

"Thanks for everything." Maya, expressing gratitude.

"So, you got home safe and sound?" Panting ever so slightly, as I tried to catch my breath. Why did I answer the phone?

"Yeah. What's wrong? You sound out of breath."

"Oh, nothing. I just walked in and ran to the phone."

"By the way, I just got your RSVP and it says you are coming with a guest. I'm a little confused."

"Why? I thought I could invite a date." Putting pinky back into the drawer. Darn it! (I'll be seeing you later.)

"You can, but not to be rude," clearing her throat, "since when did you have one to bring?"

"Since about a month ago."

"You have been holding out. While I was pouring my heart out to you last night, you don't even share with me that you have a new boyfriend."

"He's not really new, and I didn't think last night was the best time to break it down." Defending myself. "I thought it was better to focus on you."

"You did and you were beyond great, but still . . ."

"But still nothing. You're going to freak a little when I tell you who it is."

"No, I won't."

"Yes, you will."

"Just tell me already. Stop beating around the bush."

"Jonah."

"Oooohhhh!"

Great, she's shocked and going to grill me. She only enunciates like that when she's dismayed.

"I know that tone and it isn't what you are thinking." Trying to prevent the interrogation. "I already know how you feel about him."

"Jonah?" Repeating louder.

"Yep."

"What is that about? What, after he sees you he gets a change of heart?" Not even trying to be courteous.

"Lilly, what are you thinking? Is this just a ploy to have someone to bring to the wedding? I know how much you want to have a date with you."

"I'm going to pretend you did not just say that. For you to even suggest that is fucked." Raising my voice. "I know I was worried about that, but to throw it in my face is just not right."

"You're right, I'm sorry, but this just isn't registering very well with me."

"Things have changed. He's not the same and he's been amazing. The whole thing has been wonderful."

"I just think you always forgive people too easily. He was rude and disrespectful. It makes you look like a fool to go back."

"Like I forgave you after our trip?"

"So not the same thing, and I can't believe you brought that up. I have already apologized too many times for ruining our European Adventure. I know I was zero fun to be with and screwed up our plans and am so happy you got over it, but it is just that, over."

"It slipped out, sorry." I apologized. "I don't want to argue with you and trade stupid barbs. We had such a good time yesterday, and this is all weird. Why are you reacting so intensely?"

"I don't really know. It's just that you are so special. I know how hard it was for you. I had to listen to so much shit about him hurting you."

"Maya, he was involved with me, not you. This is not about you at all. Besides, yes he was a jerk and couldn't deal, but my God! I was so intense! I had us married with three-point-five kids after our second date."

"I just remember all the times you cried to me about Jonah. You were so tragic, like some Brontë character."

"I was a fucking drama queen!"

"That is true."

"Listen, Maya, can you just take a breath? If I can deal with what happened before, you should not have a problem with it now."

"Lilly, I don't know." Letting out a big sigh.

"Maya, it's not for you to know." Remaining strong and getting stronger with each breath. I am woman hear me roar! "This has nothing to do with you. You are not even listening."

There was a pause on the line, and I knew Maya had finally heard what I said. She was probably picking at her nails and wondering how to plot her next move.

"How did it all happen?" Taking the factual route.

"He called out of the blue, and we went out and that was that. We've been inseparable since."

"That was that? That's a little simplistic. If you want me to listen you need to say something."

"We went out and talked for hours. We talked about the past and the future and what we want from life and love. We caught each other up on our lives. We reconnected. He's where I wanted him to be before."

"Are you sure? You have a lot of those 'talks' with guys who then leave you high and dry."

"It's different. I can't explain it. And, no, I'm not sure. Can someone ever be sure of a relationship? You, yourself, flipped last night."

"But that's different."

"Why? Just because we are at different stages? It's all about taking chances. He's worth that to me."

"This chance could seriously fuck you up." Maya, reiterating herself.

"I know, but I believe in him." Feeling good about what I was saying. "Maybe I'm a fool, but I can't not do this. I can't live my life wrapped up tightly in a blanket of self-protection. It would make me choke."

"Okay, you do tend to get claustrophobic." Giving in a little. "I guess I'll see for myself at the wedding. You do seem rather rational about this."

"To be honest, I have not felt this clear about anything, ever."

"All right." Softening even more.

"He's really looking forward to the wedding." Wanting to switch topics. "By the way, how excited are you for Vegas again?"

"Beyond. Gambling, drinking, craziness with my ladies. Love it."

The doorbell.

"Maya, I have to go. Someone's at the door."

"Bye. Be careful please." I felt as though she were hugging me through the phone. "I'm sorry for being bitchy."

"I know and I will. See you next weekend."

I rushed to the door and opened it. Jonah. God, I loved being wrapped up in his arms. The way he smelled made me smile. The way his hands held my back and supported me made me weak in their firmness. The way he kissed me made me scatter. Every kiss should always feel like the first kiss. Full of expectation and nervousness, desire and trepidation. It's the only kiss you ever get that is a surprise. You never know when it's going to happen, what the lips will feel like, taste like. How your stomach will roll and turn with the touch. The prize is to always

260 maintain the motion, maintain the unsteadiness, the imbalance, the fluttering. Every time Jonah kissed me, I was filled with a hundred different dizzying emotions. I loved that. Maybe I loved him.

"Baby." Kissing me again. "Missed you last night."

"Me too, but as it turned out, I was rather occupied." Nuzzling into him as I pulled him into the house.

"Got another guy on the side?" Taking off his Adidas black-and-white hoodie.

"Actually, I have three. One's in the bedroom now and he is amazing." Giggling as I brought him to the couch.

"I want to meet him." Kissing me again. "Maybe he can show me a few pointers."

"He's a little a shy, but I'll ask." Kissing back.

As we sat, our arms, legs, fingers, and necks became entwined. Everything had to be touching each other at all times. He was glue and I, the wallpaper. We were a jigsaw puzzle, each completing each other's picture. Sometimes I was the edge pieces, smooth and sturdy, wrapping around him, holding the image together. Other times, he fenced me in with his sky and green grass. We lay like this for a while, just kissing, and smiling, and fitting together.

"Seriously, Maya showed up on my doorstep all bugged-out about getting married."

"Is she okay?" Stroking my hair.

"I think so, she just had a meltdown. There's a lot of pressure she is dealing with and instead of allowing herself to be nervous and scared, she's been feeling that everyone else would think she was a hypocrite for freaking."

"How so? I think it makes total sense to be phobic about getting married. Even if you are in love and confident in your partner, it is a major undertaking." Twirling me around his finger.

"It's just that she has been miss marriage girl forever, so if she was hedging then she was going against everything she has believed in."

"How do you feel about marriage?" Jonah, asking.

"In general?"

"In general."

"I'm one hundred percent for it whenever it presents itself. I can't wait to feel that permanent and safe. Have kids and build a life with someone. I'm all about the white horse and fairy tale. And you?" Tracing his cheek with my finger.

"In theory I'm the same way, minus the horse part of course, but I'm more hesitant. My parents didn't make it, so I guess I don't think anything is safe and permanent. There are too many variables trying to disrupt the fairy tale."

"I agree, but that's where the beauty is." Sitting up a bit.

"What do you mean?" Lining up with me.

"With all that threatens the fairy tale, to believe in it completely will at least allow you the confidence that you tried despite the obstacles."

"But, Lil, trying can mean failure."

"Sure, but love hurts. Wouldn't you rather feel it than stay protected forever without it?"

"Yeah, but it's nice sometimes to live with stone walls, body armor, and moats filled with sea monsters."

"Okay, enough with the medieval references." Smiling. "I'm not saying serve up your heart on a platter to the first chick in line. You still have to make good choices. But when you meet someone who you think might be worth it, go for it. Let down the drawbridge, so to speak."

"How can you be sure she is going to be worth it twenty years from now?"

"It's funny you bring up that question now. Maya and I just talked about that in regards to you." Staring at him.

"Really?" Jonah, blushing a little. "What did you say?"

"Basically, she voiced concern over you and me doing whatever it is we are doing. She wanted to make sure I was sure I wanted to get involved with you again."

"And?"

"I told her I just don't think sureness ever plays a role in relationships. However, I think you can be sure in taking a chance to see what happens. You can be sure in the decision to try and give it a go."

"And is that what you are doing with me, Lilly?"

"Probably. You may hurt me again, you may not, but I'm willing to see."

"I'm not going to hurt you." Taking my hand. "That is not part of the plan."

"I know that, but it might happen. Things happen." Squeezing his hand. "I'm okay with that if it does. No matter where we end up, you are worth the risk. I want this."

Jonah was quiet for a little while and couldn't stop staring at me. At first I was nervous that I had said too much and freaked him out. But then he squeezed my hand back, and I was afraid to blink. Something told me deep in my gut that this was one of those major life moments. A moment that lays you out naked and vulnerable. A moment that encapsulates emotion and exemplifies it in a Webster dictionary kind of way. I think our life story inevitably becomes just a patchwork quilt of these moments, the colors and patterns personifying and reflecting the nature of the time spent. This instant was screaming hot pink, bursting with a Gerbera daisy motif, and ringed with shiny silver lamé!

"Lilly, I'm falling in love with you." Jonah, whispering.

"What?" Unsure I was hearing correctly.

"I love you." Looking me right in the eyes.

"I love you too." Saying it without hesitation.

He smiled and I smiled and we got up and we went into my room and we undressed each other without averting our gazes and I truly made love for the first time. Then, we slept.

acknowledgments

So many have given me infinite support, love, and inspiration. To my agent, lawyers, and all my editors, thank you for carrying out the business of this book and taking me under your experienced wings. To all the ladies, young, old, and in between, thank you for your faith in me and for the encouragement to keep writing. To my friends, thank you for providing me a life rich with smiles and pages of material. And, to my family, Jake, Ruth, and Jason, thank you for creating a safe haven for me, a place where all my dreams come true.